Trouble always comes in threes . . .

Mary Simon hummed to herself as she rinsed some dirty dishes in the sink before putting them in the washer. Sunlight shone through the kitchen windows, which offered a pleasant view of the fields and barn outside. Country crafts and floral wallpaper decorated the tidy kitchen of the farmhouse she shared with her husband, Dale. A plump older woman, wearing an apron over a blue gingham dress, Mary marveled at the amount of dirty dishes piled up in the sink. It was hard to imagine that two people could go through so many cups and plates and silverware in just a day or two.

You'd think we were running a bed-and-breakfast, she thought.

Squeaks and scratches, coming from right behind her, startled her. Spinning around, she was shocked to discover three large, ugly rodents occupying the solid pine kitchen island across from the sink, rooting greedily through her fruit bowl. The mice or rats or gophers or whatsits were the size of tabby cats, with greasy gray fur, twitching noses and whiskers, nasty yellow teeth, tufted ears . . . and no eyes to speak of.

TOR BOOKS BY GREG COX

The Librarians and the Lost Lamp
The Librarians and the Mother Goose Chase

THE
LIBRARIANS
AND THE
MOTHER GOOSE
CHASE

GREG COX

A TOM DOHERTY ASSOCIATES BOOK
NEW YORK

THE LIBRARIANS AND THE MOTHER GOOSE CHASE

Copyright © 2017 by Electric Entertainment

A Tor Book
Published by Tom Doherty Associates
175 Fifth Avenue
New York, NY 10010

www.tor-forge.com

Tor® is a registered trademark of
Macmillan Publishing Group, LLC.

The Library of Congress Cataloging-in-Publication Data
is available upon request.

ISBN 978-0-7653-8415-7 (hardcover)
ISBN 978-0-7653-8414-0 (trade paperback)
ISBN 978-0-7653-8416-4 (e-book)

Our books may be purchased in bulk for promotional, educational, or business use. Please contact your local bookseller or the Macmillan Corporate and Premium Sales Department at 1-800-221-7945, extension 5442, or by e-mail at MacmillanSpecialMarkets@macmillan.com.

First Edition: April 2017

Printed in the United States of America

0 9 8 7 6 5 4 3 2 1

To David Hartwell,
who loved books as much as any Librarian.
Thanks for everything.

THE
LIBRARIANS
AND THE
MOTHER GOOSE
CHASE

1

※ *Washington State* ※

"Have I mentioned how much I hate toga parties?"

Colonel Eve Baird sprinted across the moonlit college campus, inconveniently draped in a rumpled white bedsheet that had been repurposed to serve as standard-issue frat party attire. A veteran counterterrorism agent formerly assigned to NATO, the statuesque blonde generally preferred more sensible clothing, particularly when in the field, but sometimes undercover work required . . . flexibility, and never more so than when employed by the Library.

"A couple of times, yeah." Jake Stone raced beside her down a tree-lined path leading away from Fraternity Row. His own makeshift toga made running for his life somewhat more difficult than usual, even as it showed off his equally well-built physique. "Greek life," he snorted in disgust. "See, this is why I got most of my degrees online."

His rugged good looks and gruff manner belied the fact that Stone was a world-class expert on art history and architecture, albeit under an impressive assortment of pseudonyms and false identities. Truth to tell, Baird knew professional spies who had fewer aliases than Stone, but, despite his abundant academic credentials, she doubted he had ever been a frat boy. A wildcat oil rigger and occasional hell-raiser, sure, but not a frat boy.

Thank heaven for small favors, Baird thought.

Loud music and raucous laughter blared behind them as they made tracks from the ill-advised revelry at the Gamma Gamma Rho House. The paved walkway provided a short-cut between Fraternity Row, which was located on a hill over-looking Western Cascade University, and the main academic buildings below. Given that it was Friday night, Baird figured most of the student body would be hitting parties instead of the books at the moment—or so she hoped. The fewer po-tential casualties, the better.

Heavy hooves pounded the pavement behind them, com-peting with the clamor from the toga party. A ferocious snort sent a chill down Baird's spine.

"It's still after us!" she said. "Keep running!"

"Great," Stone muttered, even though that was the plan after all. A gold-trimmed alabaster figurine was cradled in his arms. About two feet tall in height, the statue reeked of beer after having been "baptized" in a kegger-fueled frater-nity ritual. Lipstick and rouge defaced the figure's formerly pristine features. Stone had personally vouched for the relic's authenticity earlier, confirming that it was a genuine cultic idol from a temple in ancient Greece, which went a long way toward explaining the fix they were currently in.

The pounding of the hooves grew louder. Glancing back over her shoulder, Baird glimpsed a mountainous shape bar-reling toward them. Steam rose from a pair of large flared nostrils. Maddened red eyes glowed like hellfire. Ivory tusks gleamed in the night.

At least we're luring it away from the party, she thought. *Lucky us.*

Reaching the bottom of the hill, they dashed onto a red-brick quad surrounded by various college buildings housing lecture halls, laboratories, and libraries. Newer buildings of glass and steel squatted across from older, ivy-covered brick edifices dating back to the college's founding. A dish-shaped fountain, surrounded by low metal benches, sprayed a plume of water into the air. Canvas banners, advertising everything from a peace rally to a used book exchange, adorned the walls of the buildings. Most of the windows were dark, but a few lighted offices suggested that some of the more industrious students and faculty members were working well into the weekend. And despite all the partying on the hill, a handful of college kids were milling about on the quad, engrossed in their phones, their studies, or each other. They gaped at the sight of the two toga-clad strangers dashing onto the quad.

"Run!" Baird shouted at the kids, concerned for their safety. She had thought this part of the campus would be more deserted, but that may have been wishful thinking on her part. "Vamoose! Scram!"

She was used to giving orders, but unfortunately she wasn't dealing with trained soldiers at the moment, or even Librarians. And her ridiculous outfit didn't exactly convey a sense of authority. She tugged the top of her toga farther up onto her shoulder, even though possible wardrobe malfunctions were the least of her worries at the moment.

"You heard the lady!" Stone added. "Get out of here! It's not safe!"

A studious-looking coed bearing an armload of books peered at them in confusion. Like her fellow students, she made no move to exit the scene, promptly or otherwise.

"What are you talking about?" the student asked. "Who are you anyway?"

"We're the Librarians," Stone said, even though Baird was technically a Guardian as opposed to an actual Librarian. He held on tightly to the beer-drenched idol in his arms. "Trust me, you don't want to be here."

Before he could even attempt an explanation, a monstrous beast barreled onto the quad, trampling over an organic herb garden in front of the biology building. The glow from a couple of tall metal lampposts exposed the legendary creature in all its fabled fearsomeness.

The Calydonian Boar was at least twice the size of any mortal porker, weighing in at more than five hundred pounds at the very least. Piggy red eyes glared balefully from its massive head. Thick black bristles sprouted along its spine, while lethal-looking tusks jutted upward from its lower jaw. Froth spilled from its chomping maw. Its hot breath steamed from its snout. Once employed by the goddess Artemis to punish disrespectful humans back in ancient Greece, the Boar had resumed its mission in modern-day America, thanks to some idiotic frat boys who just *had* to employ a genuine relic in their drunken rituals.

Some people had no respect for history . . . or magic.

Intent on avenging the goddess's honor, the Boar charged at Baird and Stone, who had filched the idol from the frat house before the monster could turn the toga party into a massacre. In the bacchanalian bedlam of the party, few revelers had taken note of the narrowly averted rampage. A cast-iron bench got in the monster's way and was reduced to scrap metal beneath its adamantine hooves. The Boar noisily whet its tusks against its stumpy upper chops.

Just another Saturday night, in other words, at least as far as the Librarians were concerned.

Pandemonium consumed the quad as terrified students

dropped their books and phones and dates to run screaming in every direction. Momentarily distracted by the commotion, the Boar swung its huge head from side to side as though uncertain which annoying mortal to rend to pieces first. Baird instinctively reached for her gun, then remembered that her toga didn't come with a holster. *No matter,* she thought. *The damn thing's hide is probably bulletproof anyway.*

According to myth, only one weapon had ever brought down the Boar. . . .

"Sooooo-ie!" Stone called out. He lifted the besmirched idol above his head. "Come and get me!"

Foaming at the mouth, the Boar veered toward Stone, crossing the quad with surprising speed given its bulk. Stone dived out of the way just in time to avoid being gored or trampled, but the Boar was nothing if not persistent. Doubling back, it charged at him again, ignoring the frantic students for the time being.

That was good for the civilians, Baird observed, but not so great for her cohort.

"Stone!" She dashed away from him across the quad. "Toss me the idol!"

He got the idea. "Catch!"

The idol arced through the air before landing heavily in Baird's arms. "Look who's got the goddess now!" she yelled at the Boar. "You got a problem with that, you overgrown reject from a Harryhausen movie?"

Provoked, the Boar wheeled about and ran at Baird, who suddenly had profoundly mixed feelings about capturing its attention. Its hooves literally tore up the pavement, sending pulverized brick flying. Not wanting to call things too close, she lobbed the idol back over to Stone, who caught it with a greater degree of hand-eye coordination than you might expect from somebody with so many PhDs to his credit. He defied stereotypes, that one.

"Over here!" he hollered. "Wrong way, bacon bits!"

The Boar skidded to a halt, trashing more of the quad, and started after Stone again. Baird wondered just how long she and Stone could keep up this death-defying game of keep-away, even as she went long and got ready to receive the idol once more. Her arms were already getting tired. That statue wasn't exactly lightweight. . . .

"Back to me!" she yelled. "Hurry!"

"You don't need to tell me twice!"

He hurled the idol at her, but the throw fell short, splashing down into the basin of the fountain. Baird held her breath, hoping that the Boar would lunge after the idol, but it kept charging at Stone instead, reminding her that the monster wasn't out to retrieve the idol, but simply to punish those who disrespected it and, by extension, the gods.

"Crap," she muttered.

Stone turned and ran, but the frothing razorback was closing in on him. Baird tore one of the canvas banners down from a wall and flapped it loudly to get the Boar's attention. She held it before her like a matador's cape.

"Hey, Porky! Olé!"

"That's bulls, not boars!" Stone corrected her.

"Not helping!"

The flapping cape distracted the Boar anyway. Temporarily abandoning Stone, it thundered toward Baird, who found herself pining for the good old days when all she had to deal with was terrorists and insurgents, not mythological monsters. At the last minute, she swung the banner to one side, so that the Boar plowed into the cape instead of her, slicing it to ribbons. The force of the beast's charge tore the canvas from her grasp even as its bristly hide grazed her side, knocking her off her feet.

"Baird!" Stone shouted in alarm.

The shredded banner was draped over the Boar's head, infuriating it. The monster shook its head violently to rid itself of the annoying encumbrance, and Baird took advantage of the moment to scramble to her feet. She leaned against a tall metal lamppost, catching her breath. Her right leg was raw and sore where the rampaging Boar had scraped against it. It stung like Hades.

Now what? she thought. They couldn't just let the berserk beast keep running amuck. Back in ancient Greece, the Calydonian Boar had terrorized an entire kingdom, laying waste to everything in its path, until it was finally slain by—

"Watch out!" Stone hollered. "Here it comes again!"

He wasn't kidding. Baird could practically smell the Boar's rank breath as it bore down on her with murder in its eyes. With nowhere to run, she shimmied up the lamppost to put some distance between her and the monster. As far as she knew, boars—even mythical ones—couldn't climb.

But that wasn't about to stop the Boar, who slammed into the post hard enough to all but uproot it, with no visible damage to the beast itself. Baird clung to the post for dear life as it tilted precariously at a sixty-degree angle. Snorting, the Boar backed up for another run at the post, which was unlikely to withstand too many blows like that.

What the heck is keeping the others? Baird thought impatiently. *Anytime now would be good. . . .*

As if on cue, a blinding white flash came from the front door of the college library just across the quad. The door swung open and two more Librarians burst onto the scene. Panting in exhaustion, and looking distinctly worse for wear,

Cassandra Cillian and Ezekiel Jones arrived in what Baird desperately hoped was the nick of time. Their clothes were rumpled and torn, their hair was mussed, Ezekiel was missing one shoe, and was Cassandra wearing a pair of . . . antlers?

"We've got it!" Cassandra brandished an antique bow and arrow. The petite redhead waved the weapon enthusiastically. Large blue eyes gleamed with excitement. "We found it!"

"About time!" Baird clung to the tottering lamppost. "What took you so long?"

"Hey," Ezekiel protested. "You try robbing an ancient Greek temple that's been hidden for thousands of years—and that just happens to be guarded by some very grumpy Harpies." He flashed Baird a cocky smile, looking typically pleased with himself. An Australian accent tinged his voice. "You're welcome, by the way."

"You can tell me all about it . . . later," Baird said. "At the moment, I could use a little help here."

Although momentarily distracted by the new arrivals, the Boar rammed its massive skull against the base of the lamppost. Sparks flew where its tusks scored the metal. Baird gulped as the leaning post dropped another fifteen degrees or so, bringing her closer to the frenzied razorback. Gravity tugged on her as she tightened her grip upon the tall iron pole, holding on to it with both arms and legs. Hanging beneath the post, with her back to the demolished pavement, she struggled to get up on top of it instead.

"Right, sorry," Cassandra stammered. She nocked the arrow to the bowstring, but struggled to draw the string back as the sturdy bow resisted her efforts. "Wow, this is harder than movies make it look!"

Legend told of how the Calydonian Boar was finally brought down by an arrow loosed by the celebrated Greek heroine

Atalanta. Tracking down the long-lost arrow of Atalanta after a couple of millennia had been no easy task, but it was precisely the sort of quest at which the Librarians excelled. Now Baird could only hope that history—and myth—repeated itself.

"Gimme that." Stone ran over and claimed the bow and arrow from Cassandra, pausing for a moment to admire the artifacts. "A classic recurve bow, as employed in ancient Greece, composed of polished horn per tradition. Craftsmanship and detailing consistent with early Aetolia, fifth century BCE if not earlier . . ."

Baird rolled her eyes. *Librarians.*

As their Guardian, it was her job to protect her brainy charges, sometimes even from themselves.

"Less ogling, more shooting!"

"Technically, you loose an arrow, you don't shoot it," Stone said. "But . . . I'm on it."

His upper-body strength proved sufficient to draw back the bowstring. He let fly the arrow, which struck the Boar squarely between the shoulders. It squealed in fury and gnashed its choppers.

"Nice shot, mate!" Ezekiel said.

Stone shrugged. "Well, I've done some bow hunting in my time. . . ."

"Mind you, I could have made that shot, too," Ezekiel said, "if necessary, that is."

"Uh-huh," Stone said with a smirk. "You keep telling yourself that, pal."

Ezekiel grinned at his friend's disheveled toga. "Nice look, incidentally. Very Bed, Bath, and Beyond."

Stone scowled. "Don't even start. . . ."

"Um, guys," Baird called. "We're not done here yet."

Although wounded, the Boar was still up and about. Snorting and squealing, it furiously rubbed its back against the tottering lamppost, trying to dislodge the wooden arrow jutting from its back. Ichor trickled down its hide, but the monster seemed as preternaturally powerful as ever. The unsteady lamppost shook from the impact of the Boar's frantic activity. An exposed electrical cable, severed and sparking, hissed like an angry serpent.

"I don't understand." Cassandra looked on in confusion. "Why isn't it working?"

"Beats me," Stone said. "In the myth—" His eyes lit up as he put it together. "In the myth, the Boar was famously defeated by a *woman* warrior—after all the male heroes had failed." He shouted at Baird. "You hearing me?"

"Loud and clear." She sighed in resignation. "Guess it's up to me."

Letting go of the tilting post, she dropped onto the Boar's back. Its spiny bristles scraped her flesh, but she grabbed the jutting arrow shaft with both hands to keep from being thrown off the bucking monster. No way was she falling off the Boar and under its angry hooves. She hadn't survived magical transformations, time travel, and a couple of near apocalypses just to get trampled by an overgrown potbellied pig.

"Time to put you down for good."

Gripping the arrow with all her strength, she drove it deeper into the Boar's hefty body, aiming for where she guessed its heart should be. An anguished squeal rewarded her effort as the ancient wooden arrow pierced something soft and vulnerable deep inside the creature. A tremor shook the Boar from head to tail, almost unseating Baird, before the previously solid monster dissolved into a puff of thick gray smoke that smelled vaguely of pork chops. Baird tumbled onto the broken pavement as the beast vanished out from under her.

"Ouch!" she exclaimed. "Remind me to do that over grass next time!"

The Librarians rushed to her side. "You did it!" Cassandra blurted. "You bested the Boar . . . just like Atalanta!"

"No, *we* did it." Baird let go of the arrow, which clattered onto the ground. "It was a team effort all around, just like always."

Stone helped her to her feet. "Is that it? Are we done?"

"Pretty much." She dusted herself off before wading into the fountain to retrieve the idol. "Now we just need to get this back to the Library so Jenkins can undesecrate it somehow."

"Er, I think the word for that is consecrate," Cassandra said. "Or maybe reconsecrate?"

"Whatever," Baird said. "Just so long as it defuses this puppy."

"Hang on." Ezekiel turned toward the noise coming from the party on the hill. Fireworks exploded in the air above the raucous celebration. Explosions briefly drowned out the dance music until somebody turned the volume up to eleven. "What's the rush? Sounds like quite the blast." He rubbed his hands together in anticipation. "Which means we're talking drunk college boys who aren't paying close attention to their valuables."

A master thief as well as a Librarian, Ezekiel often had his own, somewhat questionable priorities.

"Forget it," Baird said firmly, laying down the law. Her soggy toga dripped onto the shattered pavement. "I've had all the Greek-a-palooza I can handle tonight."

Cassandra retrieved the arrow. "I'm with Baird. It's been a

long day . . . night . . . whatever." She fought back a yawn. "I'm getting jet lag from hopping from America to Greece and back again."

Ezekiel started to protest again. "But—"

"No buts." Baird held up her hand to forestall any further debate. "Home it is." She took a closer look at Cassandra. "So what's with the antlers, Red?"

Blushing, the smaller woman removed the bony tines crowning her head, as though she had forgotten about them.

"It's a long story," she said.

"Can't wait to hear it." Baird herded the Librarians toward the waiting doorway. Beyond the entrance to the college library, another Library awaited.

The Library.

2

※ *Not long before* ※
Ohio

Mary Simon hummed to herself as she rinsed off some dirty dishes in the sink before putting them in the washer. Sunlight shone through the kitchen windows, which offered a pleasant view of the fields and barn outside. Country crafts and floral wallpaper decorated the tidy kitchen of the farmhouse she shared with her husband, Dale. A plump older woman, wearing an apron over a blue gingham dress, Mary marveled at the amount of dirty dishes piled up in the sink. It was hard to imagine that two people could go through so many cups and plates and silverware in just a day or two.

You'd think we were running a bed-and-breakfast, she thought.

Squeaks and scratches, coming from right behind her, startled her. Spinning around, she was shocked to discover three large, ugly rodents occupying the solid pine kitchen island across from the sink, rooting greedily through her fruit bowl. The mice or rats or gophers or whatsits were the size of tabby cats, with greasy gray fur, twitching noses and whiskers, nasty yellow teeth, tufted ears . . . and no eyes to speak of.

Just flesh and fur where their beady eyes should have been.

She gasped in fright. A china saucer slipped from her fingers, crashing down onto the floor, where it shattered loudly, but neither the crash nor Mary's audible reaction scared the monstrous creatures away. Instead they turned their blind faces toward her, grunting and squeaking aggressively. Mary backed up against the kitchen counter, alarmed; she was no shrinking violet when it came to mice and bats and such, but for all she knew these grotesque creatures were diseased. There was no telling what they might do.

"Shoo!" she yelled at them. "Scoot, you filthy vermin!"

The rodents sprang at her instead. Vicious little teeth and claws flew at her.

Ye Gods!

Quick reflexes saved her from being scratched or bitten. She ducked out of the way just in time, so that the frenzied mice landed in the sink and on the kitchen counter, knocking over plates, dishes, Mason jars, and a coffeepot. The clatter added to the chaos, which would have surely attracted Dale had he not been out doing errands. Mary was on her own against the sightless invaders.

But not without resources.

She plucked a large steak knife from the knife rack on the counter and slashed at the nearest rodent as it scrambled out of the sink. Swinging wildly, she missed its head, but managed to slice off the tip of its tail. The creature squealed in protest, then fled in panic.

"That's right! You'd better run!" She waved the knife at the other two rodents and charged at them, shouting. "What about you? You want a piece of me, too?"

Faced with a knife-wielding Mary, who meant business, the two remaining creatures chose the better part of valor. They leaped from the counter, joining their compatriot on the floor, and all three hightailed it toward a latched screen door leading out to the backyard. The fleeing rodents tore through the wire mesh as though it wasn't there, shredding the screen, before disappearing down the back steps.

Good-bye and good riddance!

Her ire up, she was briefly tempted to chase after them, but the impulse faded before she took more than a step in that direction. Panting, she leaned back against the counter to catch her breath and steady her nerves. The rush of adrenaline subsided, leaving her shaking and still clutching the knife, just in case the nasty little creatures wanted a rematch. Broken china crunched beneath the soles of her sensible shoes, reminding her of the wrecked crockery on the floor. All that was left of the invasion was the mess, the gashed screen door— and a bloody tip of tail resting on the counter. Mary shook her head in bewilderment.

Her husband was *not* going to believe this.

❈ *Northumberland, United Kingdom* ❈

The weekly farmers' market was just getting under way, but Percy McQueen was optimistic about the day's prospects. Shoppers were already flocking to his vegetable stand, drawn not just by his generous selection of fresh produce but by the prize pumpkin on display in front of the stand. Weighing in at nearly seven hundred kilograms, the mammoth orange pumpkin was eye-catching to say the least. Percy figured it was worth its weight in free advertising.

And then it started shaking.

Out of the blue, and for no obvious reason, the pumpkin began rocking back and forth like a Mexican jumping bean.

A little boy, who had been admiring the huge gourd up close, jumped backward in alarm, while nearby passersby and browsing shoppers reacted in surprise as well. Percy shared their confusion.

"What the blooming hell?" he blurted.

Percy glanced around the market to see if perhaps he'd somehow overlooked a sudden earthquake or underground explosion, but, no, nothing else seemed to be shaking and none of the other fruits and vegetables were acting up.

Just his pumpkin, which appeared to be having a fit of some sort.

Percy scurried out from behind his stand to investigate, even as the pumpkin's antics drew a crowd of puzzled spectators, who looked to him for an explanation, very much in vain, and peppered him with questions he couldn't begin to answer.

"Make way!" He shoved his way through the crowd to get closer to the bucking pumpkin. "Let me through!"

Muffled shouting reached his ears and he realized in shock that the cries seemed to be coming from *inside* the pumpkin. Straining his ears, he thought he could almost make out the words:

"Help! Help me, please!"

"Oh my Lord," a shopper exclaimed. "There's someone inside!"

"No," Percy whispered. "That's not possible."

By all appearances, the bumpy orange shell of the pumpkin was still intact. There was no way in or out. He had to be hearing things, along with everyone else. Or maybe there was a puckish ventriloquist at work?

A fist, covered in goop, punched its way out of the pumpkin. Frantic fingers clawed at the outside of the shell, trying to tear it open. A woman's voice clearly escaped the punctured gourd.

"Help me, someone! Get me out of here!"

Galvanized by her cries, the crowd came to her rescue. Volunteers rushed forward and started tearing apart the shell with their bare hands, tossing great chunks of the shell and pulp aside in their haste to liberate whoever was impossibly trapped inside the giant pumpkin. Percy looked on in amazement as, within a matter of minutes, his prize pumpkin was torn asunder by the crowd and a distressed young woman was pulled from its pulpy innards, almost as though the gourd had given birth to her.

"Thank you! Thank you so much!" she said. "I was kicking and screaming, but I didn't know if anyone could hear me. . . ."

Gooey pumpkin guts coated the woman, obscuring her identity. Pumpkin seeds clung to her hair and skin and clothing. An oversized university T-shirt, now slimed with mashed pumpkin, protected her modesty, while a North Country accent marked her as a local, not that Percy immediately recognized her under all the gunk. Gasping for air, she looked around in confusion.

"Where am I? How did I get here?"

She stared down at the trashed remains of her former prison.

"A pumpkin? I was inside a pumpkin?"

She sounded every bit as flabbergasted as everyone else, if not more so.

"So you were, miss," Percy volunteered. "I don't suppose you have any notion as to how you came to be in such . . . an unusual predicament?"

She shook her head.

"Not a bloody clue!"

✸ *Florida* ✸

The cherry picker was parked alongside the busy highway. Up in the bucket, high above the shoulder of the road, George Cole diligently pruned a row of palm trees insulating a suburban neighborhood from the noise and activity of the roadway. A youngish black man in his mid-twenties, he wore a hard hat and work clothes. Old-school rap came over his headphones as he bobbed his head to the beat while sawing away at a dead branch that posed a potential traffic hazard. State law required that palm trees be pruned at least twice a year. Cole appreciated the job security that provided.

Thank you, Ma Nature, he thought.

To be sure, tree trimming was just his day job, to pay his bills until his true vocation brought in serious green, which he figured was any day now. In the meantime, however, he couldn't really complain about his current gig, especially on a beautiful day like today. Sunshine, fresh air, nice weather . . .

Knock on wood.

He rapped on the nearest branch, but the precaution came too late. Without warning, and in defiance of this morning's forecast, the weather suddenly went sour. Heavy gray clouds blew in from nowhere, darkening the sky. Violent winds whipped up, rattling the bucket.

"Whoa!" he exclaimed. "Where did this come from?"

The crane was built to withstand a little wind, but the elevated bucket was already shaking like a carnival ride, making Cole grateful for the safety straps holding him securely within the bucket. Putting down his pruning saw, for safety's sake, he took off his headphones. Run-D.M.C. went away, replaced by howling winds that sounded like a hyped-up crowd roaring in a packed stadium. To his alarm, the bucket began to sway back and forth at the end of the crane's extendable metal arm.

Screw this, he thought. *We're done here.*

Leaning over the edge of the bucket, he called down to the crane operator, shouting to be heard over the sudden gale.

"Hey! Get me down from—"

Before he could finish, a sudden gust hit him with the force of a hurricane. The wind ripped him straight out of his safety harness and up into the air, dozens of feet above the pavement. A scream tore itself from his lungs, but was drowned out by the ferocious wind roaring in his ears. He grabbed frantically for a treetop, but he couldn't hold on to it. The wind was just too strong.

Oh, crap, he thought. *I'm a dead man.*

The capricious wind played with him like a cat with a mouse, batting him about way up high in the air, while cruelly allowing him too much time to think about the hard landing coming up all too soon. There was no way he could survive a fall from this height. His future was . . . *splat!*

Good-bye, Miami. You don't know who you're losing.

He waited for his life to pass before his eyes, but instead he found himself wondering who was going to show up for his funeral and what they were going to say about him. He hoped he got a good turnout at least.

The wind kept toying with him. Instead of dropping him straight onto the highway, it carried him up and over the fringe of trees toward the residential neighborhood beyond. Tumbling through the air, at least sixty, seventy feet above the ground, he glimpsed rooftops, houses, garages, driveways, lawns, backyards, slides, and swing sets. He offered a silent apology to whatever unsuspecting family he was about to drop in on. . . .

The wind went away, exiting as quickly as it had arrived. No longer held aloft by the gale, he plunged toward a grassy green yard below. Closing his eyes, he braced for the impact and hoped he wouldn't feel a thing.

What a whacked-out way to go. . . .

He hit a taut surface . . . and bounced back up in the air again.

And bounced some more.

Expecting to be splattered, it took him a few moments to process that he was still alive . . . unless the Sweet Hereafter was a lot more *energetic* than he'd expected. Opening his eyes, he was surprised to find himself coming to rest on a kid's trampoline in somebody's backyard.

"You gotta be kidding me," he muttered. "What are the odds?"

There was lucky, and there was lucky, and then there was this, which was off-the-charts miraculous. *So much for me ever winning the lottery,* he thought. *I just used up a lifetime's worth of good karma in one drop.*

But where had that crazy wind come from in the first place?

A scowl crossed his face, despite escaping certain death.

Something wasn't right here. Not one bit.

3

"That's more like it," Baird said.

The triumphant Guardian looked and felt more like herself, thanks to a quick shower and change of clothes. She strode into the cozy ground-floor office of the Library's Portland Annex, which was connected to the Library proper, as well as to the rest of the world, by various magical doorways bypassing ordinary space. Antique electric lights cast a golden glow over polished wooden bookcases sagging under the weight of countless volumes, whose esoteric subject matter defied the limits of the Dewey Decimal System. A vintage card catalog ran along one side of a sweeping staircase leading up to the mezzanine. Baird was happy to see that the rest of her team had freshened up as well.

No more togas or antlers, she noted. *Works for me.*

As she entered the office, Jenkins was performing some bizarre ablutions over the liberated idol, which now rested atop a cluttered oak conference table. A dapper, silver-haired older gentleman in a conservative gray suit, he chanted in what Baird assumed was ancient Greek while anointing the cleaned-up figure with olive oil. (Extra-virgin, she assumed.)

A parchment scroll, held down by a paperweight, was unrolled for easy consultation. Burning incense tickled Baird's nose. She worried briefly about the Annex's smoke detectors and sprinkler system.

But Jenkins seemed to know what he was doing. A brilliant silver aura flared like moonlight around the idol before swiftly fading away. A strong wind, redolent of forests and fields, wafted through the office, rustling papers and pages. Baird tensed, bracing herself for action, but the unearthly wind departed without leaving any irate swine behind. Strange, ethereal music came out of nowhere, as though from an invisible lute or lyre, then died away.

"There." Jenkins flicked the last of the oil from his fingertips. Drawing a silk handkerchief from his breast pocket, he fastidiously wiped his hands clean. "I believe we can safely pronounce the gods appeased."

"So case closed?" Baird asked. "No more 'Release the Kraken' scenarios for the time being?"

"I believe so. Rest assured, however, that I will see to it that this sacred idol of Artemis Laphria occupies a place of honor in the Library's Greco-Roman gallery. Hell hath no fury like a goddess disrespected." He sighed heavily. "Trust me, I speak from experience."

Baird could believe it. Although Jenkins appeared to be in his sixties, she was well aware that his actual age could be numbered in centuries. Even with all she knew about his past, she guessed that she had still barely scratched the surface.

"Any word from Flynn?" she asked him.

"I'm afraid not, Colonel Baird." He checked to make sure his bow tie was not askew. "But, as you well know, Mr. Carsen often charts his own course."

"Don't I know it," she said, sighing.

At one time, Flynn Carsen had been the *only* Librarian in modern times, single-handedly guarding arcane knowledge and relics that were too dangerous *not* to be stored away in the Library. So when the Library had recruited four new Librarians (and a Guardian to look after them), Flynn had struggled to adjust, often preferring to fly solo and disappear on quests of his own. It was hardly out of character, Baird reminded herself, for him to drop off the radar for days or even weeks at a time.

Still, I thought he'd gotten better about checking in with me. . . .

"Well, keep me posted if you hear from him," she instructed Jenkins, trying not to let her disappointment show. She and Flynn had become more than just Guardian and Librarian; they really had something special, or so she liked to think. *And then he pulls another vanishing act like this.*

Jenkins nodded. "You may rely on it, Colonel."

He carefully lifted the idol from the table and headed off into the deeper reaches of the Library. His footsteps had fully receded into the distance when, without warning, the Clippings Book acted up. A large hardcover tome packed with old-fashioned press clippings, such as newspapers employed back in the predigital era, the Clippings Book was the Librarians' early-alert system when it came to supernatural matters demanding their attention. It thumped atop its stand as an unseen force turned its pages.

"Uh-oh," Baird said. "No rest for the wicked."

"Who are you calling wicked?" Ezekiel quipped. He was seated at the far end of the conference table, with his sneakers up on the table. A ringtone came from his phone. "Hold on, I'm getting an alert, too."

Each of the new Librarians had been gifted with their own personal Clippings Book, smaller and more portable than the hefty, leather-bound volume kept at the Annex. Ezekiel, who had little patience with old-school, analog technology, had naturally converted his Clippings Book into an app for his phone.

"Me, too," Stone announced, sitting up straight. He fished a pocket-sized scrapbook from his back pocket. Bound pages flipped themselves.

"Me, three!" Cassandra sprang to her feet. "Or four, I guess, counting the big book."

"That's unusual," Baird said, frowning. "Are we talking four different alerts, or just an all-points bulletin?"

"Good question," Stone said. "What have we got here?"

Ezekiel peered at his phone. "Mine's about some mutant rats—"

"A miraculous escape from death," Cassandra interrupted, talking over Ezekiel.

"A giant pumpkin?" Stone said. "What the—?"

"Whoa there! Not all at once." Baird held up her hands to quiet the overlapping voices. "One at a time, please, starting with the office copy."

The original Clippings Book sat open atop the table. Approaching it, she saw that, as usual, a new clipping had appeared on a previously blank page. She read the headline aloud.

"No Happy Endings. 'Mother Goose' Theme Park Scheduled for Demolition."

A quick scan of the press clipping revealed that a long-abandoned amusement park in New Jersey, Mother Goose's Magic Garden, was soon to be bulldozed over. A black-and-white photo accompanying the article showed a dilapidated fun house in the shape of a giant shoe—as in "There was an Old Lady," presumably. Baird raised an eyebrow at the word *magic.* She used to think that real magic only existed in fairy tales.

Now she knew better.

"Your turn," she told Ezekiel.

"Local Woman Assailed by Rodents," he read from his phone, before summarizing the rest of the article. "A woman, who lives in some hick town in Ohio I've never heard of, had a run-in with some bad-tempered rats. Had to fight them off with a knife, actually. But here's the freaky part: according to her, the rats didn't have any eyes. Like they were deformed mutant rats from some pitch-black underground lair or something."

"Ugh." Cassandra shuddered. "Not a big fan of rodents, eyeless or not."

"Can't blame you there." Baird made a mental note to read Ezekiel's clipping herself at some point. She nodded at Cassandra. "What have you got, Red?"

The rat-phobic Librarian, whose interests included math, science, *and* sorcery, glanced down at her own notebook.

"Lucky Tree Trimmer Survives Unlucky Fall," she recited. "Seems a tree trimmer in Miami was blown off an elevated cherry picker by a freak gust of wind, falling more than eighty feet, but, miraculously, he landed on a kid's trampoline in a neighboring backyard and walked away unharmed." She lifted her gaze from the clipping. "Wow, what are the odds. . . ."

Her gaze turned inward, and Baird could practically see her starting to calculate *exactly* what those odds were. Cassandra's brain was like a computer, but sometimes she could get lost inside it as she got carried away by the ideas and equations flooding her mind.

"Earth to Cassandra." Baird snapped her fingers in front of

the other woman's eyes. "Stay with us here, Cassie. We're going to need your help figuring this out."

Cassandra blinked and her eyes came back into focus. "Sorry. Little distracted by the various probability factors at play in this scenario, including wind velocity, rate of downward acceleration, the surface tension and structural integrity of the trampoline, and so on. There's a lot to look at here."

Baird knew Cassandra was speaking literally. When her brain kicked into full gear, Cassie could actually *see* mathematical equations and figures swirling before her eyes in the form of visual hallucinations. A grape-sized tumor in her brain gave Cassandra something called *synesthesia*, which caused her senses to get cross-wired in unique ways. Numbers were colors, math had a smell, science rang in her ears like music . . . or so Baird understood.

"I get it," Baird said, "but let's stay focused on the big picture before you go too deep into the specifics."

Cassandra nodded. "Don't worry. You have my full attention."

"I never doubted it," Baird said. In fact, Cassandra *had* gained a lot more control over her condition since her early days as a Librarian, only a few years ago. It took a lot to make her go into meltdown mode these days. "Okay, Stone, you're up. You said something about . . . a pumpkin?"

"A *big* pumpkin, apparently." He read from his notebook: "Modern-Day Cinderella? Area Woman Wakes Up in Pumpkin." He scowled as he reviewed the article. "According to this, a college professor in England went to bed one night and awoke to find herself trapped inside a prize pumpkin at a nearby farmers' market. She managed to kick and punch her way out, with some help from other shoppers who heard her yelling for help, but . . . how does something like that even happen?"

"You can still ask that?" Baird said. "After everything we've seen on this job?"

"You got me there," Stone conceded. "But . . . rats, pumpkins, a trampoline? How does it all add up, and is it even supposed to? Are we talking one big case or four completely unrelated ones?"

"My money's on the former," Baird said, "but I'm not seeing the pattern yet. What connects all these incidents?"

"The pumpkin and rats point toward Cinderella," Cassandra observed, "but I'm not sure where my lucky tree trimmer fits in."

Baird groaned. "I thought we were done with Cinderella after that business with the fairy tales a couple years ago." Embarrassing memories of her morphing into a swooning princess type surfaced from her memory. "God, I hate reruns."

"I don't know," Cassandra said with a grin. "Being Prince Charming was kind of fun for a while."

"Easy for you to say. You weren't stuck being a damsel in distress."

Stone walked over to inspect the primary Clippings Book. "Forget Cinderella," he said. "I think that's a red herring. I'm guessing that this clipping is the key to the puzzle since it was directed at all of us." He pondered the newspaper article newly pasted into the book. "Mother Goose's Magic Garden." He scratched his chin thoughtfully. "Mother Goose . . ."

"Right!" Baird sensed they were on the right track; it was the same gut feeling she used to get when she was closing in on a terrorist base or black-market WMDs. "Mother Goose, not the Brothers Grimm. Nursery rhymes, not fairy tales."

"The eyeless rodents!" Stone exclaimed. "The Three Blind Mice."

"Good! Now we're getting somewhere." Baird seized on the

electricity of the moment, urging her Librarians on. "And the woman in the pumpkin?"

"Peter, Peter, pumpkin eater," Ezekiel chimed in. "Had a wife but couldn't keep her. Put her in a pumpkin shell . . . yada, yada, yada."

"Nice!" Baird was impressed and a little surprised; Ezekiel was great at computers and heists, but was hardly the most literary of Librarians. "Good work, Jones."

"No problem." He shrugged and leaned back in his chair. "What kid didn't learn those rhymes growing up?"

Baird turned toward Cassandra. "What about your skydiving tree trimmer? Any ideas?"

"Give me a minute." Cassandra closed her eyes, the better to leaf through her photographic memory. Her hands traced odd patterns in the air, as though she was sorting through hallucinatory files only she could see, while using her amazing brain as her own personal search engine. "Heights, falling, gravity, trees, wind . . ." Her eyes snapped open. "I've got it! Rock-a-bye baby, in the treetop, when the wind blows—"

Baird saw where she was going and rushed ahead to the end of the rhyme. "The cradle will fall, and down will come baby, cradle and all!"

"Bingo!" Stone said. "That's three out of three. This is definitely a Mother Goose thing!"

"Mother Goose?" Jenkins reentered the office. His sober expression grew even more so. "Please tell me we don't have a Mother Goose situation on our hands."

There was no trace of humor or irony in his voice. If anything, he sounded genuinely dismayed.

That can't be good, Baird thought. "Mother Goose situation?"

"The details, please," Jenkins said urgently, "with all deliberate speed."

Baird quickly briefed him on the clippings and their own ingenious deductions. "I take it we should be concerned?"

"Alarmed would be the better word. Terrified works also." Jenkins remained standing, but looked as though he needed to sit down. "From what you're telling me, I can only conclude that the Mother Goose Treaty has indeed been broken."

His dire tone made it clear that this was no laughing matter.

"The what again?" Baird asked. "Maybe you should start at the beginning, especially for those of us who haven't thought much about Mother Goose since kindergarten."

"That is probably for the best." Jenkins assumed a place at the head of the table; the role of lecturer came naturally to him. "Please pay close attention. I fear there is no time for you to repeat this class."

Cassandra sat back down at the table, settling in for Jenkins's trademark exposition. Despite his ominous attitude, her eyes were agleam with excitement. "So Mother Goose is a real person, too? Like Santa Claus?"

"Not quite," Jenkins said. "Mother Goose is a not a person, but rather a title and a position: denoting a custodian of ancient wisdom, passed down from generation to generation as seemingly harmless nonsense rhymes. In the right hands, however, they are actually powerful charms and incantations with the ability to shape and alter reality as we know it."

Baird tried to wrap her head around that. "And we've just been casually teaching them to kids since forever?"

"The rhymes were never meant to be written down," Jenkins said, "let alone published. They were only to be transmitted as an oral tradition, but back in 1719, the son-in-law

of that generation's Mother Goose, one Elizabeth Goose of
Boston, Massachusetts, foolishly printed a collection of the
rhymes as a children's book, inadvertently creating a spell
book of frightening power."

"Only 1719?" Baird asked. "I would've thought that the
Mother Goose rhymes were much older than that."

"Oh, many of the rhymes, in their original forms, date back
to antiquity, but the first bound collection was in fact published as *Songs for the Nursery, or Mother Goose's Melodies* a
mere three centuries ago. And even today, tourists in Boston
flock to what's claimed to be the grave of the 'real' Mother
Goose, blithely unaware that she was actually only one in a
long line of Mother Gooses, carrying on an ancient tradition."

"Just like us Librarians," Ezekiel said, "but with a much
goofier name."

"Not an entirely inapt comparison, Mr. Jones, although I
venture to think that the Library has a much broader purview,
as well as a somewhat loftier mission."

"Whatever you say, mate." Ezekiel didn't exactly do lofty.
"So what came first, the Library or the Goose?"

"That is a matter of some dispute . . . and hardly germane
to our present situation. The events leading up to the Mother
Goose Treaty truly began in 1719 with the publication of that
first unsanctioned volume, which put all the power of the
rhymes into print for the first time in recorded history."

"Hold on," Stone interrupted. "This is coming back to me
now, from some research I did a few years ago on the subject
of early-eighteenth-century book illustration. If I remember
right, no known copies of that first Mother Goose collection
are known to exist, and there's even some scholarly debate as
to whether the book ever truly existed at all."

"Quite right, Mr. Stone." Jenkins sounded like a professor

doling out a modicum of praise to one of his less ignorant students. "Indeed, the original 1719 printing of *Mother Goose's Melodies* has been described as the most elusive 'ghost volume' in American letters. Many have sought it, but it exists today only as a puzzling bibliographical mystery . . . or so it is commonly believed."

"But it did exist?" Cassandra asked. "For real?"

"It did, but the Librarian of that era managed to round up and dispose of every copy of the book, except for a single copy, which remained in the possession of Elizabeth Goose and her family, as a professional courtesy as it were. And so the crisis was contained . . . for a time."

"Let me guess," Baird said. "One copy of the book was still one too many?"

"More like it wasn't enough for all of Elizabeth's descendants. Elizabeth Goose ultimately had six children, ten stepchildren, and innumerable grandchildren, and, over time, a dynastic struggle broke out between three rival branches of the family, with each claiming the title of 'Mother Goose' and the spell book as their inheritance. Matters turned ugly. Family turned against family, spells were invoked, livestock went missing, bathtubs were washed out to sea. . . ."

Come again? Baird thought.

"Thankfully, for the sake of humanity, all-out magical warfare was averted by the Mother Goose Treaty of 1918, which was negotiated by yet another Librarian. Said treaty called for the book to be split into three parts between the factions, with each branch of the family charged with guarding their portion and keeping it safe."

"Why three?" Cassandra asked.

"It's *always* three," Jenkins said archly, as though that went without saying. "Except when it's seven."

Baird took his word for it. She was getting used to Library logic.

"I don't understand," she said. "Why didn't that Librarian just take possession of the book and bring it back to the Library for safekeeping? Isn't that standard operating procedure?"

"Ideally, yes," Jenkins admitted, "but it was a tricky, highly volatile situation and this was judged an acceptable compromise at the time, and all the more so given that the Librarian of 1918 already had her hands full dealing with Rasputin."

"Wait a second," Stone said. "Didn't Rasputin die in 1916?"

Jenkins snorted. "That's what history wants you to believe. . . ."

Baird decided to let that one pass for now, but she understood how an overworked Librarian might need to concentrate on an ongoing threat or adversary. A Dulaque, say, or a Prospero.

"You mentioned the Mother Goose Treaty once before," Cassandra recalled. "You said something about Beatrix Potter not getting it right?"

"Forget Beatrix Potter," Jenkins said. "You might as well consult the Disney cartoon for the truth about *The Little Mermaid*. We're not dealing with cute little cottontail rabbits here. We're talking about spells and incantations of potentially game-changing scope and potency. If someone is truly violating the Treaty, after all these years, these seemingly trivial incidents could be merely the harbingers of a much greater catastrophe."

"Really?" Ezekiel asked skeptically. "It's Mother Goose. How bad could it be?"

"Need I remind you just how violent and perverse many of those 'childish' nursery rhymes are? They're positively rife with falls, accidents, drownings, amputations, decapitations, hangings, beatings, fires, theft, murder, grave robbing, and every sort of calamity imaginable, short of a meteor hitting the Earth. There's more cracked skulls and severed limbs in Mother Goose than you'll find in an entire season of cable television." Jenkins paused to let his words sink in. "Granted, as with fairy tales, many of the darker verses have been sanitized over the years, but the potential for harm still remains buried within the rhymes, just waiting to be unleashed. Don't take this matter lightly," he warned, "unless you want your tails cut off with a carving knife."

Ouch, Baird thought. "Point taken."

4

The family tree grew before Cassandra's eyes, shimmering in the air above her desk. Luminous branches, diverging in all directions, rose up and outward from the tree's roots in colonial New England, tracing the ancestral lines of Elizabeth Goose and her myriad offspring. Cassandra could hear the branches rustling and swaying over the course of three centuries; it was like music in her ears that only she was privy to. The smell of plums and pumpkins and freshly baked pies made her mouth water, even though no such foodstuffs were actually in the vicinity. Phantom feathers tickled her skin, giving her, well, goose bumps.

"Any progress?" Baird asked, looking over Cassandra's shoulder. Her voice intruded on Cassandra's attempt to track down Elizabeth Goose's far-flung descendants. "Job one is locating those three scattered pieces of *Mother Goose's Melodies* to see which one might have fallen into the wrong hands."

"I know, I know," Cassandra said a bit sharply. "Just let me concentrate. I've got three hundred years of genealogy to map, and don't get me started on the stepkids and their kids and their kids' kids' kids. . . ."

Dog-eared birth registries and census reports were piled atop the desk, while multiple windows were open on the screen of her laptop. Virtual marriage licenses and baptism records shared the screen with popular Web sites designed for tracing one's ancestry. Names and dates poured into Cassandra's brain from multiple sources, nourishing the hallucinatory family tree unfolding before her. She reached out to prune one branch that had come to a dead end during the late 1950s. Using her fingers as scissors, she snipped it off.

"Sorry." Baird backed off. "Just do your thing. I know you've got this."

Cassandra appreciated the vote of confidence. She did her best to tune out any outside distractions in order to fully immerse herself in the task at hand. The other Librarians were conducting their own research in and around the office, while Jenkins had excused himself to check on various nursery-rhyme-related papers and relics. Her gaze ascended from the base of the family tree to its upper reaches, which had proliferated at a geometric rate over the generations. Malthusian calculations danced around her head, pealing like church bells, as a slow-motion population explosion scattered Mother Goose's descendants hither and yon. Time and circumstances had cropped off a few tree limbs, making her task a little easier, but that still left plenty more branches to account for. Her mind reeling, Cassandra found herself sympathizing with a certain old woman who lived in a shoe; there were just so many children she didn't know what to do.

Did Mother Goose have to take her title quite so literally?

"Wanna bet I get there first?" Ezekiel asked. Lounging in an easy chair on the other side of the office, he swiped through various apps and Web sites on his phone. "My hacking against Cassandra's superbrain?"

"You're on." Stone leafed through an illustrated collection of Mother Goose rhymes from the nineteenth century as he

sat at the conference table. "Loser has to clean up after the
goats on Level Four."

"I'll get in on that action," Baird said, joining them. "No
offense, Jones, but this job is right in Cassandra's wheelhouse.
Tracing patterns and seeing connections is what she does
best."

"Maybe. Probably," Ezekiel said breezily, as though his ego
wasn't too invested in the wager. "Just trying to keep things
interesting, you know?"

Boredom was Ezekiel's archenemy, which he often claimed
was his only reason for accepting the Library's job offer in the
first place.

Cassandra wasn't sure she entirely believed that. Despite
the attitude he strove to project, Ezekiel always came through
when they needed him most. Still, if he *really* thought he could
beat her at unraveling Mother Goose's convoluted family tree,
he was fooling himself in a big way. Shaking off her earlier
fatigue, Cassandra dove back into the challenge with renewed
determination. Her slender hands made rapid passes in the
air, picking up the pace.

Game on, Jones.

Cassandra felt like a professional tree trimmer as she mer-
cilessly snipped away at dead branches while trying to shape
the sprawling family tree into something manageable. Identi-
fying all of Elizabeth Goose's disparate descendants was only
half the battle; the really tricky part was finding some kind
of worthwhile leads in the ever-expanding family tree. By
Cassandra's calculations, Mother Goose's family had multiplied
by several orders of magnitude since the 1700s; they could
be looking at thousands of potential suspects, assuming
there even were specific individuals at fault in this case. Just
trying to narrow the names down to a workable list amounted

to pruning an immense family tree down to a few particular branches. She was half-tempted to ask that unusually lucky tree trimmer in Miami for some tips. . . .

Hang on, she thought. *What was that guy's name again?*

Inspiration rang like cymbals in her head. Playing a hunch, she consulted her personal Clippings Book, then glanced back at the topmost branches of the Goose family tree. A single name suddenly stood out among the others, glowing incandescently now that she knew what to look for.

"George Cole," she whispered. "Got you!"

Her excitement did not escape Baird's attention. "What is it, Red? Have you got something?"

"I think so." Cassandra called out to the other Librarians. "Quick, what are the names of the individuals in your clippings?"

Ezekiel answered first, bringing it up on his phone. "Mary Simon, of Who Cares, Ohio."

Cassandra scanned the top of the family tree. Another name brightened before her gaze. Her goose bumps got bumpier.

"Found her!" She glanced urgently at Stone. "Next?"

He flipped to the end of his pocket-sized scrapbook. "Dr. Gillian Fell of Northumberland, England." He paused and scratched his head. "Hold on. Where do I know that name from?"

"It's right here!" Cassandra pointed excitedly at an illuminated name, forgetting for a moment that nobody else could see it. "It all fits. Every one of the 'victims' in the clippings is a direct descendant of Mother Goose!"

"And a possible heir to the title?" Baird theorized. "Maybe someone is trying to take out the competition?"

"Or perhaps hostilities have already broken out between

the various factions?" Stone said. "The Mother Goose Wars heating up again?"

"Also a possibility," Baird conceded. "In any event, great work, Cassandra. I knew we could count on you."

"Thanks." Cassandra powered down. With a sweep of her hand, she collapsed the illusory family tree to give her eyes (and her brain) a rest. Her wayward senses stabilized, falling back into their usual boxes. The ordinary sounds and smells of the Library replaced any more exotic perceptions. "Sorry I didn't see the connections more quickly."

"No need to apologize, Cassie. You did good." Stone smirked at Ezekiel. "You lose, pal. Get ready to pay up."

Ezekiel sighed and put away his phone. "I was almost there, really, but . . . whatever. Way to go, Cassandra." He flashed a disarming smile at her. "Just wait until next time."

"Oh, I will." She grinned back at him. "Bring it."

"So now what?" Stone asked. "Do we split up to investigate all of these incidents?"

"That appears to be what the Library has in mind." Baird laid out their battle plan. "Each of you check out your respective clippings. I'll take that defunct Mother Goose amusement park, while Jenkins mans the home front as usual. We can compare notes once we've got some firsthand intel to share."

Cassandra closed her books and stepped away from the computer. "Looks like I'm heading to Miami then." She generally preferred it when the team stayed together, but it made sense to split up this time. "Too bad Flynn isn't around to help out on this case."

"Tell me about it," Baird said.

5

Once upon a time, Mother Goose's Magic Garden had delighted generations of children and their parents with its shady, sylvan setting and charming, life-sized re-creations of classic nursery rhymes. Researching the bygone park on the Internet, Baird had turned up assorted postcards and family photos of the Garden in its heyday, when the attractions were freshly painted and the paths and gardens scrupulously maintained, and beaming visitors had been able to wander the winding wooded trails past life-sized fiberglass facsimiles of Little Bo Peep, Wee Willie Winkie, the Man in the Moon, and company. Wooden cottages, picket fences, and brightly blooming flower beds added to the colorful tableaux on display.

Times had changed, however.

Dipping attendance, bankruptcy, abandonment, vandalism, and decay had taken its toll on the once-thriving park, which had officially closed its doors over a decade before. Weeds clotted the overgrown paths and gardens. Peeling paint exposed rusty metal and rotting wood. Graffiti defaced crumbling snack bars and picnic tables. Simple Simon's head rested at the foot of his decapitated body. A spray painted "anarchy"

symbol tagged Little Miss Muffet's tuffet. Broken window
shutters had fallen off the House That Jack Built. Old Mother
Hubbard's paint job had been stripped as bare as her cup-
board. Creeping moss had turned Little Boy Blue green. The
Three Little Kittens had lost their footing as well as their
mittens, having toppled over into the underbrush. Pond scum
coated the stagnant pool surrounding the Three Wise Men
of Gotham who had gone to sea in a bowl. Autumn leaves littered the ground, leaving the trees bare and skeletal. Here and
there a bright spot of color had survived time and the elements, hinting at the park's once-festive appearance, but the
contrast only made the general dilapidation more glaring. An
overcast sky added to the melancholy atmosphere. A John
Deere bulldozer was parked by the wreckage, awaiting the demolition crew.

"Nope," Baird muttered. "This isn't creepy at all."

The Annex's Magic Door had allowed her to bypass the
chain-link fence enclosing the condemned park. She had
merely stepped through the doorway and, accompanied by
a flash of white light and the crackle of eldritch energy, emerged
from the front door of a gargantuan wooden shoe. Crossing
from Portland to New Jersey meant that it was now past noon,
local time, making a long night feel even longer. Faded "No
Trespassing" signs, posted on tree trunks and a few surviving
fence posts, had not deterred her from exploring the forlorn
remains of the park. Broken bottles and empty beer cans suggested that the deserted locale had inevitably attracted its
fair share of partying teenagers over the years, but as far as
she could tell she currently had the ruins to herself. She kept
her guard up, however, since it never hurt to keep sharp while
on a mission. Her surroundings looked safe enough, if a trifle
depressing, but the Clippings Book had alerted the Librari-

ans to this site for a reason, so there was bound to be something amiss.

Best not to take chances, she thought. *Magic can be a minefield.*

After taking a few moments to get her bearings, she got down to business and unclipped a device hooked to her belt: a handheld scanner designed to detect magical energy or its residue. The device resembled a steampunk egg beater with four gleaming steel spheres at the end of its probes. Cassandra, who was forever tinkering with the detector to improve its accuracy and reliability, had tried to explain to Baird how exactly the device worked, but most of it had flown over Baird's head. Dirty bombs and tactical maneuvers Baird understood; "etheric subfrequencies" and "transcendental ectoplasmic connectivity" had not been part of her NATO training.

Just as long as it works in the field, she thought.

She flipped the On switch and the detector powered up. An analog gauge registered a higher than usual level of background magical radiation. As Baird understood it, there was more "wild magic" at loose in the world than there had been a few years ago, thanks to the sinister machinations of a certain Serpent Brotherhood, but she thought the devices had been recalibrated to compensate for that. She reset the counter to zero, just to be sure, but got the same readings again. Mother Goose's Magic Garden was living up to its name.

She made a mental note to check to see if the park was at a juncture of mystical ley lines when she got back to the Library, where there was a globe charting the placement of the various natural magical "jet streams." In the meantime, she used the scanner like a Geiger counter to try to locate where the ambient magic was strongest. Higher readings to the east led her down an overgrown path heading deeper into the park.

It was not an easy trek. Nature was busily reclaiming the
path, which barely qualified as such anymore, forcing her to
duck beneath overhanging tree branches and stomp through
thick underbrush at times, so that Baird found herself wishing that she had brought hiking boots—and a machete. Random debris, strewn about the park, further obstructed the
way. A quaint wooden cottage, formerly belonging to Jack
Sprat and his wife, had collapsed into a heap of rotting timbers and rusty nails. Broken lengths of rebar jutted from the
debris. Discarded garden tools—spades, hoes, and rakes—
waited to trip the unwary. Baird stepped carefully, leery of
potential pitfalls buried in the bushes. She found herself trying to remember the last time she'd had a tetanus shot. . . .

The detector's probes whirred, spinning ever faster, as
climbing readings led her past more evidence of the park's deterioration. The Dish and the Spoon, once posed in the act of
running away with each other, now lay on opposite sides of
the path, half-buried beneath weeds and fallen leaves. Little
Jack Horner's corner had apparently burned to the ground;
Baird suspected smoking trespassers or an unauthorized
campfire were to blame. All that remained was a charred door
frame where a blackened wooden door was barely hanging
on by its hinges. Jack and Jill's well had tumbled down its hill,
becoming nothing more than a pile of rubble at the bottom
of a grassy slope that looked as though it hadn't been mown
since MySpace was hot.

The needle on the gauge edged toward the yellow zone,
raising her concern. If the detector had been registering actual
radiation, instead of the magical variety, she'd expect to be
entering Chernobyl by now. Instead, she rounded a blind
corner, pushing past a curtain of hanging branches, to discover . . . Humpty Dumpty.

As one might expect, he lay shattered at the bottom of a moldy brick wall. His head, which consisted of a large fiberglass egg with a friendly, smiling face painted on it, had cracked down the middle and was now in two pieces, with one eye and half a smile on each fragment. Both halves had also broken off from the rest of his body, which remained sitting atop the wall. One hand was still raised to greet approaching visitors.

Three pieces, Baird thought to herself with a grunt. *It's always three, Jenkins said.*

At first, she wasn't sure if Humpty was supposed to be lying in pieces or not, but then she remembered an old postcard that had shown the figure sitting happily intact on his wall, sometime prior to his celebrated fall. *Makes sense*, Baird thought. You wouldn't want to upset small children by showing a Humpty *after* his spill. She wondered if the damage to the mannequin had been caused by time and neglect, or if some visiting vandal had possessed a poetic sense of mischief.

"All the king's horses and all the king's men," she recited, "couldn't put Humpty together again."

There was no evidence of men or horses, sculpted or otherwise, but the excess magical energy registered as stronger here than anywhere else. Baird slowly circled the shattered egg man, scanning it with the detector. The probes whirred at an alarming rate; the needle swung much farther to the right. The readings she got from Humpty were practically off the charts; he was all but glowing with magic.

Ground zero?

She backed away from Humpty, reluctant to touch him or even get too close. That she had located the heart of the mystery at Mother Goose's Garden she had no doubt; what exactly her discovery meant was anybody's guess. She could only hope that Jenkins or her Librarians could make sense of it. Once again, she wished that Flynn was available. Unlike the new Librarians, each of whom had their own individual specialties, Flynn was more of an all-around genius, who often seemed to know a little bit about everything.

Including magical nursery rhymes?

Putting away the detector, she took out her phone to take some photos of the site that she could share with the others. She stepped backward to get a better shot.

Something crunched beneath her feet.

"Crap," she muttered. Visions of broken glass and rusty metal hinges flashed through her brain. Stooping to investigate, she warily groped through the weeds to see what she had stepped on. Bits of shiny black plastic and metallic silver glinted in the weak sunlight. It took her a moment to identify the object. A gasp escaped her lips. Blue eyes widened in surprise.

It was another handheld magic detector, similar to the one she had just employed.

"What the heck?"

Her first thought was that maybe this was evidence of some weird time-travel shenanigans, and that she was actually retracing the path of her future self who had visited the park sometime in the recent past. It certainly wouldn't be the first time she had stumbled onto a paradox along those lines. But then a simpler explanation presented itself: another Librarian had already checked out this site and left their scanner behind.

Flynn?

Worry creased her brow. Why would Flynn have come here on his own, and, even more distressing to consider, why had he left his scanner behind? That was top-secret Library tech that was probably semimagical itself. Flynn could be manic sometimes, his restless mind taking off in all directions, but he wasn't careless. He wouldn't have left without the device.

Unless he was rudely interrupted?

"Oh, Flynn, what have you gotten into now?"

Glancing around the site, she saw no obvious signs of a struggle, only Humpty Dumpy lying broken on the ground, but that didn't mean that Flynn hadn't run into trouble. Risk came with the job, as recently demonstrated by a certain mythological boar, and the Librarians often found themselves contending with ruthless secret societies, rival treasure seekers, and miscellaneous archenemies, any of which might have carried away Flynn against his will. Concerned for his safety, she reminded herself that Flynn had survived on his own as a Librarian for over a decade, which was longer than any other Librarian on the books. He could take care of himself.

Which didn't make her any less anxious about him.

"Flynn?" she called out, raising her voice. "Flynn? It's me, Eve. Are you still here?"

Her voice echoed through the desolate park, but received no answer.

"Flynn! Can you hear me? Answer me, Flynn!"

It was no use. There was no immediate way of knowing how long the magic detector had been resting in the weeds, but her gut told her that Flynn was long gone. Frustrated, she tried calling him on her phone, but his voice mail was full, as usual. She cursed under her breath as she put her phone back in her pocket. Flynn's incommunicado status had gone from annoying to alarming.

She took a closer look at the discarded detector. An embossed plastic label, of the sort made by an old-fashioned label maker, was stuck to the bottom of the device. It read:

PROPERTY OF FLYNN CARSEN. HANDS OFF.

Baird sighed. *Still working on that "team player" thing. . . .*

The label cinched it, though. Flynn had been here and now he was missing.

She decided that she had seen enough. It was time to head back to the Library and let the rest of the team know what she'd discovered. With any luck, maybe one of the other Librarians had already crossed paths with Flynn while investigating the other incidents. Taking custody of the forgotten scanner, she started back toward the Old Woman's giant shoe and took her phone back out to dial Jenkins so he could reopen a doorway back to the Annex.

"You get on your way, young lady!" a stern voice accosted her. "Can't you read the signs? No trespassing!"

Baird spun around to see someone who could only be Mother Goose herself standing atop an oversized fiberglass pumpkin that had once housed a well-known pumpkin eater and his wayward wife. The indignant crone looked as though she had just stepped out of the pages of a storybook. A conical black hat, held on a by ribbon, gave her a distinctly witchy appearance. Tight gray braids peeked out from beneath the brim of the hat, while a pair of antique spectacles rested upon her sharp, pointed nose. She wore a green peasant dress with a ruffled collar and sleeves above a pair of striped stockings and buckled black shoes. A red woolen shawl was draped over her bony shoulders. Her wizened face was craggy, her expression severe.

Startled by the figure's sudden appearance, Baird nonetheless kept her cool. She'd encountered stranger beings since signing on with the Library.

"Mother Goose, I presume?"

Or at least a *Mother Goose,* she thought.

"The one and only," the crone insisted. A pronounced Boston accent bordered on parody. "No mere pretender am I."

"I didn't say you were," Baird said diplomatically. She cautiously approached the older woman, while wondering precisely who or what she was facing. A Fictional like Moriarty, freshly sprung from the actual pages of a book, or one of Elizabeth Goose's descendants, claiming the ancestral title and identity of Mother Goose? Baird couldn't rule out either possibility.

"That's close enough," the woman atop the pumpkin said. She shook a crooked wooden cane at Baird. "Keep your distance, Guardian. This is no affair of yours, my fine beauty!"

Baird was caught off guard by being addressed by her title. She paused in her tracks. "You know who I am?"

"Aye, Colonel Eve Baird, and I know your ways. You'll not file me away in your Library, no matter how grand it may be. I have important matters to attend to and I'll brook no interference. You'd be well-advised not to meddle in my business."

Sorry, Baird thought. *Meddling is a big part of my job description.*

"Can't we just talk?" Baird raised her hands to indicate that she was unarmed. "I only want to ask you some questions."

Mother Goose snorted at the idea.

"I keep my own counsel and do not answer to the likes of you." She pointed with her cane. "Be on your way, Guardian, and trespass in my Garden no more."

"Forget it," Baird said, losing her patience. She could play Bad Cop too if she had to. "I'm not going anywhere until I get some answers." She strode toward the immense pumpkin, prepared to scale its faded orange walls as readily as she would a concrete barricade in a war zone. "Where is Flynn Carsen? What's become of him?"

Mother Goose smirked, as though at a private joke. "Wouldn't you like to know?"

"I would, actually, now that you mention it." An automatic pistol was tucked beneath Baird's jacket, but she held off on drawing it just yet; pulling a gun on Mother Goose just felt *wrong* somehow. "Are you going to get down from there or I do have to climb up and get you?"

Baird reminded herself not get overconfident. Under ordinary circumstances, she could take a gray-haired old lady, no problem, but these circumstances were about as far from ordinary as a cow jumping over the moon. And when it came to magic, appearances could be *very* deceiving.

"Don't trouble yourself, dearie," Mother Goose advised, not seeming at all concerned about the increasingly impatient Guardian. "I won't be staying long."

Before Baird could ask her what she meant, the crone cupped one hand in front of her mouth, miming a megaphone, and honked as loud as her feathered namesake. Baird fought an urge to clap her own hands over her ears.

"Not exactly what I wanted to hear!" she shouted back.

"I wasn't talking to you, Guardian."

An answering honk came from somewhere overhead. Looking up, Baird gaped at the sight of a gigantic goose—or gander—swooping down from the murky gray sky. The bird's wingspan was at least twelve feet across, making it only slightly smaller than that Native American thunderbird she and Flynn had just barely escaped in the Cascade Mountains last summer. Its snowy white plumage contrasted with its large orange beak—and the long red ribbon dangling from said beak. The wind from the goose's great wings stirred the tree branches as well as the fallen leaves carpeting the ground. Its honk put an air horn to shame.

"Okay, I didn't see that coming." Baird shook her head in disbelief. "I probably should have, considering, but . . ."

Mother Goose cackled in glee.

"Forgotten your nursery rhymes have you, Colonel?" The huge bird alit atop the phony pumpkin, landing next to Mother Goose, who climbed onto its back as though it was a pony and not the biggest goose ever. Her raspy voice took on a singsong quality as she recited: "Old Mother Goose, when she wanted to wander, would ride through the air on a very fine gander!"

Gander, not goose, then, Baird noted, although the bird's gender was not particularly pertinent at the moment. No way was she going to let Mother Goose fly out of here, not while Flynn was missing and unaccounted for.

"Don't even think about it." Baird drew her gun and took aim at the other woman. "Stay right where you are—and that goes for the bird, too."

"Really, Guardian?" Mother Goose clucked at her. "You're going to open fire on a harmless old lady who hasn't done you any harm . . . yet?"

"Harmless my foot," Baird replied, while balking at the idea of actually pulling the trigger. Despite Jenkins's warnings about the danger posed by a rogue Mother Goose, and the mystery surrounding Flynn's disappearance, she knew the old woman had her number. She couldn't bring herself to shoot Mother Goose purely on suspicion of . . . what? Trespassing in a condemned theme park? Impersonating a storybook character? Illegal possession and abuse of nursery rhymes? Having a giant goose—that is, *gander—* on call?

Damn it, she thought. "Don't test me, Goose . . . or whoever you are."

"I don't need to test you, Eve Baird. I know you too well. You're a soldier girl, not a murderer."

Calling Baird's bluff, Mother Goose took both ends of the red ribbon in her hands and pulled on them as though they were reins. Extending its wings, the gargantuan gander took to the skies. Baird realized that she could try to wing the bird at least, but she hesitated too long. She couldn't risk shooting the gander without causing the old woman to fall from too high up.

"Come back here!" Baird hollered. "What have you done with Flynn?"

"Go back to your Library, Eve Baird, and leave me and mine alone!"

Baird watched in frustration as Goose and gander ascended into the clouds, taking any answers with them. Lacking a flying carpet or air support, there was no way to go after them for now. Baird found herself alone in the deserted park, hoping that Jenkins could shed some light on what had just transpired.

'Cause, frankly, she was stumped.

6

"Humpty Dumpty?" Jenkins said gravely. "Oh dear."

Returning to the Annex via the Magic Door, Baird had briefed Jenkins on what she had discovered—and encountered—
at Mother Goose's Magic Garden. To her surprise, he appeared
even more concerned about the wrecked Humpty mannequin
than Mother Goose's actual appearance and escape.

"Is that bad?" she asked.

"More than you can possibly imagine, Colonel." Jenkins extracted a massive leather-bound tome from a bookshelf and
laid it down on the conference table in front of Baird. It appeared to be a general guide to the mythologies of the world as
opposed to a collection of nursery rhymes. " 'Humpty Dumpty'
is actually one of the oldest and most powerful rhymes in
the book . . . and there's a very good reason why Humpty
Dumpty must *never* be put together again."

Baird braced herself for the worst. "Hit me."

"Humpty Dumpty, or 'Humelken-Pumpelken' as he's
known in Germany, or 'Thille Lille' in Sweden, or many
other names in many other lands, is more than just a childish

storybook character. He is a symbolic representation of the original World Egg, from which all of Creation was hatched according to numerous ancient myths and Gnostic traditions." He opened the book and turned the pages until he reached a woodcut illustration of a cosmic egg cracking open to disgorge stars, planets, and swirling nebulae. Leafing through the book revealed similar imagery on pottery shards, temple mosaics, mystic scrolls, and alchemical texts. He paused on a photo of weathered stone hieroglyphics. A pictographic nest cradled a stylized, two-dimensional egg inscribed with mystical runes. "Interestingly enough, in the ancient Egyptian version of the myth, the Egg is said to have been laid by a divine Goose. . . ."

"Where did the goose come from?" Baird asked.

"That's another story," he said, a trifle evasively. "The relevant point is that restoring the Egg—in other words, putting Humpty Dumpty back together again—would essentially reverse the Big Bang . . . and might eventually lead to the birth of a brand-new universe, overwriting the one we know."

He closed the book for emphasis. Loudly.

"But the Humpty at the park is just a broken fiberglass mannequin," she protested, before remembering the excess magical energy it was apparently charged with, according to the detector. "Isn't it?"

"At one time, probably, but magic is all about symbolism. You should know that by now," he chided her. "Power, focus, effect. Let us assume that Mother Goose is providing the power, Humpty Dumpty is the focus, and the effect. . . . Well, fourteen billion years isn't a bad run for a universe, but I wasn't expecting a reboot quite so soon."

Baird tried to grasp the enormity of what Jenkins was implying. The fate of the world was one thing—she was getting used to that—but the entire universe? Because Mother Goose might want to put Humpty Dumpty back together again?

That was bizarre even by Library standards, which was saying something.

She held on to her sanity by getting down to brass tacks. "But that hasn't happened yet? We can still stop it?"

"I sincerely hope so," Jenkins said. "The fact that the universe does not, as yet, appear to be collapsing in on itself suggests that the individual you encountered, who claims to be Mother Goose, has yet to fully realize her aims. My current working theory—or best guess, if you prefer—is that she may need to reassemble the *entire* spell book to perform magic of such magnitude. Furthermore, legend holds that the original text contains lost verses of 'Humpty Dumpty' that may indeed hold the power to unmake reality on a cosmic scale."

"In other words," Baird translated, "we need to find those three fragments of the original book before Mother Goose does."

"If she has not already obtained one or more of them," Jenkins added, always the pessimist. "That ill-advised publication was divided in three for good reason, Colonel. Reassembling the book is a bad idea in general, even without a rogue Mother Goose on the loose."

He winced at the accidental rhyme.

"Understood," Baird said. "But why is this happening now, after all these years?"

"If I may venture a guess, the recent outbreak of wild magic, which has roused many previously dormant magical artifacts and spells, unleashing them anew upon the world, might well be the catalyst here."

Baird nodded. "Like when Prospero got his wizardly mojo back, after being powerless for centuries."

"Precisely," Jenkins said. "And one more thing, Colonel. Magic, once awakened, often *wants* to express itself, so the magic of Mother Goose, long hidden away and suppressed, may itself be at work here. The fractured spell book may long to be complete again . . . and is striving to accomplish that end via the individual you encountered at the park."

"Yeah, what about her?" Baird asked. "Where does she fit in to this theory? Is she a pawn, an instigator, or what? She can't actually be *the* Elizabeth Goose, can she?"

"Not a chance," Jenkins said. "That particular Mother Goose was a respectable Boston matriarch, not the cackling caricature you described. We're dealing with someone who has adopted the *persona* of Mother Goose for their own highly imprudent purposes."

"And we have no idea who that person might be?"

"Not as yet, Colonel."

Great, Baird thought.

"Any word from the others yet? Or Flynn?"

"I'm afraid not, Colonel. You were the first to return from your investigation. And Mr. Carsen remains unaccounted for, aside from your discovery at the park."

Flynn's discarded magic detector rested on Baird's desk, reminding her that he was still MIA. Had Mother Goose done something to him, or had he ingeniously escaped her clutches somehow? Flynn was a survivor, despite his many eccentricities. Baird refused to assume the worst until she knew for certain what had become of him.

Baird hoped her Librarians were faring better than she had. She wondered what they were up to now.

And what had become of Flynn?

7

"Sorry. My wife's not here," the farmer said. "She's at work."

This was not what Ezekiel Jones wanted to hear. It was unfair enough that he, an international man of mystery and master thief, had gotten stuck taking the Magic Door to some bucolic backwater in the middle of nowhere, but now the person he was looking for wasn't even home? If he didn't know better, he'd think that the Clippings Book had it in for him.

Mary Simon was the Goose descendant who had allegedly run into some hostile blind mice. Ezekiel had hoped to do some digging on that incident and get back to the Library in no time at all. Standing on the front porch of a predictably picturesque Ohio farmhouse, whose address he had gleaned from the Internet, he found himself tragically out of his element. Chickens clucked and pecked in a coop nearby. Barnyard smells wafted on the breeze. A silo was the closest thing to a skyscraper. A dozy hound dog was stretched out on the porch, drooling. There probably wasn't anything worth stealing in the entire county.

"And where is work?" he asked.

"The library, of course."

"Library?" Ezekiel wasn't sure he'd heard that right.

"Naturally. She's the children's librarian, isn't she?"

Of course she is, he thought, amused. Fate definitely seemed to be messing with him today. "That wasn't in the news clipping."

Farmer Simon stood in the doorway, looking Ezekiel over. "Who did you say you were with again?"

"Animal Control," he lied easily. "Looking into reports of a recent mutant rodent sighting."

"Don't know anything about that myself," the farmer admitted. "I was away at the Grange when that happened." He continued to regard Ezekiel quizzically. "You're not with the local outfit, I'm guessing. There's more than a trace of Down Under in your accent if I'm not mistaken."

"You got me, mate." Ezekiel lowered his voice to a conspiratorial whisper while making a show of glancing around to make sure no one else was listening, even though they seemed to have the farm to themselves, aside from the poultry and livestock, and only the dog was close enough to eavesdrop on the conversation. "Between you and me, and this is strictly off the record, we may have a global infestation on our hands. But keep that under your hat, okay? We wouldn't want to start a panic."

"I imagine not," the farmer said. "But just how serious a problem are we talking about here, if you don't mind me asking?"

"Hard to say," Ezekiel said with a shrug. "It's probably nothing, but it needs to be checked out. Better safe than sorry."

"That's for certain." The farmer stepped away from the front door. "Mary won't be home for a couple of hours, but you're welcome to wait inside."

"Thanks for the offer, mate, but I'm on a tight schedule. Where exactly would I find this library?"

"Smack dab in the middle of town, just off Main Street." The farmer peered at the long dirt driveway leading to a lonely country road several yards away. Cornfields stretched for acres in the distance. "Say, how did you get here anyway? Where's your car?"

Ezekiel had stepped onto the farm through the doorway of a nearby toolshed, but he could hardly explain how the Magic Door worked to a civilian. Thinking on his feet, he ad-libbed instead.

"Oh, my partner dropped me off while following up on another lead." He took out his phone. "I'll just call and tell her to come pick me up."

With any luck, Ezekiel thought, *Jenkins can fine-tune the settings on the Magic Door to transport me straight from the Library to, er, the library.*

"No need for that," the farmer said. "As it happens, I need to drive into town to pick up some fresh fertilizer at the feed-and-grain store. I can drop you off at the library on the way."

Ezekiel figured the Magic Door would be faster and less trouble. "That's nice of you to offer, but—"

"No bother," the farmer insisted, not taking no for answer. "You stay right here while I get the keys to the pickup." The hound lifted her head. "Say, you don't mind riding up front with the dog, do you? Bernice does love her car rides."

———

One slobbery, bumpy ride later, the truck rolled into Banbury, Ohio, a small rural town whose downtown area seemed to mostly consist of a single wide thoroughfare and a few side streets. A canvas banner hanging over the street advertised a country fair. The pickup pulled up to the curb in front of a tidy, one-story building just one block off the main drag. A sign out front identified it as the public library. An outdoor book drop sat by the front entrance, along with a couple of loitering teenagers.

"Here you are, young man," Farmer Simon said. "Say hello to Mary for me . . . and don't worry, mum's the word about those rodents of unusual size."

Ezekiel waited until the truck drove off before wiping a clinging strand of drool off his shoulder and taking a closer look at the library. It didn't look terribly impressive from the outside, but then again, neither did the Annex, which was tucked away under one end of a suspension bridge back in Portland. He started toward the entrance only to be interrupted by his phone. The ringtone identified the caller as Baird, so he figured he should actually answer it.

"Hello?" he said. "Please tell me you've already solved this case so I can catch a one-way trip back to the Library. I'm getting nowhere fast here in Farmville. I don't suppose you have any tips on the best way to wipe drool off silk and cashmere?"

"*Drool?*" Baird's voice asked.

"Never mind," he said. "What's up?"

He listened as Baird filled him in on her expedition to Mother Goose's Magic Garden, all of which sounded a lot more exciting than anything he'd run into yet. "So there's an actual Mother Goose running around, making trouble?"

"*Flying around, actually,*" she confirmed. "*And, according to Jenkins, we can't let her get her hands on all three segments of that original Mother Goose book.*"

"Or Humpty Dumpty gets put back together, the universe gets unhatched, and it's the end of everything as we know it," Ezekiel said glibly. "Got it."

"You don't sound too freaked out by that," she observed.

"I'm a Librarian. I know the drill by now." Freaky was their business. "But don't worry about it. You've got Ezekiel Jones on the case. No way is some Mary Poppins wannabe on a flying goose going to get to those pages before me."

"Just stay on your toes," she said. *"We still don't know entirely who or what we're dealing with."*

"Do we ever?"

Getting bored with the call, he wrapped it up before Baird could remind him one more time of how vital their mission was and how he needed to watch his back. He liked Baird, and appreciated that she took her job as Guardian very seriously, but the whole worried-den-mother thing got old sometimes. He didn't need a babysitter or bodyguard.

Especially not when dropping in on a small-town librarian.

He strolled inside the library. To his slight surprise, it actually looked more modern and up-to-date than the Annex, which, in all honesty, was a little too stuffy and retro for his tastes. It was brightly lit and airy, with computer stations instead of dusty wooden card catalogs, and an automated, self-service checkout setup. Sure, there were still plenty of dead trees crammed on the shelves, but he also saw a wide selection of games and movies on display. His opinion of the town rose a notch.

Now this is my kind of library.

He sauntered up to the front desk where a twenty-something librarian or intern was assisting the patrons too set in their ways to check their books out themselves. He waited impatiently for his turn.

"Excuse me, I need to talk to Mary Simon. The children's librarian?"

"Sssh!" The young woman at the counter raised a finger to her lips. "You're going to have to wait. It's story time."

She pointed to the children's section, where an older woman sat in a rocking chair surrounded by a pack of rug rats listening to her with rapt attention. An open storybook rested in her lap. Groaning inwardly, Ezekiel began to wonder if he was *ever* going to be able to get on with his investigation. Still, with any luck, maybe story time was just wrapping up.

"Once upon a time . . ." Mary Simon began.

Ezekiel sighed.

Still, he had to admit that Mary Simon certainly looked as though she was descended from a long line of Mother Gooses. A matronly, rosy-cheeked senior citizen (at least by Ezekiel's standards), she had neatly coifed silver hair, glasses, and a lap large enough to accommodate a grandkid or two. Watching her cast her spell over her underaged audience, as opposed to them squirming impatiently, it was clear that she had inherited a knack for keeping small children entertained. Cassandra's genealogical detective work, it appeared, had been right on the money.

Got to hand it to her, he thought. *You never want to bet against that brain grape of hers.*

Too restless to sit still for the story, Ezekiel killed time by quietly casing the library and assessing its security measures. He had figured out approximately sixteen different ways to rob the place blind and was working on a few refinements when he heard story time winding down. He wandered back toward the kids' section.

"The end," Mary Simon said, closing the book on her lap.

"One more story," a child pleaded. "Please, Mrs. Simon."

She shook her head. "That's enough for today, I think. Run along now. Your parents are waiting for you."

They're not the only ones who've been waiting, Ezekiel thought. As the kids reluctantly dispersed, he approached the librarian. "Mary Simon?"

"Yes?" She rose from the rocking chair to reshelve the storybook. "Can I help you, Mr.—?"

"Jones," he volunteered. "Ezekiel Jones." He held out his hand. "I'd like to talk to you concerning a certain rodent problem you encountered recently."

"That again?" A frown transformed her from lovable granny to stern librarian. "I've already discussed this with the police, Animal Control, *and* the local paper. How many times do I have to go over this again?"

Her uncooperative attitude momentarily fazed Ezekiel, but he figured it was nothing he couldn't handle. Heck, he'd once talked his way past the guards at the Tower of London.

"I understand," he said, feigning sympathy. "You're obviously a very busy woman and I don't want to take up one minute more of your valuable time than I have to, but I'd really appreciate hearing the story in your own words." He treated her to his most winning smile. "As a personal favor?"

She saw right through him.

"Dial it down, buster. I'm a married woman and you're too young for me anyway." She inspected him warily. "Why are you so interested?"

He briefly considered mentioning that he was a Librarian as well, albeit of a very different sort, but he figured he needed to stick to his original cover story just in case she compared notes with her husband at some point. "I'm with a global animal control organization, investigating similar reports from all over the world." He lowered his voice. "You didn't hear this from me, but your case may be only the tip of the iceberg. It's imperative that I get the full scoop . . . ASAP."

She listened, nodding, then rolled her eyes.

"Right," she said skeptically. "Tell me another one."

"You don't believe me?" Ezekiel clasped his hand to his chest, as though wounded to the heart. "What kind of friendly librarian are you?"

"The kind who has heard enough lame excuses about late or lost books to know when I'm being fed a load of bull." She crossed her arms atop her chest and looked him squarely in the eyes. "Look, Mr. . . . Jones, was it? If you require assistance researching pest control or the natural history of barn mice, I'll be happy to steer you toward the appropriate shelves and reference works. I can even direct you to our neighborhood police station where you can ask to review my previous statements, but, if you don't mind, I've just talked myself hoarse reading aloud to those kids and I've got a lot of administrative paperwork to catch up with. Story time is over, so you'll have to get your jollies elsewhere."

Leaving him dumbfounded in the children's section, she walked away from Ezekiel and past the front desk. She was about to disappear into her office when he blurted out the first thing that came to mind.

"Wait! What do you know about Mother Goose . . . and the Three Blind Mice?"

That got her attention. She froze and looked back at him.

"What did you say?"

"We need to talk about . . . Mother Goose."

Their conversation was starting to draw curious looks from the library's other patrons and staff. Looking slightly uncomfortable, Mary beckoned to Ezekiel.

"Let's talk about this in my office," she suggested. "That's a . . . fascinating topic, but we shouldn't bore the other patrons."

Works for me, Ezekiel thought.

He followed her into an office behind the front counter. She shut the door and took a seat behind her desk. Glancing around, Ezekiel spotted a framed piece of needlework mounted on a wall. Embroidered on the quaint country sampler was a nursery rhyme:

Simple Simon met a pieman,
Going to the fair,
Says Simple Simon to the pieman,
Let me taste your ware.

Ezekiel took the sampler as proof that he was on the right track. He nodded at the decorative needlework. "How about that?" he said with a smirk. "Mother Goose, right?"

"An old family heirloom, that's all." She shrugged as though it was of no consequence. "Now then, Mr. Jones, what's all this about Mother Goose?"

Ezekiel didn't feel like wasting any more time beating around the bush. "You are descended from *the* Mother Goose, right? The one in Boston way back when?"

She stared at him agape. "That's what we were told, growing up, but it's probably just a colorful family legend, passed down for the generations, the same way most every American claims to have a genuine Cherokee princess as an ancestor. I doubt if there's anything to it."

"Oh, it's no legend . . . at least not one of those legends that aren't actually true. Believe me, I have it from a *very* reliable source that you've got plenty of geese in your family tree, going back to Ye Olde Times."

"How . . . how do you know any of this?" she stammered. "And what does this have to do with those ugly vermin anyway?"

"Come on," he said. "Mother Goose . . . the Three Blind Mice. You're a children's librarian. Don't tell me you didn't make the connection?"

"The thought crossed my mind," she admitted, "but the very notion is absurd. That business with the mice had nothing to do with an old nursery rhyme. That's just an odd coincidence."

"No such thing," Ezekiel stated. "Not in my line of work."

"Which is?" she asked. "And don't give me that line about Animal Control again."

Ezekiel saw no reason to stick with a cover story that wasn't working. "I'm a Librarian, actually. Honest."

"A librarian investigating the Three Blind Mice?"

"Nailed it in one." He sat down across from her. "Now we're getting somewhere."

"But . . . but that's insane."

"Why don't you let me be the judge of that," Ezekiel suggested. "What's the real scoop on those mice?"

"Fine," she relented. "If you must know, I was in my kitchen at home, doing some dishes, when I heard this loud skittering and squeaking behind me. I spun around and, lo and behold, there were these three hideous creatures scrambling on top of the kitchen island, twitching their whiskers at me." She shuddered at the memory. "They were bigger than any mice or rats I'd ever seen, and, yes, they had no eyes. Just . . . fur."

Ugh, Ezekiel thought, glad to have missed them. "Any idea where they'd come from?"

"Not a clue. We've never had any serious vermin problems before, let alone king-sized rodents making themselves at home in my kitchen. They just showed up all of a sudden, bold as brass and ugly as sin." Mary's flair for storytelling kicked in as she got caught up in recounting the incident. "Gave me quite a start, I'm not ashamed to admit. I yelled at them, hoping to chase them away, but they sprang at me instead, all claws and teeth and spitting mad."

Ezekiel leaned forward in his chair. "And . . . ?"

"I'm spryer than I look, young man. I ducked out of the way and snatched a steak knife from a rack and slashed at them in self-defense. I nicked one of them in the tail and that, thank goodness, was enough to put the fear of God into all three of them. They turned tail, springing off the counter, and scurried out of the kitchen, tearing right through a screen door." She grimaced. "Haven't laid eyes on them since."

Ezekiel hoped that would remain the case. Freaky mutant mice were not his idea of a fun time. Shiny lost treasures and world-class heists were more to his liking. He was a Librarian, not an exterminator. Pest control was a waste of his talents.

"But don't you see? The Three Blind Mice, a carving knife, you being a farmer's wife . . . it all adds up."

"Maybe in whatever fantasy world you're living in, Mr. Jones, but not here in Ohio," she said firmly. She sat solidly behind her desk, her tone and attitude rooted squarely in reality. "Those unpleasant creatures were surely just some deformed, unusually aggressive rodents, no doubt caused by pesticides or fracking or GMOs."

"Or maybe a spell from Mother Goose's lost book of magic rhymes?"

She blinked at him in surprise. "That . . . . that's just a myth. A bedtime story my late grandmother used to tell me."

"About how the book was divided into three parts by three different branches of your family?" He enjoyed her startled expression. "I've got news for you. That's no myth, no story, and I really need to find those missing pages. I don't suppose you've got them tucked away somewhere?"

She shook her head, looking a bit dazed. "Not that I know of."

Figures, Ezekiel thought. "I should've known it wouldn't be that easy. These capers almost always involve clues and puzzles and riddles, and clues inside puzzles inside riddles. If you ask me, people in the past had *way* too much time on their hands. . . ."

"You're really serious about this," she said incredulously. "Aren't you?"

"Well, as serious as I am about anything." He pondered what his next move should be. Grilling witnesses wasn't exactly his specialty; he hoped there'd be a museum or vault to break into at some point. "You mentioned a grandmother before. She ever drop any hints about where your family's chunk of the book might be hidden?"

"Not that I recall," Mary said, thinking it over. She glanced up at the sampler on the wall. "Although that was a legacy from Grandma, and I remember her telling me, more than once, that it must always remain in the family." She shrugged again. "As far as I know, it only has sentimental value."

"Sentiment is for suckers." He walked over to examine the sampler. "What I'm looking for is a clue."

As much as he hated to admit it, Ezekiel found himself wishing that Stone was on hand to help out. This kind of boring, old-timey stuff was more Stone's thing; he could probably tell just by looking at the embroidery and thread when and where it was sewn, right down to the exact year. Ezekiel was tempted to "borrow" the sampler long enough to run it past Stone, but balked at the idea of allowing that he was stumped. He had an image to maintain, after all. Ezekiel Jones did not need backup.

Maybe the clue was in the actual rhyme?

"Pie, fair, wares . . ." He looked to Mary Simon for guidance. "Any of this ringing a bell?"

"Well, fairs and markets and pies recur frequently in Mother Goose," the librarian said. "Little Jack Horner, 'to market, to market,' and so on."

Ezekiel had trouble imaging that an old book could be hidden for generations within a soggy old pie, unless there was some kind of mathematical pun involving pi going on, in which case he might have to call in Cassandra as well, although she was presumably busy investigating that tree trimmer in Miami.

"What about fairs?" he asked. "Are there any actual fairs in the vicinity?"

"The annual Banbury Fair is the oldest in the county," she said proudly. "As it happens, it's going on right now . . . at the fairgrounds outside of town."

Ezekiel remembered seeing a banner advertising the fair.

"Well, that's not coincidental at all," he said wryly.

Mary smirked. "I thought you said there's no such thing in your line of work."

"Good point." He saw another excursion in his future. The sampler wasn't much to go on, but it was the closest thing he had to a lead. "Guess I'm going to the fair."

"Not without me you aren't." She got up from behind her desk. "If there's anything to any of this, that's my family's legacy you're looking for. Don't think for a minute that I'm not going to be looking over your shoulder the whole time."

Ezekiel found that prospect less than appealing.

"Thanks, but I work alone," he lied.

"Tough," she said. "Don't cross me, Mr. Jones. I can be quite contrary when I want to be."

A suspicious thought crossed Ezekiel's mind. Was she just being stubborn or did she have an ulterior motive? How much did she really know or believe about the Mother Goose Treaty and all that? For all he knew, she could be in cahoots with that "Mother Goose" character Baird ran across in New Jersey.

"I'm not sure that's a good idea," he said. "Those scary Blind Mice may just be the warm-up act. You'd better let me handle this."

"Not a chance. And don't even think about trying to ditch me. I'd hate to have to alert the local authorities to a con man posing as an Animal Control agent." She brushed past him on her way out. "Car's parked outside. You coming or not?"

Ezekiel sighed. "There's not a dog in the car, is there?"

Before she could reply, frantic squeals and shrieks came from outside the office.

"What in tarnation?" Mary exclaimed.

Rushing out to investigate, Ezekiel and Mary were shocked to see the Three Blind Mice rampaging through the library. The large, eyeless rodents were even more revolting than Ezekiel had imagined and had, understandably, thrown the library into pandemonium. Hysterical patrons and library staff bolted for the exits, often screaming at the top of their lungs. Books and DVDs, heedlessly dropped in the panic, were strewn across the floor.

"I don't suppose you have a carving knife handy?" Ezekiel asked.

"Does this look like a butcher shop?" Mary said tartly.

She stared aghast at the Blind Mice, who, thankfully, seemed more interested in trashing the library than chasing after the terrified patrons. They scampered madly about the premises, knocking books off shelves and shredding newspapers and magazines, while squeaking loudly enough to hurt Ezekiel's ears. He and Mary ducked behind the checkout counter.

"I don't understand," she said. "What are those awful creatures doing here?"

"Best guess? Somebody *really* doesn't want you to help me find those pages."

Their hurried conversation attracted the Blind Mice, who turned and sniffed in their direction. Ugly pink noses twitched ominously. A low growl emanated from the oversized rodents, one of whom was still missing the tip of its tail. Ezekiel hoped it wasn't holding a grudge.

"Time to get out of here," Ezekiel decided. Any good thief knew when to make a run for it and he had already clocked all the available escape routes. "Make for the fire exit."

Mary hesitated. "But . . . my library?"

"Suit yourself." Ezekiel started toward the exit. "I guess I'll just have to find those hidden pages by myself."

Mary scoffed at the notion. "Not if I have anything to say about it."

They darted for the exit, even as the mice came scrambling over the counter after them. Ezekiel hurled a bulky hardcover, which looked as though the author had been paid by the word, at the disgusting creatures to slow them down while Mary yanked open the door, setting off the fire alarm. The blaring siren struck Ezekiel as another good reason to vacate the premises; he resented alarms on principle.

He hustled Mary out the door. The mice pounced at them, but he slammed the door shut in their faces, so that their heavy bodies smashed into it with force. He heard them squeaking and scratching angrily on the other side of the door.

Could Blind Mice handle doorknobs? Ezekiel wasn't about to stick around to find out, especially since he heard police cars and fire trucks heading their way. He liked dealing with law enforcement as much as he liked noisy alarms.

Which was to say, not at all.

"You were saying something about a fair?"

8

※ *Northumberland* ※

"So you're really Jackson Dennings?"

"Guilty as charged," Stone said to the woman sitting across from him in a cozy pub in the North Country of England. Exposed oak beams held up the ceiling, while an open fireplace kept the place toasty despite the cool fall weather outside. Rows of bottles lined the shelves of a well-equipped bar, not far from the booth they occupied. Laughter and conversation echoed off the venerable stone walls, but Stone was used to chatting up pretty ladies in bars. "At least when I'm writing academic papers on the intersectionality of culture and infrastructure. But when I'm not hiding behind a fancy byline and degree I'm just plain Jake Stone, Librarian." He smiled engagingly. "But, please, call me Jake."

"In that case, you must call me Gillian." An appealing accent revealed that she was native to the region. She examined Stone by the subdued lamplight of the pub. "I have to say, you're not exactly as I envisioned you."

"Likewise," Stone replied.

Dr. Gillian Fell, professor of anthropology at Bede College in Northumberland, was an attractive woman, roughly the same age as Stone, with wavy brown hair, chestnut eyes, and a stylish pair of designer glasses perched upon her nose. A turtleneck sweater showed off her figure. According to Cassandra, she was also yet another descendant of Elizabeth Goose. That Gillian's particular field of study just happened to be folklore and oral traditions had not escaped Stone. The feather, in this case, seemed to have fallen not far from the goose.

"Is that so?" She arched a graceful eyebrow while her voice took on a teasing flavor. "And whom exactly were you anticipating?"

"The highly erudite author of *Reflections on Mirrors and the Other Self*, of course." Who had turned out to look more like Moneypenny than M. "A fascinating piece, really. Some of your insights into the psychological significance of mirrors and reflecting pools, as opposed to their practical uses, really made me think . . . and reexamine my own assumptions about form versus function."

He was utterly sincere in his appreciation of her scholarly accomplishments. Back at the Annex, it hadn't taken him too long to recall where he knew her name from. He was, in fact, quite familiar with her work, which occasionally overlapped with his own studies of traditional art and architecture. He wasn't sure that he had ever corresponded with her directly as Jackson Dennings, but they had certainly swum in the same circles.

"High praise," she said, returning the compliment, "from the mind that first postulated a link between Pennsylvania Dutch hex signs and Freemasonry, by way of Pythagorean aesthetics."

That she was acquainted with his own work—as Jackson Dennings—had proved handy when it came to wangling a meeting with the subject of his clipping. He was not above taking advantage of Dennings's academic reputation to get his foot in the door as it were, especially when that turned out to involve meeting a good-looking colleague for drinks at her favorite pub.

"Thanks again," he said, "for squeezing me in to your busy schedule."

"No worries. Hope I didn't keep you waiting too long."

"Not at all," he lied, given the urgency of his quest. In truth, the Library was in a race to beat "Mother Goose" to that hidden spell book, but that was hardly something he could just up and explain to Gillian given that he wasn't sure how much she knew about the magical secrets in her family tree. "But about your recent close encounter with a giant pumpkin . . ."

She winced at the memory. "I still don't entirely understand why you would be interested in that, beyond the sheer bizarreness of the whole episode, that is. Something about the symbolic use of pumpkins in Anglo-American folk art?"

"More or less," he said vaguely. "It's a bit more complicated than that, but I'll spare you the whole song and dance." He smiled at her. "Indulge me."

"I'll bet you say that to all the anthropologists." She let out a sigh of resignation. "All right then. Might as well get it over with, I suppose."

"Whenever you're ready," he said.

She took a sip of ale to fortify herself. "You have to understand, the whole experience was just so . . . surreal . . . that even I have trouble believing that it actually happened, and wasn't simply some phantasmagorical dream or hallucination. I went to bed one night, after a perfectly ordinary evening grading papers, and the next thing I knew I woke up

inside something dark and gooey and claustrophobic. I
didn't realize at the time that I was curled up inside an unusually capacious pumpkin of all things, only that I was
trapped inside an enclosed space with no idea how I'd gotten there." She shuddered in recollection. "I swear to God,
I hadn't taken any drugs the night before or drank anything
stronger than tea."

"I believe you," he said. "Besides, even if you had been
under the influence, that wouldn't explain how you got inside the pumpkin. But I'm still a little fuzzy on one point:
were you in any danger of suffocation?"

She shook her head. "No, not right away at least. The pumpkin was hollowed out on the inside, in a way that nobody has
quite been able to explain just yet. From what people tell me,
the pumpkin—which was on display at the local farmers'
market—appeared entirely untouched from the outside." She
threw up her hands. "Tell me, how is that even possible?"

Magic, Stone thought, wishing there was some way to explain that to Gillian without sounding like a lunatic. "So what
happened next?"

"What do you think? I bloody well panicked, kicking and
punching hard enough to crack the shell . . . and raising
enough of a ruckus that several Good Samaritans joined in
to help liberate me from the pumpkin, much to the dismay
and confusion of the fellow whose vegetable stand it was." A
wry chuckle escaped her lips. "You should have seen his
face. I swear, the poor old gent was almost as gob-smacked
as I was."

"I can imagine," Stone said. "That must have been a very
disorienting experience."

"That's putting it mildly." She stared into her drink as she seemed to open up a bit more, her voice taking on a more troubled, vulnerable tone. "To be frank, I still experience a certain trepidation every night before I go to bed, wondering if something similar—or worse—is going to happen again. I mean, how do I know that I'm not going to wake up at the bottom of a well some morning?"

Stone was tempted to let her in on the recent outbreak of nursery-rhyme-related magic, but he was afraid to scare her off at this juncture. *Maybe later,* he thought, *after we've got a better handle on the situation.*

"I wish I had some answers for you," he said lamely.

"No reason why you should." She adopted a lighter tone to offset the lingering anxieties she had just confessed to. "So, was my twisted Cinderella moment of any use to you, Mr. Stone?"

"Jake," he insisted again. "And not Cinderella . . . Mother Goose."

Her brown eyes widened. "What did you just say?"

Now it was his turn to gulp down some ale before speaking. "Like I said before, it's complicated. . . ."

He gave her a carefully edited version of the truth, leaving out the full nature of the Library, the whole Humpty Dumpty business, Mother Goose and her gander, and all the freakier stuff, stressing instead the saga of Elizabeth Goose, her trisected legacy, and the elusive first printing of *Mother Goose's Melodies.*

"My associates and I are trying to track down all three pieces of that so-called ghost volume," he explained, "and some timely genealogical research led us to you."

Confusion was written on her face. "But what does that have to do with me waking up inside a pumpkin?"

"Good question," he said, ducking that conversation for now. "But you *are* descended from Elizabeth Goose of Boston?"

"So the story goes," she conceded. "As I understand it, my great-great-grandmother served as an army nurse during the First World War, during which duty she met and married a young British soldier and ended up settling down in these parts after the war."

Which was around the time of the Mother Goose Treaty, Stone noted. "I don't suppose your great-great-grandma passed down one third of the missing book to you?"

"Not that I'm aware of," she said. "Although I suspect I owe a good part of my abiding interest in folklore and such to the stories I heard growing up about our family connection to the 'real' Mother Goose."

"Or maybe it's just in your blood," he speculated.

"A fanciful notion, but no more so, I suppose, than finding oneself inexplicably encased in a pumpkin shell." Her eyes narrowed suspiciously. "Speaking of which, why do I get the distinct impression that you're not telling me everything?"

Because you're clearly nobody's fool, he thought, even as his phone chimed for his attention, using Baird's ringtone.

"Sorry," he said, saved by the bell. "If you'll excuse me for a minute . . ."

"Go ahead," she said. "I'm not going anywhere."

Was that a promise or a threat? Stone pondered that mystery as he exited the booth and stepped outside the pub to take the call. It was early evening, Greenwich Mean Time, and the sun was already going down, taking the warmth of the day of with it. The sky was clear, though, making for a pleasant autumn night that was eight hours ahead of the Annex—or wherever Baird was calling from.

"What's up?" he asked.

"*Plenty,*" Baird said. "*I just got an update from Jones. Listen up.*"

She filled him in on what Ezekiel had learned in Ohio so far, including the bit about a nursery rhyme sampler passed down from generation to generation as a family heirloom. The idea of a secret message embroidered into a piece of folk art intrigued him.

"Interesting," he said. "Let me try following up on that lead on my end."

"*Just keep us posted on your progress,*" Baird said.

"Will do."

Stone ended the call and stepped back inside the pub. As promised, Gillian was waiting for him in their booth. He took a moment to admire the way the firelight flattered her hair and complexion before he slid back into his seat across from her. *Keep your mind on the job,* he told himself, despite the fact that he felt some definite chemistry cooking between himself and Gillian. He wondered how many of her students were nursing secret crushes on their highly distracting professor. *More than a few, I'm guessing.*

"Anything important?" she asked him.

"Possibly." He explained about how Ezekiel had found a lead to one-third of the lost book hidden in a sampler bearing a nursery rhyme. "Is it too much to hope that you inherited something similar?"

"Not one bit," she said with obvious excitement. "As it happens, I do have such a sampler proudly displayed on the wall of my flat, not too far from here. But instead of 'Simple

Simon,' mine has the first few verses of 'Jack and Jill' embroidered on it."

Stone leaned forward eagerly. "As in 'Jack and Jill went up the hill'?"

"The very same!" She pounced on the topic like any true scholar hot on the trail of a new breakthrough or discovery. "As I recall, there are various competing theories as to the meaning of the rhyme, some more plausible than others. One of the prevailing theories is that the rhyme derives from the Norse myth of Hjuki and Bil, which concerns two children, a brother and sister, who were fetching water from a well, using a pail no less, when they were snatched up by the Man in the Moon."

Taking out her own phone, she went online and called up an old woodcut illustration of two children carrying a long pole between them, upon which was suspended a wooden pail. A leering moon gazed down on them.

"From the *Prose Edda*?" Stone guessed. "The myth I mean, not the illustration."

"Precisely." She put away her phone. "Circa the thirteenth century. That's centuries before the first known references to the Mother Goose rhymes, so there's no way to prove a connection, but, as theories go, it's probably the most convincing." She rolled her eyes. "Don't get me started on the popular notion that the rhyme actually refers to the beheading of King Louis the Sixteenth and Marie Antoinette, which is utter balderdash and chronologically impossible to boot."

Stone took her word for it, as his mind struggled to connect an obscure Norse myth to his quest for the missing volume. According to Jenkins, many of the Mother Goose rhymes had roots deep in antiquity, but the segments of the spell book were not hidden away until 1918 or so, which implied . . . what? That any clues would date back to the twentieth century, not medieval Scandinavia?

"I confess that was always my favorite Mother Goose rhyme growing up," Gillian said. "To be honest, I used to think that the 'Jill' in the sampler was named after me . . . when I was very young, naturally."

"Yeah, about that," Stone said. "Jill . . . Gillian. Bit of a co-incidence, don't you think?"

Stone wondered if the hidden clue was sitting right across from him.

"Not as much as you might think," she said, dismissing the notion. "Jill—or sometimes Gill—was pretty much a generic term for a young girl or sweetheart in days of yore, dating back to Shakespeare at least. 'Jack shall have Jill; naught shall go ill,' etcetera."

"*A Midsummer Night's Dream*," Stone said, recognizing the quote. "Act three, scene two, if I remember right."

"Very good." She nodded in approval. "I'm impressed."

He was pleased to hear it, more so perhaps than was strictly necessary. *Eyes on the prize*, he reminded himself again. "Getting back to Jack and Jill, what else is there in the rhyme? A hill, a well, a pail . . ."

Gillian brainstormed along with him. "Well, wells and hills are recurring themes in folklore in general and Mother Goose in particular. 'Pussy's in the well,' 'the old woman who lived under a hill,' and so forth."

"But a well on top of a hill?" Stone said, thinking aloud. "That doesn't really make any sense. Who puts a well on top of a hill you have to climb every day? Unless maybe you're talking about some kind of fortified hilltop stronghold that required a secure source of water." Inspiration struck and he smacked his forehead for not seeing it earlier. "Of course! Look where we are right now."

"In a pub?" she asked.

"In Northumberland," he clarified. "Because of its proximity to the Scottish border, and the battles waged back and forth across that border, Northumbria has the highest concentration of old castles and forts of any county in Britain. And those hillside fortresses would have had wells or cisterns."

"Where my great-great-grandmother might have hidden her third of the book?"

"That's what I'm thinking," Stone said. "Are there any ancient structures on top of hills around here?"

She nodded. "There are the remains of an old Roman fort atop a hill just outside town, although there's not much left of it and what's there isn't very impressive, not like the bigger, more impressive Roman ruins at Vindolanda or Housesteads. You know, the ones that draw all the tourists."

"All the better to hide something in." Stone thought these hilltop ruins were sounding more promising by the minute. "And that bygone fort would have definitely needed a source of water for drinking and bathing. Hell, the Roman legions didn't set up shop anywhere without building a bathhouse or two. There's bound to be a well of some sort buried amidst those ruins."

"And where there's a well, there's a way?" she quipped.

"You're reading my mind." He glanced at his watch. The night was not getting any younger. "Is there any place in this town where I can pick up some hiking and caving gear in a hurry?"

"Caving?" A trace of alarm entered her voice. "So we can go spelunking in some crumbling, two-thousand-year-old well?"

He didn't miss the plural pronoun. "We?"

"Naturally," she said. "You can't tempt me with the possibility of finding the very first printing of *Mother Goose's Melodies*—and maybe an answer to my Pumpkin Morning nightmare—and then just leave me in the lurch. Besides, do you even know the way to the ruins? Believe me when I tell you that it's a long, difficult hike on a trail that's not exactly designed for sightseeing academics from America. You don't want to go it alone."

"Thanks for the offer, but I can manage outside the ivory towers of academia, thank you very much. I'm not exactly your typical Librarian."

"I'm picking up on that," she said, "and consider me intrigued, in more ways than one. But that doesn't change anything. I'm going with you, period."

Her tone, which was enough to put the fear of God into any errant student, brooked no further discussion, but she had no idea what she was letting herself in for if she tagged along on this quest. He couldn't in good conscience let her wander into potentially mortal jeopardy unawares.

"Look," he said, "it's not that I wouldn't appreciate the company—and your company, specifically—but my colleague and I aren't the only ones looking for those pages. We have competition and, in all honesty, I'm not sure how far they might go to beat us to the pages. We could be talking serious danger to life and limb."

"Even worse than waking up in a pumpkin with no idea how you got there?"

"Possibly," he said. "Academic politics may get cutthroat at times, but compared to treasure hunting?" He tried to get across just how serious this was. "More than reputations can be destroyed, if you get what I'm saying."

"I see." She was silent for a minute, absorbing what he'd told her. "But you still think this search is worth pursuing?"

He shrugged. "It's my job, not yours."

"But according to you, I'm Great-Great-Great-Great-Granddaughter Goose or whatever, so this is my business, too." She nodded to herself, her decision made. "Like it or not, you're stuck with me, Jake or Jackson or whatever you're calling yourself at the moment. You're not going up that hill without me."

Stone realized that there was no winning this battle, short of stuffing her in a pumpkin himself. "All right then," he conceded. "Every Jack must have his Jill, I guess."

She smiled slyly in a way that promised trouble.

"Don't get ahead of yourself, Jake Stone."

He was searching for a suitable reply when the overhead lights flickered and went out, throwing the pub into darkness. Startled gasps and exclamations replaced the general hubbub as confused customers and servers reacted to the unexpected blackout, which puzzled Stone as well. It wasn't as though there was any sort of storm going on outside.

"What the devil?" Gillian said. "This doesn't—"

The lights returned as abruptly as they left, bringing an unwelcome surprise.

A large orange pumpkin, about the size of a Halloween jack-o'-lantern, had magically appeared on the table between them. Gillian's face went pale at the sight. Stone assumed that this pumpkin was not nearly as enormous as the one she'd woken up inside, but it still had to be a very triggery reminder of her recent ordeal.

Which is exactly the idea, he guessed.

"What . . . ?" she stammered. "How . . . ?"

Stone reached across the table to take her hand, hoping to comfort her. "Hang in there," he began. "It's just a pumpkin."

"No," she said, shaking. "There's more."

She turned the pumpkin around and he saw *writing* carved into its shell in a way he recognized from his boyhood. Back home, farmers would sometimes scratch short messages—such as, say, a child's name—into the tender green skin of a freshly sprouted pumpkin. As the pumpkin matured, the message would grow, too, scabbing over to form bumpy white script across the bright orange shell, just like on the pumpkin he was looking at now.

The message scarring the pumpkin was short and to the point: THE BOOK IS MINE.

"Damn," Stone muttered.

Gillian looked understandably freaked out. "This is insane," she protested. "What's this all about?"

"It's a warning," Stone said. "To leave those missing rhymes alone."

From Mother Goose, no doubt.

She took a deep breath to steady her nerves. The color began to return to her face.

"For you or for me?"

"Both, I'm guessing." He squeezed her hand. "I'll understand if you want nothing more to do with any of this. You can just walk away."

"Like hell I will!" Her cheeks flushed with anger, suggesting that the brazen attempt to intimidate her had achieved precisely the opposite result. "I've had quite enough of being bullied by pumpkins."

She shoved the threatening gourd off the table. It crashed to the floor, splattering pumpkin guts all over the tiles.

Startled customers looked on in shock, but Gillian couldn't be bothered to explain or apologize. She rose defiantly to her feet and put on her jacket.

"Well?" she asked Stone impatiently. "Are you coming or not?"

9

❈ *Florida* ❈

"Excuse me. Sorry. No, thank you. I'm fine."

It was open mic night at Slant, a hip-hop night club in Miami, and Cassandra found herself adrift in a sea of bodies bobbing and swaying to the rhythmic beats and rhymes coming from the stage. It was hot and crowded and loud and she felt overwhelmed and out of place, not to mention daunted by the challenge of finding George Cole, the unnaturally lucky tree trimmer from her news clipping, in the midst of the densely packed club.

This was not the kind of "rock-a-bye baby" I was expecting, she thought. *And is the music* supposed *to be this loud?*

She had been running around the city for hours trying to track down Cole, and getting nowhere, until one of his neighbors had helpfully steered her toward this club. "You're looking for Georgie on a Saturday night?" the woman had volunteered before carrying a heavy bag of groceries into her own place. "Slant is the place to be."

Cassandra hoped that advice was on target, as she fruitlessly searched the faces of the crowd, looking in vain for anyone who resembled the news photo of George Cole she'd found online. Random bodies jostled her or protested being jostled. Someone offered her a drink, but she declined without hesitation, recalling her inebriated exploits at Dorian Gray's club in London not too long ago; she needed to keep her wits about her.

And I really don't need a hangover tomorrow, she thought. *Magical or otherwise.*

The noise and commotion were already giving her a headache. Rapper after rapper took their turn upon the stage, eliciting cheers and jeers from the hyped-up crowd. Cassandra paid little attention to the performances, scanning the crowd instead. Sensory overload threatened to send her head spinning; the percussive four-beat rhythm of the raps intruded on her brain, filling it with mathematical static: four by four by four, sixteen bars to a verse, snares on every second beat, rhyme and cadence forming recurring patterns, syllables synched to a staccato schema that smelled oddly like children's aspirin—

Stop it! She shook her head to clear it. *Keep it under control.*

She was tempted to turn back and stake out Cole's doorstep until he finally dragged himself back home, but who knew how long that might take, especially if he met somebody at the club. According to Jenkins, time was of the essence; she needed to locate Cole with all due speed, even if she had no idea how.

Maybe I can just step outside for minute to get a little fresh air and quiet?

She was starting to make her way toward the nearest exit, despite the raucous throng between her and the door, when the MC strode back out onto the stage to introduce the next performer:

"What's crackin', Miami? You ready for more?"

The audience whooped in response, practically shaking the building.

"All right! Then raise the roof for the slamming stylings of Miami's favorite black sheep, our own homegrown shepherd of swag . . . Bo-Peeps!"

Bo-Peeps?

Cassandra halted her exodus and spun around in time to see George Cole take the stage, decked out in an oversized T-shirt, sweatpants, and sneakers. A large gilded candy cane hung on a chain around his neck; it took Cassandra a moment to realize that it represented a shepherd's crook. Claiming the mic from the MC, Cole confidently turned toward the audience and launched into his rap:

They call me Bo-Peeps 'cause I tend to my flock,
I walk the walk, not just talk the talk.
No man is an island. Gotta watch for the strays.
You mess with my peeps, you best mind your ways!

Cassandra was no expert on rap music, but her heart pounded in excitement. She was clearly on the right track: Cole was trumpeting his Mother Goose roots for all the world to see and hear. She didn't need to retrace his ancestry back to Elizabeth Goose to know that she had gotten it right the first time.

You want a good shepherd, you're talking Bo-Peeps.
I keep watch in the night; them wolves never sleep.
No eyes are sharper, my name's in the book.
I keep my sheep safe . . . by hook or by crook!

Waiting anxiously for "Bo-Peeps" to wrap up his performance, Cassandra caught herself tapping her foot in time to the beat, getting into the rap. She was almost disappointed when he finally surrendered the mic and exited the stage on the right. Bouncing on her tiptoes, she peered over the heads and shoulders of the crowd, desperately trying to keep him in sight.

"Mr. Cole? George Cole?" she called out, struggling to be heard over the general hubbub. She shoved her way through the crowd, wishing she had Eve's Amazonian height and physique. Dirty looks and grumbling followed her as she squeezed her way forward, feeling like a salmon fighting its way upstream. "Mr. Peeps! Bo-Peeps!"

Her frantic shouting caught his attention. Surrounded by some friends or admirers, with whom he was chilling after his act, he stared at her in curiosity. She couldn't blame him for looking puzzled; she wasn't exactly dressed for clubbing. What with her Peter Pan collar, pink floral dress, and leggings, she appeared neither hip nor hop.

"Yo!" he called back. "You lost, little sheep?"

Not anymore, she thought. "If I could please just have a moment of your time . . . !"

He gestured for his fan club to let her through. Gasping in relief, she burst from the pack to get up close to him. Her voice was hoarse from shouting.

"Mr. Cole?" she said. "My name is Cassandra and—"

"Call me Georgie," he said, grinning broadly. He was a big, muscular guy who made her feel even more petite than usual. His shaved skull gleamed beneath the club lights; an amused expression was less intimidating than his imposing physique. "As in Georgie Porgie, you know?" He looked her over again. "I kiss the girls and make them cry."

Cassandra feared he might have the wrong idea. She was a Librarian, not a groupie. "I'm sure you do, but I really need to talk to you about an important matter."

"Are you a talent scout?" he asked. "Did you like my flow? 'Cause I've got even crisper rhymes where those came from."

"No, no, nothing like that." Cassandra decided to cut to the chase to avoid any further confusion. "It's about . . . Mother Goose."

His whole face lit up. "Hell, girl, why didn't you say so? I'm all about Ma Goose, obviously." He patted his chest. "Where do you think I get my mad rhyming skills from? Cross my heart, you're looking at a genuine descendant of the original Ma Goose, the most old-school rapper of all!"

He was obviously proud of his illustrious roots.

"I know!" Cassandra said. Elizabeth Goose's luminous family tree flashed briefly before her eyes. "That's what I need to speak with you about." A stray customer shouldered past her, bumping her to one side. She found herself standing in a puddle of spilled beer. "Any chance we can relocate to someplace a little less . . . distracting?"

Cole nodded. "I know just the place." He made his goodbyes to his assembled fan club before guiding Cassandra toward a rear exit backstage. "Let's bail."

The exit led to a crowded parking lot lit up by glowing lampposts. The cool night air came as a relief after the overheated atmosphere of the club. Cole's car—an eggshell-blue convertible—was easily identified by his vanity plates, which spelled out "BO PEEPS." He chivalrously opened the passenger side door. "Welcome to my crib away from crib. Make yourself at home."

Cassandra hesitated only briefly. There was a time when she would have never gotten into a car with a strange man, but that was before she became a Librarian. She'd stepped through a dimensional vortex into a Lovecraftian hell dimension and, at various points in her new career, faced off against the likes of Morgan le Fay, Professor Moriarty, *and* the Big Bad Wolf. She figured she could handle a parked convertible in Miami.

Besides, she was getting a good vibe from Cole.

"We going somewhere?" she asked.

"I don't know. You got any place you need to go?".

"That kind of depends on what you can tell me." She took a deep breath before diving in. "I'm a Librarian and I'm looking for a certain book. . . ."

"Mother Goose's spell book? The one that got split three ways?"

Cassandra blinked in surprise. "You know about that?"

"Damn straight. Case you didn't figure it out already, I'm all into my family history. Gotta know where you came from if you want to know where you're going, right? I know the whole deal backwards and forwards, and can break it down for you beat by beat: the spells, the book, the Treaty. . . ." He pointed his thumb at his heart. "The Goose is strong in this one."

Cassandra wasn't used to it being this easy. "You're not all skeptical about . . . magic?"

"Hell, no. The world's full of seriously freaky stuff that can't be explained. All you gotta do is open your eyes and look around." He gestured at the glittering sky above them, just as a shooting star streaked by overhead. "Don't believe it? Just wait until you hear about the totally insane thing that happened to me on my day job."

"Your miraculous fall onto that trampoline?"

Now it was his turn to be caught off guard. "You heard about that?"

"That's what called you to my attention in the first place," she divulged. "Maybe you can tell me exactly what happened, in your own words?"

"My favorite kind," he joked. "Sit back and let me enlighten you, little lamb." He held an imaginary mic up before his lips. "So I've got this tree-trimming gig, just to pay the bills until my raps blow up big, and one day I'm up in the bucket, pruning some limbs, when, right out of the blue, this extreme wind comes out of nowhere—like Auntie Em, it's a twister!—and tears me right out of the bucket and tosses me into the air, up, up, and away." He shivered in recollection. "Now I can handle heights, no problem, but I'm not too proud to admit that I was screaming like a baby, convinced that it was all over for me. Understand, we're talking *altitude* here, like at least eighty feet above the pavement. I was looking at a *hard* landing."

He slapped the dashboard for emphasis, making Cassandra jump.

"But then, just as I was saying my prayers, that same crazy wind carried me away from the road and out over somebody's backyard, then dropped me onto some kid's trampoline." He threw up his hands in disbelief, marveling at his own survival. "Wild, right? Don't tell me there's no such thing as luck or magic in this big, wide world!"

"I wouldn't dream of it," she said.

"But what's that got to do with Ma Goose?" he asked.

"Rock-a-bye, baby," she prompted him. "When the wind blows . . ."

Understanding dawned on his face. "Damn! How did I miss that?" He stared at her in amazement. "You saying that somebody whammied me with an honest-to-gooseness curse?"

"That's one way to put it, I guess." She admired his colorful turn of phrase. "And you weren't the only target. My colleagues and I have reason to believe that someone posing as Mother Goose—probably one of the other heirs to the title—is trying collect all three sections of the book in order to unlock its full power . . . and misuse it."

She figured she didn't need to explain the whole Humpty Dumpty business, which was bizarre by several more orders of magnitude. Even she was having trouble wrapping her head around the idea that putting Humpty Dumpty back together again would reboot all of Creation.

"That's whack," Cole said, nodding gravely. "So one of my distant relations is making a major power play, like on *Game of Thrones* or something?"

"More or less," she said. "Or at least that's our best guess as to what's going on."

He let that sink in for a minute. "What kind of librarian did you say you were again?"

"The kind that tracks down dangerous magical books and that, no offense, doesn't have a lot of time to spare." She hoped that Cole's knowledge of his family's past included the location of their share of Elizabeth Goose's legacy. "You don't happen to know where I can find those missing pages?"

"Sorry, lamb chop. According to my folks, that secret was buried six feet deep on purpose. Mother Goose's spell book is like the Holy Grail or the Lost Ark: it's not meant to be found."

She refrained from mentioning that both those relics were currently under glass at the Library. "Does that mean you're not going to help me locate it?"

"Did I say that?" He laughed at the notion. "Sounds to me like the ball is already in play and the game is on. Count me in!"

Cassandra was glad to hear it. "Did you inherit any family heirlooms? Such as samplers perhaps?"

She doubted he had any such item in his car, but if he remembered the specific rhyme, that might be all she needed to figure out the clues.

"Gotta hand it to you, little lamb. You know your business. Get an eyeful of this."

He tugged on the bottom of his T-shirt, pulling it up over his head.

"Whoa there!" Cassandra held up her hands to fend him off if necessary, while peeking through her fingers. "Not where I thought we were going with this!"

"Chill, lamb chop." He turned his back toward her, revealing a nursery rhyme tattooed across his skin in crooked black script. "Just wanted to give you a wink at my ink."

"That's the rhyme from your sampler?" she asked. "On your back?"

"You know it. Like I said before, I never want to forget where I came from . . . and this is a bit more hardcore than great-granny's needlepoint if you know what I mean." He shrugged. "Got a reputation to maintain after all."

Cassandra didn't argue the point. Personally, when it came to preserving her family history, she would have gone with a nice scrapbook or photo album, but to each their own. Overcoming her initial surprise, she read the rhyme inked into Cole's back.

There was a crooked man, and he walked a crooked mile,
He found a crooked sixpence upon a crooked stile,
He bought a crooked cat, which caught a crooked mouse,
And they all lived together in a little crooked house.

Cassandra searched the familiar verses for clues, but came up blank. "Crooked man . . . well, that covers a lot of ground. A sixpence, a stile, a cat, a mouse. Are there any particularly crooked houses in the vicinity?"

"Crooked as in felonious," he asked, "or crooked as in askew?"

"Don't ask me," she said, growing frustrated. "Ask your tricky ancestors. Did any of them ever live in a house that might be described as . . . crooked?"

Cole scratched his chin, thinking it over, while Cassandra pondered her next move should Cole be stumped as well. Was there some deeper meaning in the rhyme she was missing? Arts and poetry were more Stone's thing, or Jenkins's, or Flynn's. Why couldn't this branch of the Goose family have left her a nice chewy math puzzle instead?

She was on the verge of calling Jenkins for help when Cole had a brainstorm. He snapped his fingers loudly.

"The Puzzle House! My great-grandpa didn't live there, but he sure as hell ran the construction team on the Puzzle House, which is about as crooked a crib as they come."

Cassandra gave him a blank look. "Puzzle House?"

"Seriously? You've never heard of the Wilshire Puzzle House? Where have you been hanging out, little lamb? Under a rock?"

"Under a bridge, to be exact," she said. "But you were saying . . . ?"

"Let me lay some wisdom on you." Cole pulled his shirt back on before launching into his explanation. "Ezra Wilshire was this 'crooked' robber baron who swindled a whole lot of people back in the boom years after the First World War. Story is he made a deal with the Devil, selling his soul for wealth and luxury, but there was a catch: the Devil couldn't collect his soul until Old Man Wilshire finished building his mansion. So the sneaky old man tried to keep the construction going forever in order to outsmart the Devil."

"Doable," Cassandra said, speaking from experience, "but probably best left to professionals." Memories of a certain infernal contract crackled like hellfire across her brain, smelling distinctly of brimstone. "I'm guessing this didn't work out well for Mr. Wilshire in the end?"

Cole shook his head. "You could say that. All they ever found was some ashes in the shape of his shadow."

"Oh." Cassandra gulped, deciding she didn't need all the grisly details at the moment. "Anyway, I get that the late Mr. Wilshere was 'crooked' in a way, but, aside from its colorful history, was his house all that crooked, too?"

"Crooked, crazy, *mondo loco* . . . it's all of that and more. Seems Old Man Wilshire didn't entirely trust the Devil to play fair, so he made his crib as confusing as possible so that even Old Nick couldn't find his way around or tell whether the house was done yet. It's all dead ends and weird angles and secret passages and wacked-out doors and stairways that go nowhere in particular. You have to see it to believe it. It's not a house; it's a six-story Rubik's Cube with no straight edges."

And possibly an ideal spot to hide those missing pages, Cassandra thought, intrigued and encouraged by what she was hearing. "You say your great-grandfather used to work there?"

"No lie. He was the construction chief on the whole freaking job, or so I always heard growing up. His sweat and blood went into building the Puzzle House, working there day after day for year after year, and his fingerprints are all over it," Cole bragged, his pride in his heritage once more evident. "In fact, my dad snuck me in there a few times back when I was a kid. . . ."

A crooked man's crooked house, Cassandra thought. And a giant puzzle box built by one of Elizabeth Goose's heirs around the same time that the Treaty went into effect. It all added up, at least according to the peculiar calculations of Library work.

She eyed Cole speculatively.

"Just how well do you know this house?"

"How well? he said boastfully. "Why I know that house like I know—"

But before he could finish, thunder boomed directly overhead, despite the fact that the night sky had been clear only moments before. Stormy black clouds rolled in from nowhere and a howling wind invaded the parking lot as though intent on breaking up the conversation. Violent gusts swept the lot, hurling every nearby scrap of litter into the air. Fast-food wrappers, concert flyers, cigarette butts, and other debris flew about erratically. An empty beer can whizzed past Cole's head, nearly winging him. Cassandra batted away a flapping sheet of newspaper that kept trying to wrap itself around her head, even as she assumed that the grimy paper was the least of their problems. The odds against this sudden change in the weather being a natural occurrence were too small to bother calculating. She knew magic when it wailed in her ears.

When the wind blows . . .

"Déjà voodoo!" Cole said, reaching the same conclusion. "I've bounced to this beat before!" The convertible began to rock from side to side. Cassandra felt the hostile wind tugging on her, trying to tear her away from Cole and the car.

"Buckle in!" she shouted over the gale, securing her seat belt and shoulder strap in hopes of foiling the wind long enough for them to get away. "And drive!"

"You know it!" Cole buckled in and fired up the convertible. A flying beer bottle crashed into a headlight with great force, shattering both itself and the light. "Time to ditch this party!"

Cassandra searched the sky, watching out for Mother Goose, but the churning black clouds could have hidden an entire flock of giant geese and ganders. Or maybe Mother Goose was wielding her magic by long distance instead?

Splat!

A ridiculously large bird dropping, as in at least a gallon's worth, hit the windshield. Greenish-white glop smeared all over the glass.

Or not so long distance, Cassandra thought.

Cole gaped at his grossly defiled windshield. "You have gotta be kidding me!"

"Just drive!" she yelled. "Hit the gas!"

"But my windshield's all messed up! I can barely see where I'm going!"

"You're just going to have to make do! Get going!"

More king-sized droppings fell from the clouds, splattering all around the convertible and despoiling the other cars in the lot. There were going to be a lot of upset drivers when the club let out, but Cassandra couldn't worry about that. The car peeled out of the parking lot, its windshield wipers getting a workout. Cassandra hoped the car was as fast as it looked. They needed to get away from Mother Goose and get to the Puzzle House in time to find the lost pages.

Preferably without being pooped on.

10

※ *Oregon* ※

"What's this?" Baird asked.

Jenkins had plopped an old color photograph onto her desk at the Annex, where she had been attempting fruitlessly to contact Flynn or at least track down some hint as to his current whereabouts. Texts, e-mails, and social media had proven a bust, while his appointment book and personal planner hadn't yielded any actionable intel either. She knew when his dental appointment was, but not what had led him to Mother Goose's Garden in the first place—and where he had ended up afterward.

"A souvenir? A mystery? A clue?" He stood solemnly before the desk, offering little in the way of answers. "Your guess is as good as mine, Colonel."

Baird inspected the photo, which appeared to have been taken at Mother Goose's Magic Gardens back in its heyday. A mop-headed young boy, no older than seven or eight, smiled and waved at the camera as he posed in front of Humpty Dumpy, who was in much better condition than it had been when Baird had visited the park only hours ago. Humpty's fresh paint job was not yet faded or peeling. The lawn and gardens in the background looked neatly trimmed, not over-grown and infested with weeds. A sunny blue sky provided a fine day for a carefree family outing.

A vacation photo from days gone by?

Probably, Baird assumed. She had stumbled onto plenty of such photos online while researching the defunct theme park. "Where did you find this?"

"In a dusty file folder," he said, "where the Library's copy of the Mother Goose Treaty should have been." He brushed some lint from his sleeve. "I thought it best to consult the original document, but when I finally unearthed the correct folder, which required a certain degree of excavation, all it contained was this lone memento."

She squinted at the photo. "Well, this certainly doesn't look like it was taken in 1918 when the Treaty was drafted." The boy in the photo, she noted, was wearing standard kid attire: a T-shirt, shorts, and sneakers. His face struck her as vaguely familiar, but she couldn't quite place it. "Any idea who the kid is?"

"I don't believe so," Jenkins said. "I thought at first that I knew him from somewhere, but I could very well be mis-taken. I avoid children on principle, due to their general im-maturity and lack of decorum, yet I've encountered enough of them over the years that their raw, unfinished faces tend to blur in my memory." A hint of melancholy entered his voice, if only for a moment. "Aside from that brat Mordred, that is. Now there was a holy terror, even as a child. . . ."

It occurred to Baird to wonder if Jenkins had ever been a father and, if so, how many children of his own he might have outlived over the course of his ageless existence. She couldn't think of a polite way to ask, however, that wouldn't risk re-opening old wounds and it was none of her business anyway.

Plus, there are more pressing questions facing us at the moment, she thought. "So where is the actual Treaty?"

"I am at a loss to explain its absence," he admitted. "Mind you, given the unusual turbulence of the last few years, with the Library being lost, then found, then losing its memory, then regaining its faculties, it's entirely possible that the document is simply misfiled."

"At the same time that we've got a real-life Mother Goose up to no good?" Baird didn't buy it and she doubted Jenkins did, either. "You don't really believe that for a minute, do you?"

"No," he said dourly. "I do not."

"Great," she said. "Just what we needed: another mystery."

Rising from her desk, she paced restlessly around the Annex as she considered her next move. She trusted her Librarians to handle themselves in the field, but she was not content to hold down the fort at the Library during this crisis. That was Jenkins's job.

"I feel like I ought to head out to assist one of the others," she said to Jenkins, "but which one? Stone? Ezekiel? Cassandra? Or should I be out searching for Flynn? Hard to say who might need backup . . . or where 'Mother Goose' could pop up next."

"Indeed." Jenkins began to straighten up the office, perhaps just to keep busy. "Might I suggest that—"

A blaring siren cut him off before he could finish. Baird looked up in alarm, a jolt of adrenaline priming her for action. The siren was a new security measure they'd installed after the Library had been infiltrated one too many times in the last few years. Prospero, Moriarty, the Queen of Hearts, and Frankenstein's monster had been the last straws as far as she'd been concerned.

"Jenkins," she began.

"On top of it, Colonel."

Jenkins clapped loudly to silence the piercing siren. Crossing the room, he yanked away the curtain veiling a magic mirror capable of monitoring assorted locations throughout the Library. Instead of his reflection, the image in the standing wood-framed mirror reflected a large chamber furnished with multiple bookcases, tables, and antique desk lamps: the very iconic image of a library. A sepia tone tinged the vision, which was the enchanted equivalent of a closed-circuit TV transmission. Baird had never quite figured out why they couldn't just install some nonmagic security cameras, but Jenkins could be quite set in his ways sometimes. And, in any event, that was a debate for another day. For now, the magic mirror had news for them.

"The disturbance appears to be in the main Reading Room," he reported, surveying the scene. Fallen books and a toppled lamp, strewn across the floor of the Reading Room, suggested that the siren was no false alarm. "Again," he added dryly. "We may need to consider charging admission."

Baird joined him before the mirror. "Mother Goose?"

"*A* goose," he replied "but not that goose."

A large white goose flapped across the silvered glass, flying wildly back and forth around the Reading Room as though searching for the best way out of the spacious chamber. The magic mirror did not provide audio, so Baird could not hear the goose honking, but she could easily imagine the racket the frenzied bird was making. Peering at the screen, it took her a moment to identify the out-of-place avian.

"Is that—?"

"The Goose That Laid the Golden Eggs," Jenkins confirmed, nodding, "which, according to the old nursery rhyme, once belonged to Mother Goose and her son Jack." He cited the relevant passage from memory:

Jack found one fine morning,
As I have been told,
His goose had laid him
An egg of pure gold.

Baird watched the fabled goose; the bird had been in the Library's custody for as long as she'd been a Guardian, but had always behaved itself before. "Never heard that one," she admitted.

"It's like the national anthem," Jenkins said. "Everybody knows the first part, but the rest . . . ?" He shrugged as though there was nothing to be done about such a lamentable gap in the general public's knowledge. "In any event, I surmise that this recent spike in Mother Goose magic has agitated our goose, which may be frantic to return to its original mistress."

"Or her gander," Baird said.

"Also a possibility," Jenkins conceded. "She doesn't get out much."

Ordinarily, the goose resided placidly in its pen elsewhere in the Library, but something certainly had the goose riled up, as though it had been, well, goosed. Baird winced as the berserk bird knocked over another vintage banker's lamp in its wild flight about the Reading Room. The lamp crashed to the carpeted floor.

"Great," Baird said sarcastically. "As if we don't already have enough on our plate right now."

"Multitasking is often a prerequisite when it comes to the Library," Jenkins said. "Don't get me started on the turn of the millennium. Having to deal with Y2K, the Seventh

Awakening of the Marsupial Lords, *and* the Omega Comet made for some very long days, believe me." He stepped away from the mirror and started toward one of the doors leading deeper into the Library. "Step lively, Colonel, it seems we have a rogue goose to round up."

Baird questioned his priorities. "Do we really need to deal with that now? Shouldn't we be concentrating on Mother Goose instead of a runaway bird?"

"You may be underestimating the severity of this situation, Colonel." Jenkins paused in the doorway to expound. "We cannot risk that goose escaping the Library, not with its propensity for laying golden eggs. Not only does this particular bird pose a major threat to the stability of the gold standard, and ergo to the entire world economy, but magic gold in itself has an unfortunate tendency to provoke bloodshed, betrayal, and even warfare out in the world. Just ask Wagner . . . or Tolkien."

My precious, Baird thought. "I get the picture."

"In addition," he said, ticking off his points on his fingers, "a loose goose running amuck throughout the Library is a potentially explosive situation, given that it might well disturb far more dangerous relics, creating yet more chaos and conceivably setting off a chain reaction of escalating disasters . . . not unlike that time Maxwell's Demon escaped the Theoretical Bestiary, got drunk on the literal Grapes of Wrath, and nearly opened Pandora's Box." His somber tone hinted at the most dire of consequences. "Moreover, I for one have no desire to have to clean goose droppings off the Ark of the Covenant or the actual Mona Lisa."

"Enough," Baird said. "You made your case. Let's get that goose."

Sorry, gang, she mentally apologized to her Librarians.

*Looks like you're on your own, while Jenkins and I go on a wild
goose chase . . . literally.*

———

Jenkins locked the interior entrance to the Annex behind
them, to help ensure that the goose did not escape out into
the wild. Baird let Jenkins lead the way to the Reading Room,
where the goose had been last spotted. She was starting to
know her way around the main sections of the Library, more
or less, but Jenkins probably knew its byzantine byways,
shortcuts, and subsections better than anyone else on Earth,
including Flynn, so Baird was more than willing to let him
take point. The sooner they caught up with the misbehaving
bird, the better.

"So does the rhyme say anything about how to catch this
goose?" she asked him as they hustled down long hallways
lined with bookshelves and display cases. "Anything useful,
I mean."

"Depends on how you define 'useful,' Colonel." He brandished an oversized butterfly net that he had commandeered
from the Unnatural History wing. "In the rhyme, the errant
goose is ultimately caught and reclaimed by . . . Mother Goose,
which is probably not the outcome we would prefer." He
recited the verses:

> *Jack's mother came in and caught the goose soon,*
> *And mounting its back, flew up to the moon.*

Baird recalled Mother Goose departing the abandoned
theme park atop the back of the giant gander. She decided she
didn't want to see the crone launching her own space program
anytime soon.

"Yeah, let's not ask her for help."

Arriving at the Reading Room, they found that the goose had already flown the coop, leaving behind a frightful mess—and a gleaming ovoid souvenir. A large golden egg rested on the bright-red carpet, reflecting the light from the overhead lamps. It was the size and shape of an ordinary goose egg, but its metallic gold sheen was no mere decoration or trickery. This was the real thing: an actual golden egg, freshly laid.

"That's our bird all right." Baird picked up the egg, which was heavy enough to be solid gold all the way through. It was also, somewhat disturbingly, still warm to the touch. "And I don't think she's gone far."

"Let us hope not," Jenkins said. "The Library is almost un-limited in its breadth . . . and I'm not wearing my running shoes."

Baird took a moment to admire the lustrous egg. "Gotta wonder how many of these little beauties Ezekiel has made off with."

"Not a one," Jenkins stated with confidence. "I maintain a tight inventory of the goose's output and there are no discrep-ancies, at least not in this century. I suspect Mr. Jones con-siders thieving from the Library insufficiently challenging to excite his interest . . . thank goodness. My own impression is that, ultimately, his criminal exploits are driven more by ego than avarice."

"In other words, it's all about the bragging rights," she said, thinking it over. "Yeah, that sounds about right." She turned her attention back to the task at hand. "Where do we look next?"

"It's quite simple, Colonel." Jenkins located a second egg at the other end of the Reading Room, before the far exit. "We follow the eggs."

Jenkins knew whereof he spoke. Departing the disordered chamber, they found a trail of eggs leading them on a circuitous path through the Library, with a new egg turning up every hundred feet or so. Baird gave up trying to collect them all, at least for the time being, but they'd soon located enough golden eggs to fill a decent-sized basket, assuming you were strong enough to lift it.

"This is a lot of eggs," Baird observed. "She usually this . . . prolific?"

"Hardly." Jenkins continued to grip the handle of his butterfly net, which had reportedly been used to catch a Mothman or two in the past, although that had been well before Baird's time. "No doubt the same magical upheaval that excited the goose in the first place has increased her productivity as well. All the more reason to get her safely penned up again before—"

A worried expression worried Baird as well.

"Before what?" Baird asked. "Everything's cool as long as the eggs stay inside the Library, right?"

"Not necessarily." His saturnine countenance went from concerned to pained. "Centuries of unbridled human desire and adoration have imbued gold with a certain mythical cachet that transcends its merely physical beauty and rarity. I'm concerned that the presence of this much scattered gold might . . . provoke a response . . . from certain other items in the collection."

Baird didn't like the sound of that. "What items? What kind of responses?"

Before he could elaborate, a loud thumping noise came from somewhere up ahead. The clamor, echoing down the corridor toward them, didn't sound remotely like an overstimulated goose in flight, but more like a heavy object being knocked about. Jenkins released a weary sigh.

"See for yourself," he said.

Rushing forward to investigate, Baird found herself in a wood-paneled gallery she wasn't sure she had ever stumbled onto before. Shelves and pedestals displayed a variety of arcane relics, but her gaze was instantly drawn to the source of the ruckus: a large eighteenth-century treasure chest rocking back and forth atop an X-shaped pedestal.

As in X marks the spot?

The chest, which was built of sturdy oak timbers reinforced by iron, looked like something straight out of *Treasure Island* or an Errol Flynn movie. A metal padlock held the lid shut, even as the entire chest bounced violently upon its perch as though possessed. The unseen contents of the chest rattled as well, shaken up by the chest's inexplicable perturbations.

Baird eyed the rambunctious chest as cautiously as she might have once viewed a possibly live WMD back in her counterterrorism days. She skidded to a stop, uncertain if she needed to "defuse" the chest somehow—or dive for cover.

"Now what?" she wondered.

A violent tremor dislodged the chest from the pedestal, causing it to crash down onto the hardwood floor of the gallery. The padlock came loose, clattering onto the floor as well, and the lid sprang open, revealing a treasure of gold doubloons, jewelry, plates, and goblets. The smell of gunpowder emanated from the interior of the chest, evoking images of pirate ships firing broadsides at Spanish galleons, or perhaps the burning fuses Blackbeard was said to have woven into his eponymous facial hair to make himself look even more demonic. As Baird gaped wide-eyed, the lid of the chest opened and closed repeatedly, making it look like a pair of snapping jaws.

"I was afraid of this." Jenkins came up behind her. "All these loose eggs, scattered carelessly about, have awakened the Dead Man's Chest . . . and its voracious appetite for gold."

Baird spotted another shiny golden egg lying at her feet. She picked it up.

"It's after these?" she said. "But it's just a wooden chest. How can it—?"

Peg legs sprouted from the base of the chest, lifting it up off the floor.

"Never mind," Baird said, as the chest scuttled toward her like a crab, its "jaws" snapping hungrily.

"Watch out, Colonel!" Jenkins said. "It's after that egg!"

Heeding his warning, she lobbed the heavy egg at the oncoming chest to keep from getting gobbled up with it. "Here you go, Cap'n Pac-Man."

"Wait!" Jenkins cried out too late. "You never want to feed an enchanted treasure chest!"

Now he tells me, Baird thought. She watched helplessly as the animated chest caught the egg in its open maw. Its lid clamped down. Crunching noises emerged from inside the chest as it apparently chowed down on the golden egg.

"And *why* do you never feed a treasure chest?" Baird asked.

"The more gold it consumes, the hungrier it gets," Jenkins explained. "Soon the eggs alone will not be enough to satisfy it."

"Can't get enough booty, huh?" she said. "Typical."

The lid of the chest sprang open again, revealing no trace of the captured egg. Still hungry, the chest spun about like a hound after a scent and took off into the bowels of the Library as fast as its peg legs could carry it.

Which turned out to be pretty damn fast.

"Oh, dear," Jenkins said. "What did I say before about escalating crises?"

Baird braced herself for more bad news. "Don't hold back. How much does this suck?"

"More than Vlad Tepes's family reunion," Jenkins replied. "This is not just about the goose anymore, Colonel, or the eggs. There is no shortage of priceless, irreplaceable relics in the Library's care, and they are all in danger as long as that ravenous chest is on the prowl."

"So how do we stop it?" she asked. "A magic cutlass? An old-fashioned ship's cannon?"

Jenkins shook his head. "I'm afraid it's more complicated than that."

"Isn't it always?" Baird said.

"We can't risk destroying the chest," he exposited, "for fear of releasing the evil spirits trapped within it."

"Evil spirits?"

"You've heard of the fifteen men on a dead man's chest?" Jenkins treated the question as rhetorical, continuing, "Well, it's actually more *in* than *on*, and they were very, *very* bad men. . . ."

She took his word for it. "The fun never stops, does it?"

"Not in my experience, no." He contemplated the direction in which the ambulatory chest had vanished. "At the risk of stepping on your toes as our resident strategist, I suggest we divide our forces. I'll continue after the goose while you pursue the chest . . . and prevent it from consuming any of our more precious treasures."

"Works for me," she said.

"Good luck then, Colonel," he said solemnly. "I can't impress upon you enough the vital importance of the task you've taken on. The Library does not merely hide its collection from the world; we also have the considerable responsibility of preserving it for posterity. The unique documents and relics in our keeping belong to all of humanity and history, even if many of them need to be kept under lock and key for any number of compelling reasons."

"Which is why we don't simply destroy them all just to be safe," Baird said, nodding. The rules of engagement were clear: stop the chest without wrecking it, and before it wrecked the Library. "Any idea where that four-legged luggage is heading?"

"The largest concentration of golden artifacts is in the Antiquities section," he advised. "I strongly recommend you get there first."

"But what do I do when—?"

An elephant trumpeted somewhere behind them. Whale song inexplicably echoed in the distance. A dinosaur roared.

"If you'll forgive me, Colonel, I fear the goose has stirred up the specimens in the Large Animals Room." He rolled his eyes before rushing off with his next breath. "I swear, it never rains but it pours. . . ."

Baird was left alone in the gallery, facing the empty X-shaped pedestal and the unexpected challenge that just had landed squarely in her lap. "So much for the briefing," she muttered. "This mission is a go."

Yo, ho, ho, a pirate chest for me.

11

※ *Ohio* ※

The Banbury Fair was in full swing when Ezekiel and Mary arrived at the fairgrounds. Throngs of locals crowded the fair, which was spread out over several acres and buildings. Sawdust carpeted the midway, where food stands hawked corn dogs, caramel apples, cotton candy, and funnel cakes. A Ferris wheel offered a bird's-eye view of the surrounding countryside. Prize cattle, sheep, and other livestock loitered in the stables. Games of skill and chance, almost assuredly rigged, fleeced the suckers, while offering teenage boys an opportunity to impress their dates by winning them an oversized stuffed animal. Fresh fruits and vegetables were displayed in elaborate arrangements. Calliope music issued from a vintage merry-go-round. A sunny afternoon cooperated with the festivities, providing a blue sky and pleasant fall weather. A chainsaw carving exhibition drew a crowd.

"I figure we can start with the pies." Mary strode forward through the crowd, leading the way. "Baked goods are this way."

"Aye, aye, ma'am." Ezekiel had resigned himself to the bossy librarian tagging along for the time being. *Who knows,* he thought. *Maybe a native guide will come in handy.*

It wasn't as though he'd had a lot of experience prowling country fairs. Lost tombs, pricy mansions, world-class museums, and high-security installations, sure, but some dinky small-town jubilee? These were not his usual thieving grounds and for good reason. What was there to heist except piglets, chintzy sideshow prizes, or a blue-ribbon eggplant or whatever?

"No problems with me leading the way, Mr. Jones? Glad you finally see things my way."

"It's not like you gave me much choice." He wondered again about her motives and decided that perhaps there was another good reason to keep her close by. *If she is up to something, better that I know where she is. Keep your gooses close, or something like that.*

He lifted a helium balloon from a souvenir stand, just for practice. It bobbed along in the air as he followed Mary to the pie display, which was set up in an open-air pavilion not far from the amusement park rides. Rows of freshly baked pies were arrayed on picnic tables beneath a log roof, while milling fairgoers admired them. Red, white, and blue ribbons singled out certain desserts for special honors. A cool autumn breeze carried the mouth-watering aroma of the pies. Ezekiel's stomach grumbled, reminding him that he hadn't eaten for hours. He saw some individual slices on display as well, protected by plastic wrap. Fancying a particularly tantalizing slice of pumpkin pie, he sidled over to it and positioned his body to block any inconvenient eyes. Deft fingers reached toward the slice.

"Keep your hands to yourself, Mr. Jones."

Busted, he thought, withdrawing his hand. *Never underestimate an alert librarian.*

"I was just admiring the fine quality of these baked goods," he insisted.

"Uh-huh, right." She steered him away from the tempting treat. "Refreshments are elsewhere *after* we find out if there's anything to these crazy theories of yours."

"Yes, ma'am."

Getting down to cases, he scanned the wooden pavilion, which hardly seemed like someplace you'd hide a lost copy of *Mother Goose's Melodies* or even one-third of it. The structure was solidly built with a concrete floor, sturdy wooden supports, and a log-cabin-type roof. He rapped one of the timbers with his knuckles but heard no answering echoes; it was solid through and through.

Something's wrong here, he thought. It was possible that there was a hidden compartment somewhere in the pavilion, but his gut was telling him that they were looking in the wrong place—and his instincts about such things were seldom wrong. "I'm not feeling this." He looked beyond the pie pavilion to the rest of the fair. "Are there any other attractions here that might have something to do with a pie . . . or a pieman?"

Mary mulled it over. "Well, there's probably a bake sale or two being put on by some civic group or another. Their booths would be over in the community hall, next to the art show."

"Bake sales?" Ezekiel shook his head. Those didn't sound permanent enough to hide a magic tome for umpteen years. "Anything else?"

"Come to think of it, the baking competition used to be held in the old Hobbies & Crafts building, but that burned down in the big fire of '75, along with most everything else."

His ears perked up. "Fire?"

"Oh, yes." Mary was apparently a fount of local history. "A

fireworks accident back in 1975 started a blaze that pretty much burned the entire fairgrounds to the ground. About the only thing that survived was the old carousel."

Ezekiel grinned. Mental tumblers clicked into place.

"And how old is the carousel?" he asked.

"Let me see." She gazed upward, not unlike Cassandra, as she peered back into her memory. "1919? 1920? Sometime shortly after the war."

In other words, Ezekiel thought, *around the same time the Mother Goose Treaty went into effect.*

"Come on," he said. "We need to ride that merry-go-round."

He didn't need Mary to guide him. She hurried behind him, struggling to keep up, as he followed the calliope music to an old-fashioned carousel in the center of the amusement park. Carved wooden horses, painted in shining colors, pranced in a circle, accompanied by a few more exotic beasts like whales and lions and unicorns. Laughing children, and more than a few adults, bounced atop the antique ride, which had obviously been kept in first-rate condition. Ezekiel generally preferred more high-tech amusements, but he had to admit that the carousel was pretty impressive. It was practically a collector's item in its own right, which made him wonder just how much he could get for it on the black market . . . strictly in theory, of course.

First things first, he thought. "This has to be it. If what you're saying is true—"

"Are you questioning my command of the facts, Mr. Jones?"

"Not at all," he assured her. "I'm just saying that this is the only part of the fair that's old enough to be hiding those pages. And the carousel is just the right age for someone to have built a secret compartment into it." His eyes widened as he examined the ride. "And check out that canopy!"

The top of the carousel was crowned by a peaked circus tent featuring alternating red and yellow stripes. Or, to be more precise, *wedges*.

"What about it?" Mary asked.

"Don't you see?" He felt even more pleased with himself than usual. "The tent is divided into wedges. Pie slices!"

She looked unconvinced. "You don't think that's a stretch?"

"Nope! It's all coming together now." He circled the carousel, walking counter to its own rotation. "Let's see, if I was going to hide a magic book in a merry-go-round, where would I put it?"

Decorative panels hid the machinery at the heart of the carousel, but seemed too thin and flimsy to hide the missing pages. Ezekiel's eyes zoomed in on the galloping wooden horses on their poles, as well as the other carved beasts populating the ride. Booth-shaped chariots were interspersed among the prancing steeds for younger or more timid riders. One such chariot he observed was in the shape of a goose.

Mary also spotted the goose chariot as it spun past them. "There!" she said, pointing. "You think that's where my family's inheritance is hidden? If there's actually anything to the stories, that is."

"Maybe," Ezekiel said. "But is it just me, or is that just a little *too* obvious?"

She gave him a look. "Hiding a long-lost book of nursery rhymes inside a carved wooden goose on a century-old carousel is your idea of 'obvious'?"

"Compared to some of the tricky treasure hunts I've been on?" Ezekiel chuckled. "Absolutely." He couldn't resist trying to impress her. "You think that sounds devious? You should have seen the Book of the Fourth Magi. Every page held a different maze and you physically couldn't turn each page before solving it, but, in the end, it turned out that the actual route to the lost treasure of Prester John wasn't hidden inside the book at all, but stitched into the binding." He puffed out his chest. "I'm not going to say that I'm the Librarian who figured that out, but I absolutely was."

Mary still looked dubious. "You'd better not be pulling my leg."

"Who, me?" He slowed to a stop and watched the carousel rotate past him. "Is there anything else in that rhyme that might be a clue?"

"Just the lines on the sampler," she asked, "or the rest of the rhyme?"

"There's more?"

"Oh yes! Everybody knows the beginning of 'Simple Simon,' the part about the pieman, but there are actually several more verses." She took a deep breath before reciting them.

> *Says the pieman to Simple Simon,*
> *Show me first your penny;*
> *Says Simple Simon to the pieman,*
> *Indeed I have not any.*

Ezekiel had not noticed any coins or coin slots on the carousel. "Keep going," he said to Mary, who continued with the rhyme.

> *Simple Simon went a-fishing,*
> *For to catch a whale—*

"Wait!" he interrupted her. An ornate chariot fashioned in the shape of a spuming white whale rushed past him. "Why is there a whale on a merry-go-round? Unless. . . ."

Very sneaky, he thought, figuratively tipping his hat to some long-dead Goose heir. *You need to know the whole rhyme, not just the part on the sampler.*

"You think the pages are hidden in the whale?" Mary asked.

"I'd bet the farm on it, or my name's not Ezekiel Jones." He congratulated himself for solving the puzzle without any help from the rest of the team. "Now I just need to check out that whale." He glanced up at the sky, which was still inconveniently bright and blue. "What time does this fair close for the night?"

"I'm not sure," Mary said. "Ten or eleven, probably."

"That late?" He frowned and shook his head. "So much for sneaking in after closing time. Guess I'm going to have to do this in broad daylight."

Mary looked apprehensive. "Do what?"

Ezekiel grinned in anticipation. "Just sit back and watch a master at work."

A distracted tween walked by, clutching a long string of paper tickets. Refusing on principle to pay for a ride on the merry-go-round, Ezekiel adeptly detached several tickets from the string without anybody being the wiser, aside from Mary, who frowned in disapproval. As the carousel came to a halt, he handed the tickets over to the ride's pimply-faced teenage operator and made a beeline toward the whale.

Thar she blows, he thought. *That's a whale thing, right?*

Unfortunately, a little girl got there first. Ezekiel was no good at estimating kids' ages, but she looked like a munchkin in pigtails. Freckles peppered her chubby cheeks.

"Great," Ezekiel muttered, wondering why an investigation into Mother Goose had to have so many inconvenient ankle biters getting in the way. "Excuse me, kid. Are you sure you wouldn't rather ride one of the horses . . . or the unicorn maybe?"

"I like whales." She planted herself squarely on the bench inside the chariot.

"What about the lion?" he asked. "Lions are cool."

"I like whales."

"Look, kid. How about I buy you some ice cream or cotton candy if you let me ride the whale instead?"

She regarded him suspiciously, her pudgy arms crossed atop her chest.

"Are you a stranger? 'Cause my mom told me never to talk to strangers."

Ezekiel realized that he was fighting a losing battle. "Okay, okay," he said, backing off. "Suit yourself."

Claiming a gleaming painted stallion directly behind the whale, Ezekiel was forced to endure one entire ride on the carousel before it finally slowed to a halt again. He spent the time planning his next move, while pocketing the brass ring at the end of a wooden arm suspended alongside the carousel. As the passengers disembarked, he hastily ran forward to claim the whale chariot.

Finally!

More tickets bought him another ride. Tapping the bench suggested that there was indeed a hollow space beneath the seat. Feeling around beneath the edge of the bench, his expert fingers located what felt suspiciously like a hidden release button. A triumphant grin betrayed his success.

Ding, ding. We have a winner.

Now he just needed an opportunity to crack the bench open and inspect its contents. Fortunately, he knew just how to make that happen. Extracting the small brass ring from his pocket, he covertly hurled it through a narrow gap between the wooden panels at the center of the carousel and into the mechanical guts of the ride. As anticipated, a loud grinding noise came from the motor, along with puffs of oily black smoke, as the merry-god-round lurched to a sudden stop. Alarmed passengers, gasping and crying out, hastily disembarked. The carousel's operator pulled back on a lever, shutting the ride down.

"Nobody panic!" he called out. "Please exit the ride in an orderly fashion!"

Ezekiel went into action. "Excuse me!" he said, getting in the operator's face. "I'm a special inspector with the Rides and Attractions Regulatory Commission." He held up his phone to display some false credentials from his extensive collection of same. "I need to conduct an immediate investigation of this incident."

"Hang on," the operator said. A name tag on his shirt identified him as "Jimmy." He seemed predictably discombobulated by the sudden crisis. "Let's not overreact. I'm sure it's nothing."

"I'll be the judge of that!" Ezekiel hopped back on the ride. "This ride is shut down until I say so. Secure the perimeter and keep out of my way."

"Hold on there!" Jimmy started to follow after him. "You can't just go barging—"

"Jimmy Doggle!" Mary said sharply, running interference. "You let this nice man do his job. We need to take this matter seriously."

"Mrs. Simon?" Jimmy sounded cowed by the librarian. He looked young enough to have attended story time not all that many years ago. "But—"

"But nothing," she said. "I'll vouch for the inspector here. You just do as you're told and I'm sure we can straighten this whole situation out in no time."

She winked at Ezekiel.

Never mess with a librarian, he thought again. Grateful for her intervention, he ignored the sabotaged motor and headed straight for the whale. The concealed switch yielded to his fingers and he heard a lock click open. A familiar thrill quickened his pulse as he closed in on his prize. Squeaky hinges protested as the top of the bench swung open to reveal a thin leather-bound volume tucked inside the hidden compartment. Embossed golden type on the front cover read:

"Mother Goose's Melodies, Book One of Three."

12

The trail up to the ruins was just as rough as Gillian had promised, making for an arduous hike. A brisk autumn wind added a nip to the air now that the sun had gone down, although the strenuous physical activity helped to keep the chill at bay. The dark of night further impeded their progress, forcing them to tread warily, using flashlights to guide their way. Stone liked to think that he was in good shape, but he had worked up a sweat by the time they neared the top of the rocky green hill. Backpacks laden with gear commandeered from the college's geology department weighed both hikers down, although he was impressed by the way Gillian had managed to keep up with him, even leading the way most of the time. She was clearly in good shape, too, as his eyes kept reminding him.

Thank you, Clippings Book, he thought. *I owe you one.*

Pausing to take a sip of water from a canteen, he took a moment to enjoy the view of the rugged, rolling countryside below, where the colors of fall added variety to the wild brush and bracken. Leafy trees displayed rustic reds and yellows, while the murky waters of a deep black pool rippled at the base of the hill, reflecting the moonlight. Lifting his gaze,

Stone spied the picturesque roofs and towers of the small college town not far away. Some of the older stone buildings looked to date back to the 1600s at least, as he could tell from their design and materials.

"Beautiful country," he observed.

"Don't I know it," she agreed, taking in the view as well. A cheery red scarf kept her neck warm, while adding a spot of color to her outdoor ensemble. The vigorous exercise seemed to have lifted her spirits; if she was still scared or angry about that spooky business with the pumpkin back at the pub, she wasn't letting it show. "I can't imagine living anywhere else."

"Really?" he asked out of curiosity. "Not that I don't see the appeal of this corner of the world, but it seems to me that an individual with your brains and expertise would have no shortage of options and opportunities."

"What can I say?" she replied. "I love this place. It's like I'm bound to the land, as silly as that sounds."

Maybe not so silly, Stone thought. It was entirely possible, of course, that there was nothing more to what she was saying than a natural affinity for the place where she'd grown up, but could it be that there was also some mystical force or connection keeping her here, not far from the potent spells entrusted to her branch of the family? She *was* an heir to the legacy of Mother Goose, after all. . . .

"Can't say I blame you, considering." He took another swig from his canteen as he contemplated the steep, irregular, and ill-maintained trail ahead. He estimated that another fifteen minutes of solid effort would get them to where they were going. "You ready for the final push to the top?"

"Try and stop me."

A short but strenuous climb brought them to the crest of the hill and what remained of an old Roman fort that once guarded an embattled empire against the fierce "barbarians" to the north, some two thousand years ago. As Gillian had warned, time and history had all but wiped away most traces of the former stronghold, leaving behind only a few crumbling stone walls and foundations, none more than knee-high at most. Half-buried stumps were all that were left of a bygone colonnade. Weeds and moss had overgrown the ruins, camouflaging much of the locale. Stone wasn't surprised that few visitors flocked to the site; to the untrained eye, the ruins offered meager rewards after such a demanding hike.

"Here we are," Gillian said. "Such as it is."

"So I see."

Stone's own eyes were far from untrained. Although little remained of the once-imposing fort, he could easily reconstruct the ancient frontier outpost in his mind, based on the general layout of the ruins. He walked the perimeter of the site, putting the pieces together.

"From the look of things, this was a relatively minor outpost, probably dating back to roughly 200 CE or so, with some modifications and additions over the course of the next century." He picked up a loose stone and examined it. "This variety of mortar, made of lime, sand, gravel, and water, allowed the Romans to build the first real stone fortresses in Britain, which endured for centuries." He tossed the stone aside. "During the Dark Ages, many of their abandoned structures were torn apart by stone robbers in need of construction materials." He nodded toward the town in the distance. "I wouldn't be surprised if some of your older college buildings are constructed of stones pillaged from the fort many centuries ago."

He couldn't conjure up actual hallucinations like Cassandra, but in his mind's eye he could see the bustling military base in its prime, superimposed atop its paltry remains. Armored legionnaires, wearing metal breastplates over their woolen tunics, guarded the sturdy stone walls and gates. Watchtowers, long collapsed into rubble and ransacked, had once looked out over the conquered territory below, as well as the thriving shops, taverns, and markets that invariably sprung up outside a fort's walls. Stone traced the outline of the base's defenses and interior structures.

"Okay," he said, conducting a guided tour of the ruins, "this would have been the commander's house or *praetorium*, those look like the foundations of the barracks over there, and that used to be the granary. Bathhouses were typically built outside the main walls, because the furnaces used to heat the water posed a fire risk, but a fort would still need a protected well or cistern in the event of a siege, which were often located right about . . . here!"

Sweeping aside the surrounding weeds and vines, he exposed a rusty metal plate, about twice the size of a modern manhole cover, bolted atop a ring of heavy stone blocks, half-buried in the ground. He rapped the plate with his fist and heard an answering echo.

"Bingo."

Gillian, who had lagged behind him, exploring the ruins, hurried to join him. "Is that it?" she asked. "The well?"

"I'd stake a couple of my degrees on it." He tugged on the metal plate, which refused to budge. "This is hardly original to the site, of course. I'm guessing somebody ordered the well shaft covered up for safety reasons."

"That sounds familiar," Gillian said. "Now that you mention it, I seem to recall something about that in the papers a few years ago. There was some concern about liability, in case a careless visitor took a tumble down the well. . . ."

"All of which makes me think we're on the right track." Stone stepped away from the capped well and shrugged off his backpack. "Good thing this isn't my first rodeo." He retrieved a compact acetylene torch from the pack. "Just the thing for getting past this sort of complication."

"Naturally," she said dryly. "I never go anywhere without one."

Her sarcastic remark elicited a chuckle from Stone. "Seriously, the Romans were already employing lead and ceramic pipes in their waterworks by the time this fort was built. Figured it couldn't hurt to be prepared in case we had to cut through some old pipes to get to wherever. Or maybe even an old iron vault."

"All this and a Boy Scout, too." Gillian arched an eyebrow. "You're a man of many dimensions, Jake Stone."

"Don't I know it," Stone said. "But it's been a long time since anybody called me a Boy Scout."

"Duly noted," she said. "I'll bear that mind."

He was enjoying the banter, but there was still work to be done and that plate wasn't removing itself. He donned a pair of tinted safety glasses.

"Stay back," he said before igniting the torch. A steady blue-hot flame issued from the nozzle of the cutting torch as he knelt and got to work on the steel bolts holding the rusty plate in place. A fountain of brilliant sparks spewed from where the flame met the bolts, which heated rapidly to cherry red. The harsh smell of iron oxide let Stone know he was making progress. "Funny thing," he said. "You can actually make one of these torches in the field, using only an oxygen tank, a cucumber, and some prosciutto."

"And you know this how?" Gillian asked, maintaining a safe distance.

"Long story, but I figured why take chances? Can't always count on having some prosciutto on hand at some old Roman ruins. . . ."

Years of laying pipes in Oklahoma paid off as he worked carefully but efficiently to burn through the bolts. Switching off the torch, he gave the plate sufficient time to cool before wrenching it loose and shoving it to one side. It landed with a clatter onto the rocky soil, exposing a deep shaft descending into the earth. Moonlight penetrated only the top few feet of the shaft, where rotting wooden timbers, which had seen better centuries, reinforced the plunging walls of the well in a manner favored by Roman engineers of the era. Inky darkness concealed the bottom of the shaft.

"Well, well," Gillian quipped. "How deep do you think it goes?"

"Only one way to find out."

Watching his step, Stone extracted some rappelling gear from his pack, along with a caving helmet with a built-in headlamp. The prospect of descending into the well did not intimidate him; as a former oil rigger, he had long ago grown accustomed to working underground in excavations, and that was before his new calling as a Librarian routinely led him into long-buried catacombs and hidden temples. Compared to that nasty hell pit in Salem, an abandoned Roman well ought to be a cakewalk.

"You stay here," he said as he anchored a climbing rope to what seemed a fairly sturdy block of stone. "Just in case I run into trouble."

"You're joking, right?" she replied. "Are we seriously having this conversation again?"

"Look, I appreciate all your help," he said. "I wouldn't have gotten this far without you, but—"

"But nothing. I didn't hike all the way up this bloody hill just to cool my heels while you do all the exploring." She rescued a headlamp from her own pack and joined him at the brink of the abyss. "And I know enough about spelunking to know that going solo is the very definition of foolhardy. Suppose you fall and, well, break your crown way down there, all on your own?"

"And suppose you tumble after?" he countered. "Then we'd both be stuck down there, with no one to go for help."

"A fair point," she conceded. "Perhaps we should let somebody know what we're doing before *we* go down there." She crossed her arms atop her chest. "Note emphasis on *we*."

"Hard to miss."

Her insistence of accompanying him provoked unwanted suspicions in his mind. What if she was actually after the spells herself? Another classic nursery rhyme shoved its way into his thoughts:

I do not like thee, Doctor Fell,
The reason why I cannot tell,
But this I know and know full well,
I do not like thee, Doctor Fell.

The problem, however, was that he *did* quite like this Dr. Fell, maybe more than he should, given how little he actually knew about her and her motives. Was she also out to be the next Mother Goose? He couldn't let his growing attraction to her blind him to the possibility that she had her own secret agenda. The long-lost spell book was prize enough to tempt any number of heirs to Mother Goose's legacy and power.

"Bugger," she said, looking at her phone. "No signal."

Contemplating their remote surroundings, she sighed and put the phone away. "Where's an ancient Roman cell tower when you need one?"

He checked his own phone. "Same here."

"So now what?" she asked.

He glanced around the ruins. No trace of a doorway remained, so there was nothing for the Annex's Magic Door to latch on to. They were cut off from the Library for the time being.

"We do this the old-fashioned way . . . sort of." He recorded a brief message into his own voice mail and stuffed his phone into a chink in the ancient masonry, marking the location with Gillian's bright red scarf. "I left a message with my colleagues letting them know where we're going. They'll be able to track us this far if they have to. If we get trapped, we'll just have to wait for them to come get us."

"But we're not likely to get trapped, correct?" Gillian asked. "You know what you're doing?"

He tried to strike the right balance between confidence and caution. "There *is* an element of risk. Are you sure you wouldn't rather keep watch over things up here instead of poking around down below?"

"And if that 'competition' you mentioned earlier comes calling, like maybe whoever snuck that threatening pumpkin onto our table in the dark . . . what then?" She glanced back over her shoulder at the way they'd come. "Under no circumstances are you leaving me alone and exposed on top of this hill. Safety in numbers, I say."

Stone figured they could keep debating this until they were both as old as the ruins or he could just give in and get on with the expedition.

"Fine," he agreed. "But I'm going first. No argument."

She peered down into the forbidding depths of the old well. She dropped a loose stone down the shaft. A faint splash came from the darkness far below.

"Suit yourself," she said.

He rappelled cautiously down the side of the well. It was a tighter squeeze than he would have liked and the neglected timber supports did not exactly fill him with confidence. His descent shook loose bits and pieces of the wall, which raced him to the bottom. Despite his expertise and experience, he held his breath until he touched down in what seemed to be a shallow pool of water, about knee-deep. He mentally kicked himself for not procuring rubber waders as well, although he would have had to lug the heavy boots all the way up the hill. He was going to need some dry socks later.

"Jake?" Gillian called down from above, an edge of concern in her voice. Peering upward, he saw her head and shoulders silhouetted against the moonlit sky. "Are you all right? Is it safe?"

"Give me a minute," he hollered back to her. "Just to look around."

The beam of his headlamp exposed what appeared to be a largish underground cistern designed to capture and hold rainwater that could be hauled up via the well shaft, perhaps to replace or supplement a spring that had gone dry at some point during the fort's existence. Scum-coated water filled a half-empty reservoir the size of a private swimming pool. Ceramic tiles and mortar sealed in everything around him, preventing the collected rain from seeping into the earth. Thick wooden beams supported the vaulted ceiling of the cistern, which looked to have been carved out of a preexisting cavern pressed into service by some enterprising Roman engineers. Mold and algae coated the walls and a few fallen timbers. Stale air reeked of mildew, while cobwebs hung like tattered curtains all around the chamber. A narrow paved walkway ran along the edges of the reservoir; Stone clambered up onto it, out of the cold, mucky water. Spiders and bugs scurried away at his approach; Stone counted himself lucky that he hadn't spied any rats yet.

Unlike that one time in Sumatra. . . .

Lifting his gaze, he spotted the cracked and crumbling remains of a decorative mosaic border running just below the edge of the ceiling, partially veiled by gray webbing and green slime. Water sloshing in his boots, he stepped forward to get a better look, only to hear something splash down behind him.

"What is it?" Gillian asked eagerly, having rappelled down on her own. "Have you found another clue?"

He turned toward her, annoyed. "I told you to give me a few moments to check things out first."

"I got impatient," she said, not at all repentant. "You didn't think I was going to wait up there forever?"

"It was only a couple of minutes!"

"Be that as it may, it's water under the bridge . . . or fort." She waded through the stagnant water toward the walkway where Stone was standing. She extended her arm toward him. "Do be a gentleman and lend a lady a hand."

He helped her up onto the raised walkway, but her foot slipped on the slimy tiles and she started to tumble back into the reservoir. He tugged hard on her arm and pulled her toward him, so that she fell against him as opposed to into the drink. He wrapped an arm around her waist, gripping her tightly . . . just to help her maintain her balance, of course.

"My hero," she said, catching her breath. She grabbed hold of him to steady herself. "How very gallant of you."

"Shucks, ma'am," he said, playing up his Americanness. "T'weren't nothin'."

Time slowed for a moment as they clung to each other deep beneath the earth. Rippling water cast shifting shadows onto the dismal stone walls surrounding them. The subterranean cistern was hardly the most romantic of settings, but Stone wasn't complaining. Gillian fit very nicely against him.

I do like thee, Doctor Fell. . . .

After a moment that felt both too long and too short, she glanced down at his hand which had somehow migrated to the curve of her hip. "You can probably let go of me now," she said, with what he wanted to think was a trace of reluctance.

"You sure?" he asked, in no hurry to release her.

"We *are* on a treasure hunt, aren't we?"

Right, he thought. *Mother Goose, Jack and Jill, Humpty Dumpty, saving the world. . . .*

"Yeah, we are," he grumbled. "Just my luck."

"Luck can be fickle," she said teasingly. "Every folklorist knows that."

"And what's that supposed to mean?"

She smiled cryptically. "I thought you were supposed to be good at figuring out clues?" She glanced again at his hand on her hip, which had yet to budge. "In the meantime. . . ."

"You first," he said.

"If you insist."

Letting go, she pulled away from him and swept her gaze (and headlamp beam) over their unusual surroundings. "Oh

my, I can't believe I've never been down here before. Mind
you, I'm no archaeologist, but to think that all this history has
just been waiting here, albeit a bit moldy and worse for wear."

Her beam fell on a round opening at the far end of the
cavern, just above the lip of the reservoir. Thick white cobwebs all but obscured the open gap, which looked to be about
fifty inches in diameter. A rusty metal grate, which had probably once guarded the opening, was half-sunken in the reservoir a few feet away.

She pointed at the opening. "What's that?"

"Probably a storm drain," Stone guessed, pulling his head
back into the game. "To keep the chamber from flooding."

Gillian regarded the drain a tad apprehensively. "We're not
going to have to go crawling around in there, are we?"

"I doubt it," he said. "You wouldn't want to hide anything
valuable where it might be washed away." He turned his attention instead to the fragmented mosaics running along the
top of the walls, searching for some sort of clue or hidden
message. The mosaics, made up of countless minute shards of
stone and glass called *tesserae*, were in sorry shape, which
possibly explained why they had been largely neglected in the
modern era. Entire sections of the mosaic were missing more
tiles than remained, so that they resembled jigsaw puzzles
with most of the pieces gone astray, and what was left of the
surviving mosaic was obscured by grime and mold and cobwebs. The art historian in Stone winced at the woeful condition of the mosaic, while the Librarian examined it for clues
to the hiding place of the lost spells.

"Find anything?" Gillian joined the light of her own lamp
to his.

"Still looking," he confessed.

Despite the damage done by time, Stone observed that the

mosaic seemed to have a celestial theme, featuring constellations and figures from Greco-Roman mythology: Orion the Hunter, Castor and Pollux, the moon gazing down from the sky with a broad smile on his face. . . .

His face?

"Hang on," he said excitedly. "Romans of the imperial era saw the moon as Luna, a goddess, so why does that moon up there look distinctly masculine?" He turned toward Gillian. "Didn't you say something earlier about the Man in the Moon?"

"That's right," she said. "In the original Norse myth, Hjuki and Bil—aka Jack and Jill—are captured by the Man in the Moon and carried off into the heavens instead of falling down the hill." She stared up at the grinning, white moon. "You think that means something?"

He nodded. "Sometimes it's the piece of the puzzle that *doesn't* fit that you need to look at the most closely." It struck him that the moon mosaic appeared to be in slightly better condition than some of the fragments around; unfortunately, it was also at least ten feet above their heads and out of reach. "The question is, how do we get up there to take that closer look?"

"Don't think you're climbing up on my shoulders," she said. "In case you haven't noticed, I'm hale but not husky."

"Not my plan." He looked around speculatively. "Maybe if we can pile up enough rubble and debris . . ."

Gillian's gaze fell on a fallen wooden beam lying nearby.

"You know," she said, "there's another verse of 'Jack and Jill' that's often forgotten or omitted. It comes after Jack gets patched up and Jill gets a whipping from their irate mother:

Now Jack did laugh and Jill did cry,
But her tears did soon abate,

Then Jill did say that they should play
At seesaw across the gate.

Stone didn't get it. "So?"

She indicated one of the fallen timbers. "Care for a game of seesaw?"

13

The Wilshire Puzzle House was a sprawling Victorian mansion crouching at the end of a long private drive lined by a half dozen palm trees. High hedges and shrubberies kept the outside world at bay, but the mansion's various spires and turrets climbed even higher. "No Trespassing" signs, faded and weather-beaten, discouraged visitors, but Cassandra and Cole snuck onto the grounds anyway, having parked the soiled convertible a few blocks away. Peering upward, Cassandra noted the clock tower rising above the upper gables. It was past one, but the clock in the tower seemed stuck at midnight. She assumed that wasn't a coincidence.

"So the house is empty now?" she asked.

Cole nodded. "Old Man Wilshire died without a will, and his heirs have been squabbling about what to do with the place for generations now. From what I hear, they do just enough maintenance to keep the house from falling down, in order to preserve its value, but otherwise it hasn't changed since the Devil finally caught up with Wilshire back around the Crash of '29."

"I see," Cassandra said. "Not unlike the Goose family feuding over that spell book way back when."

"Word." He made a gesture she was unfamiliar with. "Family fights are the worst fights."

Cassandra made a mental note to make sure her own will was up to date and in order. "So how exactly did the late Mr. Wilshire die?" she worked up the nerve to ask.

"Spontaneous combustion," Cole said, "or so they say."

Cassandra gulped. That certainly sounded like the Devil's MO, at least in her experience. Memories of a scorched ceiling and an occult sigil charred into the woodwork elicited a shudder. "I can believe it."

Using their phones as flashlights, they made their way around to the rear of the mansion, which was shielded from view by dense, overgrown shrubbery. Cassandra almost tripped over a loose paving stone, but she managed to keep her balance. A cool autumn wind gave her goose bumps. She hoped that was a good sign.

"Are you sure you know the way in?" she asked.

"Trust me," he replied confidently. "You came to the right Brother Goose. After my dad showed me how, I used to explore this place all the time as a kid, mostly to prove to my friends that I wasn't afraid of no devils or curses."

"And you never ran into anything particularly . . . demonic, did you?"

"Nope," he assured her. "But I did get lost inside a few times, for reasons you'll understand when you see the place."

Cassandra didn't find that particularly encouraging.

A flight of rickety wooden stairs led up to an elevated back porch. Following closely behind Cole, she climbed the steps to reach the back door, which was a sturdy oak barrier boasting a brass door knocker that bore the face of a leering demon. She wondered if any entity in particular had posed for the ornament; the face didn't resemble any particular devil she had run into lately, but you never knew. . . .

"Try the door," Cole said with a smirk. "Ladies first."

Cassandra didn't understand. "It's not locked?"

"See for yourself."

Puzzled, she took hold of the doorknob and tugged. To her surprise, the door swung open easily to reveal a solid red-brick wall identical to the rest of the house's exterior.

"There . . . there shouldn't be a wall there," she protested.

He chuckled at her confusion. "You can't trust the doors in this place. Some of them aren't even doors."

"Then how do we get in?"

He pointed down. "This door's just a decoy. The real entrance is hidden under the porch."

He guided her back down the stairs and into a shadowy space under the porch, where their flashlight beams exposed a large stained-glass window angled like basement doors beneath the stairs.

"But this doesn't make any sense," she said. "Why put stained glass where the sun can't get to it? That's just crazy."

"Now you're getting the picture."

Undoing a small, inconspicuous latch, he swung the window inward, exposing another set of steps leading down below ground level into a basement. He scooted aside to let Cassandra pass.

"Watch your head," he advised. "And don't take anything for granted."

Ducking low, Cassandra descended the steps into a murky vestibule facing a third set of stairs leading back up to the first floor. A skylight was improbably installed in the ceiling, some stories beneath where it might let in any sun.

"See what I mean?" Cole joined her in the vestibule, sweeping his flashlight beam around. "The whole place is like this.
Wait and see."

"You're the tour guide," she said. "Lead the way."

She followed him upstairs, where she rapidly discovered
just how "crooked" a house Ezra Wilshire had built. Outdoor
windows were installed in indoor walls, making it feel as
though the house had been turned inside out. A Persian carpet was nailed to the ceiling. The skylight occupied the center of the floor like a rug. Cassandra detoured around it to
avoid crashing through the glass. Zigzagging corridors led off
in various directions. Stairways went straight up to the ceiling. Hallways tapered and widened randomly. A trapdoor
hung open in front of a fireplace, offering a view of the cellar
below. An oil portrait mounted above the fireplace showed a
shifty-looking old man with a distinctly haunted expression.
Wary eyes seemed to peer anxiously from the painting, watching out for the doom that awaited him. Dark pouches under
those eyes hinted at sleepless nights.

Ezra Wilshire, Cassandra presumed. *Precombustion*.

And sixes . . . everywhere, sixes. Wilshire seemed to have
been obsessed with the number six and its multiples. Once
Cassandra saw it, she couldn't stop seeing it: six panels in each
window, six-sided floor titles, six arms per chandelier, six cor-
ners to a room, six steps to a stairs or twelve or eighteen or
twenty-four. Thinking back, she realized that there had been
six palm trees lining the front drive, six gables on the house's
facade, six stories, counting the towers. . . .

"Six, six, six," she murmured, her head swimming. Mathematical progressions shimmered before her eyes. Geometry
rang in her ears. "Six squared, six cubed, sing a song of sixpence . . ."

She tottered unsteadily on her feet. The crooked house was disorienting enough without glow-in-the-dark multiplication tables whirling around her head like satellites. Reaching out, she placed a palm against the wallpaper to steady herself.

"You okay, little lamb?" Cole asked.

"I'm fine," she lied. "Just let me get my bearings."

She closed her eyes to block out the house's myriad eccentricities and proliferating sixes. Breathing exercises, taught to her by Baird, gradually brought her cascading synapses and scrambled senses back in line. There had been a time when something like the Puzzle House would have caused her brain to go into full meltdown mode, incapacitating her, but she'd learned to harness her unique gifts rather than fear them. She was a Librarian now and it would take more than a glorified carnival funhouse to throw her off her game.

You can do this, she thought. *You're stronger than this.*

The intrusive equations calmed down. The six-string chorus in her ears faded to background noise. She opened her eyes and let go of the wall.

"Sorry about that," she said. "Felt a little dizzy for a moment."

"You and everybody else who sets foot in these screwy digs," Cole said. "Don't beat yourself up about it."

They found themselves at a juncture splitting off in six directions. A six-armed chandelier hung unlit above their heads. A dusty parquet floor offered no obvious hints on how to proceed. Cassandra glanced about in bewilderment, at a loss as to where to even begin looking for the missing pages in the rambling old mansion.

"Just how many weird nooks and crannies are there in this house?"

"No way to say, due to the cray-cray." Cole shrugged and

threw up in his hands. "Back in the day, Old Man Wilshire had crews working 24/7, 365 days a year. Carpenters, painters, glaziers, decorators . . . you name it." He wandered over to inspect some ornate mahogany wainscoting. "Good work if you could get it. Our crooked man paid twice the going rate, so people put up with his nuttiness in exchange for a steady paycheck. By the time you add up all the additions and expansions and remodels . . . the Devil only knows how many rooms and closets and secret compartments there are."

Cassandra had no idea, that was for sure, but she was willing to bet that the Number of the Beast was involved somehow. The task before them was daunting, but she refused to let that discourage her. Jenkins and the others were counting on her, not to mention reality as they knew it.

"Well, we *are* looking for a book," she said.

"So?" he asked.

"So we start with the library."

Cole insisted he knew the way there, despite the house's bewildering layout, but Cassandra soon realized that he might have been overstating matters slightly. The mansion was a maze that made the Library easy to navigate by comparison. Despite her best efforts, Cassandra soon lost track of what floor she was on. Dead ends and trick doors confounded them, forcing them to backtrack and try to figure out where they went astray. By the time they passed what she was pretty sure was the same stained-glass window for the sixth time, she was starting to lose faith in her helpful guide.

"I thought you knew your way around this madhouse?"

A disturbing possibility crossed her mind. What if he was deliberately misguiding her for ulterior motives? What if he wanted the book for himself, or was working in cahoots with somebody else? Just because somebody had sicced that rock-a-bye wind on him earlier didn't mean that he couldn't have his own agenda that he wasn't sharing with her.

"Keep the faith, little lamb," he said, looking a trifle abashed. "This house is a little more off the wall than I remembered, but we're almost there." They rounded a corner, which was not remotely built at the right angle, to find another dead end. Two wooden doors faced each other at the end of the corridor. Cole paused for a moment, glancing back and forth between the right and left doors, before nodding to himself and decisively picking the former. He strode forward and took hold of the knob.

"You want the library? Here's the librar—"

He tugged open the door to reveal a three-story drop to a concrete patio below. A cool breeze invaded the hall from outdoors. Cole threw himself backward, away from the precipice, and slammed the door shut again.

"That didn't look like the library," Cassandra observed.

"My bad." He approached the opposite door instead, somewhat more cautiously this time. "Now that I think of it. . . ."

The second time was the charm. The door opened onto a private library that suffered in comparison to *the* Library, but looked impressive enough in its own right. Cassandra counted six walls boasting six bookcases of six shelves each; she held off on counting how many books were on each shelf, but guessed that those numbers were probably divisible by six as well. The mere thought made her start to feel a little loopy again, but she gritted her teeth and soldiered on.

"What now?" Cole asked.

"Start scanning the shelves for anything Goose-related." Cassandra doubted that the missing pages themselves would be readily on display, but who knew? Perhaps they were hidden in plain sight, like Poe's Purloined Letter. "Maybe we'll get lucky."

They started at opposite ends of the library, working toward each other. Cassandra swept her flashlight beam over the spines of the books, crooking her head to read their titles. No surprise, Wilshire had an extensive collection of occult volumes, on topics ranging from astral projection to necromancy, none of which had apparently saved him in the end. Just reading the titles of some of the books made her skin crawl, while others looked slimy to the touch. A musty smell, laced with something unnamable, turned her stomach.

Just what was *Mysteries of the Worm* about anyway?

She suspected that Jenkins would not approve of Ezra Wilshire's collection, and might even want to confiscate a few of the volumes at some point down the road, but that was a matter for another day. She kept on scouring the shelves by the light of her beam, while wishing that Wilshire had been into Beatrix Potter or dirty limericks instead. "Would it have killed him to have read *Little Women* once in a while?"

"What's that?" Cole asked from across the room.

"Nothing," she answered. "Just making an observation."

"Okay then. I thought that maybe you had . . . hey, look at this!"

The excitement in his voice set her pulse racing. Abandoning her own search, she darted across the library to join him.

"What is it? Did you find something?"

"Maybe. Scope this out."

The beam from his phone illuminated a hardcover book resting on a shelf in front of him. Cassandra peered at the title on the spine:

The Compleat Mother Goose.

"Yes! Now we're getting somewhere." She threw up her

hand, uncertain whether a high five or a fist bump was considered cool these day, and somehow managed to make a fumbling attempt at both. "Good peepers, Bo-Peeps!"

"You know it. Told you I had this covered."

Cassandra pulled the book down from the shelf. A quick glance at the copyright page indicated that this particular volume had been printed in 1916, which meant that this wasn't *the* Mother Goose book they were looking for, unless maybe the missing pages had been slyly bound into it at some point? She started to flip through it, then noticed that one page, about midway through the book, was jutting out slightly as though it had come loose or perhaps been bound incorrectly, so that it almost resembled a bookmark.

"What is it?" Cole asked, noting her interest.

"This page, it's . . . crooked." She opened the book to the "marked" section, where she found two illustrated nursery rhymes sitting beside each other. On the left-hand, or *verso*, page was that same rhyme about the crooked man, while the right-hand (*recto*) page—which was the one that was actually set in crookedly—displayed another familiar rhyme:

Hickory, dickory, dock,
The mouse ran up the clock,
The clock struck one,
The mouse did run,
Hickory, dickory, dock.

Cassandra placed the book down on a desk, the better to examine it. Cole peered over her shoulder, shining his own beam on the pages. Cassandra pulled the cord on an old banker's lamp which, to her surprise, lit up to give them a better view of the book.

"The crooked man again," Cassandra noted, indicating the page on the left. "That can't be an accident."

"You think that page was messed up on purpose . . . as a clue?"

"I'm sure of it." She felt like she was following a trail of bread crumbs, although that was more of a fairy-tale thing. "Now we just need to figure out what we're supposed to be seeing here."

"What about the other rhyme?" Cole asked. "That's the one that's out of whack, like the crooked man is pointing at it."

"Good point." She compared the two rhymes to each other, reading from left to right. "Well, both rhymes mention a mouse. 'Caught a crooked mouse,' 'the mouse ran up the clock,' etcetera. Maybe that means something?"

A horrifying thought struck her. "Please tell me we're not looking for a mouse hole in this rat trap. We could be here all night!"

"More like all week," Cole said. "We're talking rooms on rooms, remember?"

Cassandra looked for some way to narrow the search. "What about your great-grandfather?" she asked. "He's presumably the one who hid the pages in the first place. Was there any one particular room or section of the house he worked on?"

Cole scoffed at the idea. "Where didn't he work? Old Man Wilshire was constantly remodeling things. Soon as a room was finished, he'd tear it down to build it back up again, different from before. There's not an inch of this house that wasn't redone a couple of times at least—except for the Hell Room, of course."

"The what?" Cassandra asked.

"Forgot to tell you about that part. Story is, Old Man

Wilshire had a secret room up in the clock tower where he met with the Devil every night to discuss business."

"I thought he was hiding from the Devil?"

"Hey, I'm just passing along what people say. Maybe the Hell Room was a safe space for some reason, where he and the Devil could meet to haggle over the terms of their deal, or exchange stock tips, or play poker, or some crazy shit like that. Nobody knows for sure, since Old Man Wilshere kept that secret to himself, but that's where he died finally, right up there in the clock tower."

"Clock tower!" Cassandra pointed at the rhyme on the crooked page. "That's it. 'The mouse ran up the clock.' The crooked man leads us to the mouse which leads us to the only room in the house that your great-grandfather could count on not to be altered." Holding on to the book just in case, she hurried back toward the hall. "Quick! Which way to this Hell Room?"

"Your guess is as good as mine."

"Huh?" Cassandra slowed down. "What are you saying?"

"Supposedly there's a secret stairway hidden somewhere in the house, but if my family ever knew where it was, they never told me." He caught up with her. "Probably didn't want me poking around in any Hell Room . . . for obvious reasons."

Cassandra sighed. "Then I guess I'm going to have to do this the hard way."

"How's that?" he asked.

"By working my brain, Librarian-style."

Using her phone to search the Internet, she called up several exterior views of the house, including some handy bird's-eye views that gave her a good look at the layout of the roof around the clock tower. She committed them to memory before putting away the phone and throwing out her hands to

summon up a hallucinatory model of the house, which shimmered before her eyes in three dimensions. Ethereal music
played in her ears, orchestrated by the brain grape that was
bound to kill her one of these days if her risky job didn't do
the trick first. Moving her hands as though conducting an
orchestra, she rotated the model before her, examining it
from every angle.

"Er, what are you doing, little lamb?"

"Trying to solve this Puzzle House, and you can call me
Cassandra, by the way. I haven't been a lost little lamb for a
long time now." Determination steeled her voice. "Now be
quiet and let me concentrate."

"But—"

"Sssh!" she said, sounding like a proper Librarian in more
ways than one. "This isn't going to be easy."

Cole got the message and piped down, even as she talked
herself through the problem at hand.

"Despite all the tricks and decoys and distractions, the
physical geometry of the house is still a matter of volume,
area, and height. Taking into account these practical realities,
there are only so many places where that hidden stairwell can
be located . . . unless Old Man Wilshire found a way to warp
space itself somehow." She made a face. "I really hate that."

But she'd cross that non-Euclidian bridge if and when she
came to it. For the present, she chose to work on the assump-
tion that conventional math and physics applied, because the
alternative was just too discouraging to contemplate.

"We just need to map the interior layout of the house onto
its outer shell to determine where the hidden spaces are," she
said. "Of course, this would be simpler if the house itself made
any sense whatsoever. . . ."

Part of her brain had been charting the house during their

uncertain explorations. Turning her gaze to one side, she attempted to construct a 3-D map of the mansion floor by floor, despite all the confusing irregularities and misleading window dressing. The illusory floor plans were incomplete or fuzzy in places, but they slowly began to come together in a coherent fashion, more or less.

"Right. Those back stairs connect with the sliding doors hiding that one freaky corridor which doubles back through the upside-down fireplace, crisscrossing itself, to bring you right back where you started. . . ."

Her outstretched hands manipulated the images glowing before her eyes, allowing her to shift walls and doorways and windows about as needed. Her gestures were hesitant at first, but grew bolder and swifter as the puzzle gradually revealed itself to her. Virtual blueprints smelled like paste and lemon-scented glass cleaner.

"And this landing goes there . . . no, *here*!That's it."

She wondered whether Stone would be better equipped to handle this challenge than she was, or would he be even more confounded by the house's architectural insanity, which didn't conform to any logical design or principles? Which of them would find it the most frustrating, she or Stone?

Doesn't matter, she decided. *He's not here. I am.*

Once she had the house's interior mapped out to the best of her abilities, she shifted it to the left, superimposing it onto her immaterial model of the exterior walls and roof, while looking for a concealed route to the upper reaches of the clock tower. The answer to the puzzle practically leaped out at her, chiming red and flashing like cymbals.

"There it is!" She pointed eagerly at a diagram Cole couldn't see. "That negative space. That's where the hidden stairwell has to be!"

He stared at her incredulously. "What are you tripping on, lady? Or are you working some kind of spooky librarian magic here?"

"Not magic, *math*!" She grabbed hold of his hand. "I know exactly where to go now. Follow me!"

Her mental map floated before her eyes like the HUD in one of Ezekiel's video games, keeping pace with her as she used it to navigate the mansion's relentless mysteries with increasing speed and confidence. As she raced through the house, and up and down its winding staircases, she deftly erased its assorted lures and deceptions from the model to create a clearer picture of the way ahead. False doors and detours popped like soap bubbles as she deleted them from view, while dragging Cole along for the ride.

"Hey, I thought I was conducting this tour?" he said. "You sure you know where you're going?"

"I can see it all now, bright as day! Just stick with me and try to keep up!"

Two floors, three rooms, eight halls, and a cunningly concealed walk-through closet later, Cassandra came to a halt in front of a short flight of irregular wooden steps jutting out into the hall, which climbed straight into a wall, ending right below a large stained-glass portrait of a cat, distorted in the mode of a Cubist painting. No light passed through the colored glass.

"This is it!" Cassandra collapsed her shimmering model with a wave of her hand. She squeezed Cole's hand in excitement while pointing eagerly at steps leading up to the art. "The crooked stile . . . and the crooked cat . . . rendered in a crooked style!"

"I guess," Cole said, trying to keep up. "So where's the crooked mouse?"

"Let's find out." She remembered the stained-glass window hiding the entrance to the basement. "See if this opens up somehow."

Cole found a latch with little difficulty. He pulled open the window to expose a spiral staircase exactly where Cassandra had calculated it had to be. The stairwell led upward toward the clock tower.

"Damn, girl," Cole said, impressed. "Your math *is* magic."

"I like to think so," she said, grinning. *Take that, Puzzle House.*

She couldn't help counting the steps as they climbed the hidden staircase. Six, twelve, eighteen . . . ultimately, thirty-six steps brought them to a door at the top of the stairs, which boasted a stained-glass depiction of a crooked mouse, matching the cat at the bottom of the stairs.

Thirty-six, Cassandra thought. *Six by six . . .*

14

The Large Animals Room was a zoo, in more ways than one. Pens, enclosures, pools, and tanks held a variety of exotic beasts from myth and legend, including myriad leviathans, chimeras, shape-shifters, and hybrids, all of whom appeared to be in an uproar as Jenkins arrived at the menagerie after traversing the Library with unseemly haste. Ordinarily, the animals resided as peacefully as on the Ark, but the goose's erratic antics had clearly stirred them up, as evidenced by the golden egg resting on the floor in front of Nessie's tank. A chorus of roars, howls, barks, wails, trills, chirps, hisses, lows, whinnies, and miscellaneous caterwauling assailed his eardrums and his patience. He hadn't heard such a hubbub since that time the banshee clans had challenged the Sirens to a sing off. It was going to take a considerable quantity of bones, biscuits, sugar cubes, and chew toys to calm this troublesome brouhaha, not to mention precious time that he could ill afford to spare at the present moment. Not for the first time, he wished that the Library's budget allowed for a full-time zookeeper.

But if wishes were horses, he thought, *I'd probably be tending them, too.*

"Hush! HUSH!" he called out in his most stentorian tone. "Everyone settle down. Nothing to see here." He placed the offending egg in an empty nest while making his way toward the well-stocked feed cabinet. "Everyone be patient and we'll get this all sorted out in no time. Just wait your turn."

A Questing Beast yipped vociferously.

"I said, patience . . . and that means you, Glatisant."

The Beast sulked petulantly in its stall. Its elongated neck retracted.

"That's better." Jenkins was wondering where just to begin when he noticed belatedly that two of the pens were missing their occupants. The King of Beasts no longer presided over his regal den, while the Unicorn had vacated his stall, leaving a feed bucket full of oats and honey. Neither animal had been caged, as this had never been necessary before, so Jenkins was at a loss to explain them wandering off—until he remembered another nursery rhyme:

The lion and the unicorn were fighting for the crown . . .

"Oh dear." He chided himself for not anticipating this; as with the errant goose, the Lion and the Unicorn had clearly been affected by the breaking of the Mother Goose Treaty, which meant that they had almost surely bolted from the Large Animals Room in pursuit of a crown.

No, he corrected himself, *not merely* a *crown*. The *Crown*.

There were many priceless examples of royal headgear in the Library's custody, from the helm of Hades to Anastasia Romanov's cursed tiara, but for Jenkins, a one-time Knight of the Round Table, only one crown was truly *the* Crown:

Arthur's Crown.

The other animals would have to wait. A more immediate

priority moved to the top of his to-do list as he hurriedly exited the Large Animals collection and proceeded with all deliberate speed toward another wing of the Library, where the Crown occupied a position of honor.

If anything happens to that Crown, he fretted.

No. Not on my watch.

Even before he came within sight of the Crown, the noise from another ruckus confirmed that his fears were wellfounded. Furious growls and roars warred with agitated neighs and whinnies. The commotion vexed as well as worried Jenkins; there had been a time, not too long ago, when the Library had largely been a place of quiet contemplation and scholarship . . . before wild magic was let loose into the world once more.

Damn you, Dulaque. You just had to spoil everything . . . again.

The unmistakable din of conflict drew him to the Camelot collection, where he found that the Lion and the Unicorn were indeed fighting for the Crown, which, to his vast relief, still resided on a marble pedestal between the mythical animals. Jenkins's ageless eyes instantly took in the principals of the donnybrook.

The Lion was the archetypal King of Beasts: the Lion of Androcles and Daniel and Babylon and Judah, the Lion of medieval heraldry and architectural grandiosity. Tawny and majestic, with golden fur and a shaggy black mane, the beast bared his fangs and slashed at the unicorn with his claws. His mighty roar shook the rafters. Some believed him to be the model for the sculpted gold lions guarding the steps at the front entrance of the Library, but their true pedigree was actually a bit more complicated than that. . . .

The Unicorn was straight out of a medieval bestiary, complete with a spiral horn, a pristine white hide, and cloven hooves. Contrary to spurious rumors, it had indeed made it onto the Ark in days of yore, but the miraculous powers of its horn had caused it to be hunted relentlessly, rendering it something of an endangered species and forcing the Library to provide it sanctuary centuries ago. Rearing up on its hind legs, the Unicorn battled the rampant Lion, pitting its gleaming horn and hooves against the Lion's fearsome fangs and claws, as they chased and feinted with each other around the pedestal bearing their prize.

The Crown of King Arthur rested beneath a glass dome atop an ermine pillow. The Crown, lost for centuries, had been recovered only a few years ago by Flynn and the Librarians on their first joint mission together. Flawless blue sapphires and bloodred rubies adorned an ornate silver circlet that had once rested upon the very brow of Arthur Pendragon, the Once and Future King. As ever, Jenkins felt a pang of bittersweet nostalgia at the sight of the Crown, but more pressing matters precluded any indulgent trips down memory lane. By all appearances, neither the combatants nor the Crown had been seriously harmed as of yet, but he could not count on that to remain the case for much longer. Both the Lion and the Unicorn were giving no quarter, making bloodshed all but inevitable.

Moreover, the Crown itself was more than just a priceless relic. It was an object of power, imbued with arcane charms and spells that were old when Avalon was young, making it far too dangerous to fall into the possession of any untamed individual—or animal. Should the Lion claim the Crown, adding its mythical potency to his own, it might well become the King of Beasts *and* Men, threatening humanity's fragile dominion over the planet. And if the Unicorn should take the Crown . . . well, no virgin would be safe.

Best to avert both eventualities, Jenkins realized, *but for that I'm going to require some assistance.*

He placed two fingers to his lips and let out a resounding whistle. Occupied with each other, the quarreling beasts ignored the signal, as Jenkins had expected, but another denizen of the Library did not.

The Sword in the Stone, on display across from the Crown, awoke from its slumber. Responding to the command, Excalibur yanked itself free from its petrified housing and came flying through the air to Jenkins's aid.

As well it should, he reflected. *What better to defend Arthur's Crown than Arthur's own trusty sword?*

Granted, Excalibur was not now what it had once been. Having been destroyed in battle against the Serpent Brotherhood some time ago, the legendary sword had only recently been returned to the world via the abstruse machinations of the Ladies of the Lake and some convoluted time-travel shenanigans. As a result, it was still regaining its strength and skill, but Jenkins judged that even a recuperating Excalibur was better than none.

"Protect the Crown," he ordered, "in Arthur's name!"

Defying gravity, the magic sword zipped across the chamber to engage the Unicorn. Bright golden sparks flew as Excalibur fenced with the beast, pitting its shining blade against the Unicorn's equally silvery horn. The clash of the weapons, as they parried and thrust, chimed like a crystal cave.

Jenkins was relieved to see that the floating sword was employing the flat of its blade and not attempting any fatal blows, but he fretted that the immature blade might get carried away in the heat of battle. He wasn't sure if a magic sword *could* slice through a magic horn, but he had no desire to find out.

"That's Library property," he reminded Excalibur. "Take care not to damage it!"

A metallic ring acknowledged the caretaker's command.

With the Unicorn distracted, the Lion pounced for the Crown, but Jenkins was ready for him. In one hand, he held the back of the antique Windsor chair, while his other hand brandished his own leather belt, which he had adroitly removed after summoning Excalibur. The belt was rather longer than he usually cared to admit, but at the moment it made a useful whip. He cracked it like a lion tamer to get the animal's attention.

"Down, Your Majesty," he addressed the King of Beasts. "That Crown does not belong to you."

The Lion roared defiantly, but Jenkins kept him at bay with the belt and chair, employing a technique he'd taught Clyde Beatty back in the Roaring Twenties during an ill-advised flirtation with circus life. He cracked the belt repeatedly and blocked the Lion's claws with the chair.

"Back!" he ordered. "Mind your manners!"

A swipe of the Lion's great paw nearly knocked the chair from Jenkins's grip. His arm was already tired from holding it up. He was immortal, but he wasn't indefatigable. A subtle distinction, to be sure, but not an insignificant one.

This is all Mother Goose's fault, he groused. He pined for the good old days when you could win over the Lion just by removing a thorn from its paw. *What would Judson say at a time like this?*

"Hakuna matata?"

A second swipe reduced the chair to splinters, driving

Jenkins backward toward the Crown's royal perch. Claw marks shredded the front of the caretaker's neatly pressed suit and shirt, much to his annoyance.

"Excuse me, I just ironed those."

His clothes were in worse shape than he was, however. There were precious few things on this Earth that could actually harm him, and a mere scratch from an overgrown tabby cat was not among them. Of much greater concern was the fact that he was making scant progress in resolving this situation and that while he dallied here a certain goose was still running amuck, the Dead Man's Chest was on a feeding frenzy, and, oh yes, there was still the little matter of Mother Goose trying to put Humpty Dumpty back together again.

I simply do not have time for this nonsense.

Seeking inspiration, he recalled the rest of the rhyme:

The lion and the unicorn were fighting for the crown.
The lion beat the unicorn all around the town.
Some gave them white bread, some gave them brown.
Some gave them plum cake and drummed them out
   of town.

"Well, that does me absolutely no good," he muttered. He fancied himself an accomplished cook, with a sophisticated palate honed by generations of fine dining throughout the known and unknown world, but he hardly had time to raid the pantry for the proper ingredients for a plum cake, of all things. By the time he baked said dessert, the Crown would be lost, the Library would be in even greater disarray, and a fresh Creation might very well hatch from the World Egg.

In other words, it was not a good time for baking.

His belt cracked loudly against the Lion's snout, forcing the beast to retreat, if only for a moment. Jenkins dared not look over his shoulder to check on Excalibur, but his ears informed him that the sword was still dueling with the Unicorn. The clash of steel against horn (and vice versa) rang out like the music of the spheres.

Music . . .

It was often said, Jenkins reflected, that music had charms to soothe the savage beast. This was actually a mangling of the original Shakespeare, which had instead spoken of a "savage breast," but sometimes there was more truth to be found in a misprint or accident of translation than in the original text, as in the case of, say, Cinderella's famously impractical glass slippers. A frankly brilliant strategy popped into his head.

Yes, he thought. *That just might work, provided I can somehow find a way to absent myself from my current predicament long enough to secure the necessary relic.*

Alas, he doubted that the Lion would be willing to grant him a time-out.

Which left him only one other option.

Wincing at the prospect, he brought his elbow down on the glass dome protecting the Crown, shattering it to pieces. Still wielding his belt as a whip to fend off the Lion, he took hold of the Crown with his free hand while silently apologizing to his late, lamented liege.

Forgive the indignity, sire.

He hurled the Crown with all his strength and shouted to the sword.

"Excalibur, catch!"

Unlike Flynn, he could never bring himself to abbreviate the sword's name to Cal, but what was in a name? The sword responded at once, breaking off from its duel with the Unicorn to zip after the Crown like a dog chasing a Frisbee. Catching up with the flying circlet, Excalibur caught the silver hoop on the tip of its blade, skewering it, and tilted itself upward so that the Crown slid farther down the length of the blade.

"Good catch!" Jenkins praised the sword. "Now . . . run! Keep away!"

The Lion and the Unicorn both protested audibly as Excalibur whizzed out of the chamber, taking the Crown with it. The beasts took off after the fleeing sword, leaving Jenkins alone in the now-empty gallery. Broken glass crunched beneath his heels. The splintered remains of the chair also needed to be swept up at some point. The empty pillow offended his sensibilities.

"Exit . . . pursued by the Lion and the Unicorn."

So far, so good, Jenkins thought, putting his belt back on. If Fortune was with him, Excalibur would lead the obsessed animals on a merry chase, buying him time enough to find a more efficacious means to remedy the situation. *Provided I take brisk advantage of this temporary respite.*

Lifetimes spent in the service of the Library meant that he knew its ever-expanding layout better than literally anyone alive, so he set off in the right direction without hesitation. The Library had sometimes been compared to a work of origami, folding space itself in ingenious and creative ways. Jenkins took advantage of a few such folds to reach the Music History section in record time. Historic lyres, lutes, war drums, rattles, harps, and theremins occupied wooden racks, alongside shelves of collected sheet music, lost compositions, forbidden librettos, and enough vintage vinyl albums to make any knowledgeable audiophile drool uncontrollably. Ignoring the vast panoply of rare musical artifacts on display, Jenkins headed straight to one specific item in the collection: a set of panpipes dating back to ancient Greece and the glory days of Mount Olympus.

The age-old instrument hung on a hook beside a foot-tall marble statue of the great god Pan himself, complete with goatish horns and hooves. A basket resting below the pipes held a supply of fresh beeswax collected from an apiary elsewhere in the Library. Jenkins helped himself to two small wads of wax which he used to plug his ears just as Odysseus had once done on his protracted voyage home from Ilium. Suitably prepared, he snapped his fingers and addressed the pipes.

"Rise and shine," he said. "It's show time."

The pipes stirred and lifted off their hook, levitating much as Excalibur did. Legend had it that Pan's pipes had once been a nymph named Syrinx whom Zeus had transformed into hollow reeds in order to protect her from Pan's lustful advances; that had always struck Jenkins as a trifle extreme, but who was he to judge? That had been rather before his time as well, and he was not inclined to take idle gossip as gospel. All he knew for certain was that the pipes had a personality of their own—and that their music had some very special qualities.

The pipes danced in the air before him, eager to perform.

"Let me summon your audience," he promised the flute.

He whistled once more for Excalibur, who soon came racing back toward him, pursued by the Unicorn and the Lion. The former was slightly ahead of the latter, but the Lion was only a few paces behind, bounding between the stacks. Despite his plan, and his immortal constitution, Jenkins experienced a moment of trepidation at the sight of the berserk animals bearing down on him. Holding his breath, he waited until they were solidly within earshot before cueing the pipes to commence playing.

"A lullaby, Madame Syrinx, if you please."

The mythic pipes obliged readily, playing themselves without need of mortal hands or breath. Even through the wax shielding his ears, Jenkins could still hear the unearthly melody emanating from the flute. The music was preternaturally soothing, almost hypnotic. Jenkins caught his own world-weary eyes beginning to droop, but roused himself before he dozed off entirely.

In retrospect, perhaps I should have been slightly less stingy with the wax.

The Lion and the Unicorn lacked any such protection, however, as Syrinx's music truly soothed their savage breasts. Slowing to a halt, the wild animals forgot their rhyme-dictated pursuit of the Crown as they fell under the spell of the irresistible lullaby. Jenkins watched with relief as the beasts settled down onto the floor and drifted off to dreamland, snuggled up against each other. Within moments, they were both sleeping soundly. The Lion's snore also managed to penetrate Jenkins's waxen earplugs to a degree. The caretaker took a moment to admire the tranquil scene. He had to admit it: they did look angelic when they slept.

"Bravo, bravo." He quietly feigned applause to avoid rousing the slumbering wildlife. The pipes flitted about above their captive audience. "Now if you can just keep playing for the time being, that would be divine, thank you."

To be honest, he hadn't been entirely sure that the pipes' soporific melodies would be enough to overcome Mother Goose's pernicious influence, but it seemed that the pipes' immediate presence had won out in the end. It was a shame, he mused, that he couldn't employ the pipes to tranquilize the runaway goose as well, but he needed Syrinx here, keeping the Lion and the Unicorn dormant, while he dealt with the other urgent items on his agenda.

One thing at a time, he thought. "Excalibur, kindly return the Crown to its throne. That's a good sword."

The weapon took off on its errand.

A honk echoed down the endless halls and corridors of the Library, pointedly reminding Jenkins that he still had a goose to catch. As it happened, he had finally formulated a plan of action regarding the elusive waterfowl, but that scheme first required that he borrow a couple of key items from the Library's diverse collections.

And the sooner, the better.

"Play on," he whispered to the pipes as he tiptoed away from the sleeping beasts. "Encore."

He regretted losing so much time to this detour. He could only hope that Colonel Baird was carrying out her own mission with her customary aplomb and efficiency.

No doubt she has the matter completely under control . . . or not.

15

The Antiquities section was possibly the oldest part of the Library, dating back to its original location in Alexandria millennia ago. Relics and scrolls and tapestries from ancient Greece, Rome, Egypt, Babylon, Sumer, Atlantis, Lemuria, and other bygone realms and empires filled several adjoining rooms, grouped more or less geographically. Dashing into the section, after taking a shortcut in the hopes of beating the Dead Man's Chest to the spot, Baird noted that Jenkins had not been exaggerating when he'd said that Antiquities was home to an impressive amount of gold artifacts, including a pharaoh's golden sarcophagus, a priceless golden Buddha, the Golden Fleece, the Golden Camel of Marrakesh, a pair of golden sandals, and even the transmuted form of King Midas himself. The latter still sat upon his equally auric throne, his very flesh and garments converted to solid gold by his infamous curse. According to Flynn, Midas had once been displayed in the Library's main entrance hall, but he had since been relocated for reasons that didn't really matter at the moment.

The ancients really liked their bling, Baird thought. *Guess not much has changed over the centuries.*

A quick survey confirmed that she had indeed reached

Antiquities before the hungry treasure chest, but she barely had a moment to catch her breath before she heard wooden legs clattering toward her and the gleaming relics. Turning toward the noise, she spied the chest bearing down on Antiquities, its iron-edged "jaws" snapping eagerly. Two pairs of matching peg legs carried it briskly down the hallway toward an open doorway.

Good call, Jenkins, she thought. *Wonder if this chest has gone on a feeding frenzy before?*

With no time to lose, she sprinted though the Greco-Roman collection to manually activate a last-ditch security measure. A heavy iron portcullis slammed down into place, blocking the doorway. Baird hoped that would be enough to deter the ravenous pirate chest.

No such luck.

The chest started chomping through the metal gate like a woodchuck would chuck wood. Sparks and sharp metal splinters flew in all directions as it tore into the portcullis in its relentless hunger to get to the gold.

"Crap," Baird said.

Snatching a Bronze Age spear from its mount upon a wall, she positioned herself between the chest and King Midas, who was first in line to be devoured. The legendary king may have been famously greedy, but Baird figured he deserved better than to be gobbled up by a glorified foot locker. And then there was the whole unique historical being thing. . . .

Shredded iron screeched in protest as the chest made it through the gate into Antiquities and made a beeline for King Midas, despite the determined Guardian barring the way.

"Not so fast, buster!"

She poked at the chest with the spear, frustrated by her adversary's lack of any obvious vital spots. Maybe she couldn't destroy the chest without releasing those fifteen evil spirits, or so Jenkins said, but perhaps she could discourage it from eating the relics?

"Back off, chesty! Go suck another golden egg."

She had underestimated the chest's stubbornness, however. Springing forward on its peg legs, it caught the point of the spear in its jaws and bit it clean off, leaving Baird holding on to a truncated metal shaft that was steadily being whittled down by the hungry pirate chest. Bronze shavings sprayed onto the floor as the chest advanced on Baird, devouring the remainder of the spear inch by inch.

"Okay, time for Plan B," she muttered. "Which would be . . . ?"

Letting go of what was left of the spear, which she hoped hadn't been *too* valuable, she scanned Antiquities for another option. Clearly, she needed some sort of weapon or defense that operated at a distance, out of reach of the chest's clacking jaws, but what?

Jupiter's thunderbolt? No, that was too destructive. Chances were, she'd blow the chest to pieces or else set it on fire. Vulcan's golden net, the one he'd once used to snare his cheating wife and her lover, the God of War? No, that would be nothing but a heap of tasty pasta to the gold-hungry treasure chest. Pluto's helmet? No, invisibility was not going to help her in this crisis. Cupid's arrows? Nope, not going there. Neptune's trident?

A grin broke out on her face.

That I can work with!

While the chest was finishing off the last of the spear, Baird plucked the forged metal trident from its pedestal. It was cold and wet to the touch, as though dredged from the bottom of the sea. The sound of ancient waves crashed in her ears.

Getting between the chest and Midas, she aimed the barbed tines of the trident at the chest just as it charged at the golden king and his throne again.

"Cool it," Baird said.

Responding to her will, three high-pressure streams of seawater shot from the trident, converging into a single blast that smashed into the treasure chest, driving it back. The salty smell of the brine filled Baird's nostrils as she kept up the barrage. Water flooded the floor of the section, but that was a small price to pay to keep Midas and the surrounding relics safe from the rampaging chest.

But would the firehose treatment be enough?

The chest didn't seem to think so. Despite the punishing salt spray, it pushed forward against the power of the trident. Nothing, it seemed, could douse its appetite, not even the wrath of the Seven Seas. The force of the spray was such that Baird had to hold on to the trident's handle with both hands to keep it under control, but the chest kept advancing, slowly but inexorably, toward the delectable golden figure. King Midas was about to become an entrée, followed by who knew how many other courses and desserts.

"*Paging Colonel Baird.*" Jenkins's voice emerged from a nearby lyre, which he was somehow employing as an intercom. The strings of the lyre gave his voice a peculiar twang. "*Have you managed to secure the Dead Man's Chest yet?*"

"Still working on that," she shouted back. "How about that goose?"

"*Elusive,*" he confessed, "*but I am taking measures to remedy the situation. I simply wanted to stress once again how imperative it is that you do not damage the structural integrity of that chest. . . .*"

"Doing my best," she said tersely.

"I'll leave you to it then, Colonel." A goose honked noisily in the background. *"Over and out."*

Baird grunted in exasperation; she was all for the left hand knowing what the right hand was doing, strategically, but not while she was trying to fend off a ravenous treasure chest with a divine trident that was already starting to lose its punch.

To her dismay, the water pressure began to slacken. Gritting her teeth, she tried to will the trident to keep spraying, but she was only a mortal Guardian, not a sea god. There was a limit to how much water she could summon through the trident and apparently she was nearing it, while the chest was still as hungry and persistent as ever. It seemed you couldn't drown a treasure chest, so how in the name of Robert Louis Stevenson were you supposed to—

The answer struck her like a broadside from a pirate ship. *Of course,* she thought. *That has to be it.*

She had a plan. Now she just had to implement it. Still holding the chest at bay with the trident, she swept her gaze over the artifacts at hand, searching for a suitable lure. The Golden Fleece, once stolen by Jason and his Argonauts, glittered a few yards away, occupying a place of honor on the wall. The mythical ram's skin had famously enticed the Argonauts to cross the Black Sea in quest of it; with any luck, the Dead Man's Chest would find it equally irresistible.

Time to play matador again, she thought. *Olé.*

Had it really only been a day or so since she had resorted to the same stunt to distract the Calydonian Boar? She was going to need a long nap, and maybe even a stiff drink, when this Goose business was over, assuming that the universe was still around.

One last blast of pressurized ocean sent the treasure chest tumbling backward. The effort drained the trident, reducing the spray from the tines to a trickle, but it bought Baird a few precious moments. Discarding the dripping trident, she took advantage of those moments to hurtle over a pedestal and yank the Golden Fleece off the pegs supporting it. The wooly golden sheepskin, shorn from a sacred ram thousands of years ago, was just as heavy as one might expect, but Baird had once carried a wounded comrade across miles of rugged mountainside in Afghanistan after a raid on a terrorist training camp had gone south; she figured she could transport a sparkly gold fleece from one end of the Library to another. The trick was going to be not getting eaten by the chest first.

"Yo!" she shouted at the chest. "Ho, ho!"

The treasure chest had landed on its back after being knocked over by the trident's final blast. Its peg legs failed uselessly in the air and, for a moment, Baird dared to hope that maybe it was stuck like an upside-down tortoise, but then it righted itself by using its hinged jaws to flip itself back onto its legs again. Baird flapped the fleece to get the chest's attention.

"You want this? Sure you do!" She waved the fleece enticingly. "Come and get it!"

The chest vacillated, torn between Midas and the fleece, but, as Baird had hoped, the glittering skin proved too tempting to ignore. Rum trickled like drool from its jaws. Abandoning Midas and the other treasures for the moment, the chest charged at Baird, who draped the fleece over her shoulder and took off running, with the chest in hot pursuit. Peg legs splashed through large puddles of brine.

"That's it!" she shouted back at the chest, urging it on. "Catch us if you can, you greedy safe-deposit box!"

She liked to think she could outrun a treasure chest, even carrying a heavy fleece, but, as it happened, this was not something she had ever really attempted before. History, she suspected, was full of doomed merchant vessels, laden with precious cargo, that had thought they could outpace a relentless pirate ship, only to lose their treasure to greedy buccaneers.

Baird hoped she wouldn't be sunk like those ships. Jenkins was counting on her.

And so was the Library.

16

※ *Ohio* ※

Ezekiel was mildly surprised to find an actual book hidden in the antique carousel, as opposed to a stack of loose pages. *Guess the family must have rebound their third of the original volume to help preserve it.* He couldn't complain. *Makes life easier for me.*

"Oh my Lord." Mary appeared behind him, looking over his shoulder. "That's really it? This isn't some sort of complicated scam?"

"Nope. Just another lost relic liberated by Ezekiel Jones . . . with, okay, a little bit of help," he conceded.

He started to reach for the book but was interrupted by the operator, who chose that moment to check on Ezekiel. The teen gaped at the confusing tableau before him.

"Wait just one minute," he protested. "What's going on here? What's with that book?"

"The inspector has accidentally stumbled onto a bit of town history." Mary shoved past Ezekiel to claim the book. "Which I'm taking custody of on behalf of the Banbury Public Library."

Ezekiel opened his mouth to protest, then realized that

now was not the time. He could use the local librarian's clout to walk the book right out of the fair without too many questions asked. "Naturally," he agreed. "A find of this nature needs to be handled by someone who knows what they're doing. Good thing you just happened to be on hand."

She smirked at him. "Yes. I'd call that a fortuitous coincidence, wouldn't you, Mr. Jones?" Clutching the book to her chest, she strode past Jimmy toward the ride's exit. "If you'll excuse me, I should get this historically valuable document safely tucked away in the library where it belongs."

Hey, I thought that was my job, Ezekiel thought. He kept a close watch on the departing volume as he hustled after her, leaving Jimmy and the breached whale chariot behind.

"Hey," the confused operator called out. "What about the inspection? You didn't even look at the motor."

"Not my department, mate. Get yourself a good mechanic."

"But—"

Jimmy's befuddled queries were swallowed up by the general clamor of the fair as Ezekiel caught up with Mary, who was striding decisively back the way they'd come. He eyed the *Mother Goose* book greedily, while wondering if he was the first Librarian to recover one of the hidden volumes. He hadn't heard anything about Stone or Cassandra finding their targets yet.

"Good work back there," he complimented Mary. The leather-bound tome looked distinctly out of place on the midway, where everyone else was carrying popcorn and sodas and plush cartoon characters. Jubilant throngs pushed past them, heading deeper into the fair; Ezekiel stuck close to Mary to avoid losing her in the crowd. "But you can let me have the book now."

He reached for the slender volume.

"Nothing doing." She clutched the book more tightly to her chest. "I certainly hope you don't think that you're just going to gallivant out of here with my family's legacy."

"But you didn't even know it was real until a few hours ago! You thought it was just a bedtime story!"

"Well, now I know better, don't I?" She quickened her pace. "And I'm not about to hand over this book to a shady, fast-talking hustler who lies as easily as he breathes."

"But I told you, I'm a Librarian. This is what I do." His fingers itched to snatch the book from Mary's grasp, but that wasn't his style; he was a thief, not a thug. "Trust me, that book is too dangerous to be loose in the world."

"Trust you?" Mary scoffed. "You're shifty to the core. You think I can't tell that? You're as much a librarian as I'm the Loch Ness Monster."

"Actually, the Loch Ness Monster is much more cooperative, at least when it's not spawning season, but that's another story." He shoved some very scaly memories out of his mind to stay focused on the task at hand. "I promise, I'll see to it that book ends up in the right hands."

"Yours?" She paused in front of the pie pavilion, the better to give him a piece of her mind. "Don't make me—"

A wild cackle coming from somewhere above interrupted their squabble. Glancing up in surprise, Ezekiel was dismayed to see Mother Goose herself, looking like something right out of a kids' book, perched atop the log roof of the pie pavilion. Her appearance drew startled gasps and laughter from the crowd, most of whom seemed to assume that the black-hatted crone was performing for the fairgoers. Parents held up toddlers to get a better look. Scattered applause greeted her arrival. A few scared children hid behind their guardians.

Mary's eyes bulged. "Is that—?"

"Yep!" He figured this had to be the same Mother Goose that Baird had run across earlier. She had made good time getting from New Jersey to Ohio, making him wonder just how fast a magic gander could fly, or if perhaps she had some kind of Magic Door or teleportation spells of her own. He glanced up at the sky but didn't spy any departing wings. "Give me the book . . . now!"

Mary still refused to surrender the volume. "I . . . I don't understand. What's happening?"

"Don't quarrel, children," said Mother Goose, gazing down on them. She beckoned for the collection of nursery rhymes while leaning on a gnarled wooden cane. "I'll be taking my book back now, if you don't mind."

Ezekiel shook his head. "Not happening." He nudged Mary. "We need to get out of here. Who knows what that Mother Goose wannabe is capable of."

This was easier said than done, however, with the crowd hemming them in and yet more fairgoers flocking to take in the "show" atop the pavilion. "Excuse me," Mary murmured as she and Ezekiel tried to push through the packed men, women, and children. "Excuse me."

"Coming through!" Ezekiel said, much less politely.

"Not so fast, kiddies!" Mother Goose raised her voice to be heard above the hubbub, like someone accustomed to regaling listeners with stories and rhymes. She shook her cane at the fleeing librarians. "You'll not be getting away with my book, not if I have anything to say about it."

Here it comes, Ezekiel thought, knowing too well how these things almost always went. *The freaky magic part.*

"Sing a song of sixpence," the crone recited. "A pocket full of rye. Four and twenty blackbirds baked in a pie . . . !"

Ezekiel sighed knowingly as, sure enough, flocks of blackbirds burst from the dozens of pies on the display in a flurry of flapping wings and feathers. The shrill keening of the birds competed with screams and gasps from shocked onlookers as the agitated birds flew out of the pavilion into the crowd, which instantly turned into a panicked mob. Ezekiel was buffeted by the shrieking fairgoers shoving past him. It was like Mother Goose meets Alfred Hitchcock. . . .

"Watch out for your nose!" he shouted at Mary, remembering what happened to a certain unlucky maid in the rhyme. Throwing craft and subtlety to the wind, he grabbed for the book, even as a furious cloud of birds enveloped them both, forcing him to throw up his hands to protect what he had always considered to be an exceptionally handsome face. Oodles of small, feathered bodies smacked against him, while the flapping and keening created a deafening racket. Twenty-four birds per pie times a few dozen pies equaled a quantity that Cassandra could have surely calculated by now; all Ezekiel knew was that there were way too many of the bloody birds flapping in his face!

This is stupid, he thought. *Who bakes birds into a pie anyway?*

The storm of birds dispersed as swiftly as it arrived, taking the precious book with them. One minute Ezekiel was being suffocated beneath the avian onslaught, the next he was standing amidst a frightened mob, checking to make sure his nose was still all there and watching helplessly as the blackbirds latched on to Mother Goose's outdated garments with their beaks and lifted her up into the sky. The crone cackled merrily, brandishing the stolen book, as she ascended. Her triumphant voice taunted Ezekiel from on high.

"Better luck next time, Librarian!"

Ezekiel watched her vanish into the clouds before lowering

his gaze to survey the disorderly scene around him. Ruptured pies had sprayed their fruity guts all over the pavilion, creating a sticky mess, even as freaked-out fairgoers fled from the vicinity in droves. As nearly as he could tell nobody's noses had been pecked off; he guessed that he and Mary had been the flock's sole targets. Visibly shaken and shaking, the gray-haired librarian had managed to hang on to her nose as well, although her hair was mussed and tiny black feathers clung to her rumpled attire. She stared in shock at her empty hands.

"The book," she whispered. "The blackbirds took the book."

"No kidding." He was not looking forward to informing Baird and Jenkins that he had lost the prize to the competition. "This is *so* not the way this was supposed to go."

He hoped that Stone and Cassandra were having better luck than he was.

17

Working together, Stone and Gillian assembled a crude see-saw out of the wooden beam and a convenient pile of rubble. "Good thing for us that this fallen beam happened to be here," she observed.

"That might not be by accident." Stone adjusted the position of the beam to compensate for Gillian's lighter weight. "Now that I think of it, any of the original timbers from the Roman era would have long since rotted away, especially in this damp environment. Somebody has replaced and water-proofed the original woodwork, probably in the last century or so."

"Perhaps sometime after 1918, when you say those Mother Goose pages were supposed to be hidden?" Gillian clearly saw where he was going with this. "You're thinking that my ancestor left this beam for us to find?"

"Could be," Stone said. "I've seen even more elaborate puzzles left for future generations, some dating as far back as Atlantis."

"Atlantis?" she echoed. "Now I know you're pulling my leg. Atlantis is just a fable."

You wouldn't say that if you'd been on the business end of Neptune's trident, Stone thought, but he didn't press the point. He was still reluctant to push all the heavy-duty magic stuff on Gillian, for fear of sounding like a nutcase. "Let's just say that there may be more to that 'fable' than you think."

He sat down at one end of the seesaw, facing the wall where the moon mosaic was. Gillian clambered onto the other end and, sure enough, he was lifted up toward the waiting mosaic.

"It's working!'" she said as her end of the seesaw hit the floor of the walkway with a thump. "I wouldn't have thought that I was heavy enough to lift you."

"Leverage," Stone said. "You just need to provide . . . leverage."

Face-to-face with the mosaic at last, he examined it by the light of his headlamp. "Okay," he called down to Gillian. "As I suspected this segment of the mosaic is an *emblema*, a prefabricated panel assembled elsewhere before being inserted into the larger mosaic at this location." He took a closer look at the panel containing the leering lunar countenance. "And this particular *emblema* . . . it's a forgery, or at least it's not original to the site and, by all indications, was added to the design centuries later."

Gillian gaped in surprise. "How can you tell?"

"Little things," he explained. "For one thing, traditional Roman mosaics always featured a thin white outline around the figures." He turned the beam of the lamp onto a barely intact portrait of Cassiopeia a few feet to the right. Much of the mosaic had fallen away, exposing bare concrete and patches of dried mortar, but you could still make out the narrow white outline around a surviving arm and foot. "But there's no outline around the Man in the Moon."

"Maybe because he's already made up of white tiles?" she suggested. "Just to play devil's advocate."

"Nope. The Romans were sticklers when it came to form. They would have used two different shades of white to create the mandated outline." He turned the beam back on the moon, which gleamed in places just like the real thing. "And there's another thing. Some of these *tesserae* are tilted slightly, the better to catch the eye by reflecting any available light. That's a Byzantine technique, developed long after the Roman legions departed from Britain. No way was this panel placed here back when this fort was a going concern. It's a fake, meant to blend in with the actual Roman mosaics—to a degree."

"But what does that mean?"

"That's what I want to find out." He ran his hand gently over the *emblema*; even though it was not entirely authentic, he didn't want to damage the artwork if he could help it. And was it just his imagination or was this particular panel placed just a hair lower than the adjacent portions of the border? "I wonder . . ."

He wasn't the master thief Ezekiel was, but Stone had picked up a few things after a couple of years poking around for hidden manuscripts and secret compartments. Placing his palms against the recessed panel and cautiously exerting a bit of pressure, he tried sliding it left, then right, then . . .

"Eureka."

The entire *emblema* slid beneath the rest of the mosaic, revealing a concealed niche holding a latched cedar box that looked to Stone to be just the right size to hold, say, one-third of a certain ghost volume. Reaching in, he drew the box from its cubbyhole.

"I've got something!" he said. "Let me down . . . slowly."

"Roger that."

She slid gradually off her end of the seesaw, but not quite gracefully enough. Stone's end dropped abruptly, slamming into the floor with a jolt. The beam bounced against the stone walkway.

"Hey!" he protested, along with his indignant tailbone. "I said slowly!"

"Sorry!" she said. "That was trickier than I expected."

"Tell that to my bruised behind!"

She craned her head. "I don't know," she said with a smirk. "Looks fine from where I'm standing."

Her flirty tone took a lot of the sting out of his bumpy landing. He would've responded in kind, except that he was more anxious to find out what was in the box. Undoing a latch, he lifted the lid to find a slender, leather-bound book inside. An embossed title leaped out at him:

Mother Goose's Melodies. Volume Two of Three.

"Bloody hell, it's real," Gillian whispered in awe. "We found it." She looked up at Stone. "Upon consideration, I may have to rethink my views on Atlantis. . . ." A note of suspicion entered her voice. "Unless this is all some sort of scam and *you* placed the book here for us to find."

He couldn't blame her for considering that possibility, especially after he'd questioned her motives not too long ago. "You're the one who figured out the seesaw thing," he pointed out, "*and* brought up the Norse connection."

"Well, that theory's been around since the nineteenth century at least, and I am a folklorist, so it might be reasonable to expect that—"

"Look," Stone interrupted. "Trust your gut. Do you really think I'm scamming you?"

She looked him in the eyes. "No, I can't say that I do."

"Then let's get out of this hole." He closed the lid on the box for safekeeping. "We can inspect the goods someplace drier and more hospitable."

He was dying to examine the book, but he didn't want to linger too long at the bottom of the well, especially with Mother Goose still in the wind. Granted, Baird had run into her in New Jersey, thousands of miles away, but magic had a way of making time and space somewhat rubbery, as the Magic Door at the Annex proved every time he stepped through it. If he could make it from the USA to the UK in no time at all, maybe Mother Goose could as well?

Let's clear out of here before company shows up.

Getting back to the well shaft meant hopping back into the reservoir and wading again through the filthy water. Stone kept a tight grip on the box as they approached the exit. He figured he'd let Gillian climb up and out of the well first before following right behind her. The sooner they got back to somewhere he could contact the Library, the better.

This is one volume Mother Goose is not getting her hands on.

"After you," he began. "Ladies fir—"

To his alarm, the climbing rope, which had been waiting for them, was abruptly yanked upward, disappearing from sight. He grabbed for it, almost dropping the box into the water, but he was too late. Their way out of the well vanished before his eyes.

"What the—?"

A mischievous cackle came from high above. Peering upward, Stone saw Mother Goose looking down at him, just like Gillian had earlier.

"Going somewhere, children?" the crone taunted them.

Startled, Gillian looked from the stranger to Stone. "Let me guess," she said with admirable coolness. "The competition?"

"Right on the money," he said. "Meet Mother Goose."

Her jaw dropped. "*The* Mother Goose?"

"More like *a* Mother Goose . . . we think." He shrugged. "It's a mystery."

"Enough chatter!" Mother Goose demanded. "Give me that book. It belongs to me."

"Not according to the Treaty of 1918," Stone said, "or so I've been told."

"To perdition with that treaty! It's null and void!" She lowered a pail on a rope. "And I've already claimed the first volume from your friend the thief, so you might as well play nicely, too."

"You mean Jones?" Stone wanted to believe that the crone was lying, that she hadn't managed to wrest another set of missing pages from Ezekiel, but he feared that was wishful thinking. He'd been a Librarian long enough to know that the bad guys had an irritating tendency to get their hands on what they were after. "What happened to Jones? Is he all right?"

"The thief is hale and hearty, not that it matters," Mother Goose said. "Now be a good Jack and put the book in the bucket."

"Or what, we get the hose?" He was tempted to grab on to the crone's rope instead, but he doubted that she could support his weight—or wouldn't let go if he tried. "Worst reboot of *The Silence of the Lambs* ever," he muttered under his breath.

"Or you stay where you are," Mother Goose said. "Turn over the book and *maybe* I'll lower your own rope back down to you."

"Sorry. Not happening."

If Jenkins was to be believed, and Stone had no reason to doubt him, letting Mother Goose get another piece of her book could have seriously apocalyptic consequences. And Stone cared too much about history to want to see it end before its time.

"We'll stay put if you don't mind. We're in no hurry."

Gillian gave him a look. "We're not?"

"Trust me," he said.

Stone had faith in Baird and his fellow Librarians. Given time, they'd surely track him down and maybe even find a way to open up the Magic Door to come get him. Plus, there was always that drainage tunnel. . . .

"Perhaps a little company will change your minds," Mother Goose said. "You know what they say, three's a crowd. . . ."

"Company?" Gillian asked, looking around. "What does she mean by that?"

Stone wished he knew. "Stay sharp," he warned her. "Be ready for anything . . . and I do mean *anything*."

Up above them, the crone began to recite an incantation in a singsong voice:

The itsy-bitsy spider climbed up the water spout,
Down came the rain and washed the spider out,
Out came the sun and dried up all the rain,
And the itsy-bitsy spider came up the spout again!

A loud, scuttling sound came from the drainage tunnel behind them. Stone contemplated all the cobwebs draping the ancient cistern. Glancing up he saw that the night sky was already beginning to lighten high above the well. Dawn was approaching here in the UK.

Out came the sun . . .

"Oh, crap," Stone said.

Gillian clutched his arm, scooting closer to him. "That doesn't sound very itsy-bitsy."

"Poetic license," Mother Goose said with a shrug. "I'm afraid our eight-legged friend has grown somewhat larger . . . and hungrier." She cackled merrily. "Are you sure you wouldn't like your climbing rope back?"

Stone was torn. Suddenly, waiting it out underground wasn't looking like such a viable option anymore. The scuttling sounded louder and closer as something climbed up the old drainage tunnel toward them. Turning his light on the entrance, Stone glimpsed a large brown shape through the hanging cobwebs. Some forgotten guardian of the treasure, he wondered, or something conjured up by Mother Goose? *Probably the latter,* he guessed.

"The torch!" he said. "Get the torch from my pack!"

Gillian nodded, getting it. "You don't have to ask me twice!" Hurrying behind him, she extracted the acetylene torch and, showing impressive presence of mind under the circumstances, the safety glasses as well. "Now what?"

Before he could answer, the not-so-itsy-bitsy spider burst through the webbing into the underground chamber. Conditioned by old drive-in movies, Stone had expected some kind of giant tarantula, but then he remembered that those were hardly native to Great Britain. Instead he saw an immense brown house spider roughly the size of a German shepherd. Eight long hairy legs supported its bristling brown thorax and abdomen. Four pairs of eyes fixed on Stone and Gillian. Furry palps twitched ominously. Venom dripped from its oversized fangs as it scurried across the surface of the reservoir toward them.

"Light it up!" he shouted, averting his eyes.

Gillian ignited the torch. A brilliant blue flame lit up the cistern, deterring the spider, who retreated up a rear wall and onto the ceiling, where it scuttled back toward them with alarming speed.

"Watch out!" Stone shouted. "It's almost on top of us!"

"I see it!"

She swung the torch upward just in time to keep the spider from dropping down on them. Alas, the cutting torch was not a flamethrower, so it was only good for short-range defense. The spider darted away from the six-inch flame into a shadowy corner of the ceiling before taking another run at them from a different direction. Again Gillian barely managed to ward it off with the torch in time. The spider sprung backward without getting singed.

"I'm not certain how long I can keep this up," she confessed, with a slight quaver in her voice. "This wretched beast is bloody fast!"

Stone could see that. He also had his doubts about how long the torch would hold out; he had used up much of its fuel cutting through those steel bolts earlier. The torch was by no means a long-term solution, as Mother Goose surely knew as well.

"Well?" she asked from atop the well. "Is my little book worth your life, Librarian? Or your Jill's?"

Flame or no flame, the hungry spider showed no sign of abandoning its hunt. Spiders were carnivores, and this particular specimen seemed to have its cold, arthropod heart set on gobbling up him and Gillian. Little Miss Muffet, he recalled, simply ran away from her spider, but he guessed that hers hadn't been quite so aggressive. This spider was playing for keeps.

"Bugger!" Gillian swore as the monster tried to bypass her

to get to Stone instead, forcing her to shift position to defend him. The slippery floor of the reservoir threatened to undo her, dooming them both. "It gets past me just once and someday they'll be digging up our bones here!"

"Damn it," Stone swore. His own life was one thing—Librarians weren't known for their long life expectancies—but he wasn't about to let Gillian get turned into spider chow. Scowling, he placed the box in the pail. "Fine. Have your freaking book!"

"There's a good boy!" Mother Goose tugged the rope up, cackling all the while. "I knew you'd make the right choice!"

Stone watched, fuming, as the pail ascended, taking the precious volume out of his reach. By now, Gillian's back was pressed against his as she waved the torch back and forth in front of her to buy them more time. The spider's ghastly shadow capered across the walls in accompaniment to its ceaseless attempts to get past their defenses. The determined predator was not letting up, and the torch was going to give up the ghost anytime now.

"Jake?" Gillian asked. "Between you and me, I think we've outstayed our welcome."

"Working on it." He shouted up at the crone. "Hurry it up! You've got your damn book, now throw us that rope!"

"Oh, you don't want that boring old rope," Mother Goose replied. "I've got something even better for you!"

Claiming the book, she placed something else in the pail and lowered it back down to them. Stone grabbed it as soon as it came within reach and hastily inspected its contents. Hoping for something—anything—they could use to escape the spider's lair, he found instead . . . a bottle of malt vinegar and a roll of brown construction paper?

"Hey!" he yelled at Mother Goose. "What gives?"

The crone vanished from sight, but Stone could still hear her chanting up among the ruins:

Up Jack got and home did trot,
As fast as he could caper,
And went to bed and bound his head
With vinegar and brown paper!

Her voice trailed away, leaving Stone stuck at the bottom of the well with nothing but some useless props from the nursery rhyme. He raised the glass bottle, tempted to hurl it at the spider in frustration, then reconsidered. Perhaps there had been a method to Mother Goose's maddening gift?

"Vinegar," he murmured. "Of course!"

"What did you say?" Gillian asked as the blue flame from the torch started to sputter. "Jake?"

"Vinegar! It's a natural spider repellent." He uncapped the bottle and, without asking, dumped half its contents over her head. Growing up back in Oklahoma, he'd learned a thing or two about warding off brown recluse spiders while enjoying the great outdoors. He splashed the rest of the vinegar over himself. "Trust me!"

Gillian shook her head, spraying vinegar in his face. She spit the spilled brown liquid from her lips. "You could've warned me."

"No time!" He shoved her toward the entrance to the drain tunnel, several feet away. "Make for the drain . . . quickly!"

With any luck, the reeking vinegar fumes would dampen the spider's appetite for them while they dived down the waterspout. He had no idea what was waiting for them at the end of the tunnel, but it had to beat sticking around to be devoured. He wasn't sure what exactly the brown paper was for, probably just to be true to the rhyme, but he jammed it into his pocket anyway.

"Move!" he shouted. "We're getting out of here!"

They clambered out of the water and dashed toward the gaping entrance. Tattered webbing shrouded the opening, making it impossible to see what lay beyond. The spider, seeing its prey on the verge of escaping, shot a thick strand of fresh webbing from its rear, snaring Stone's leg just as he and Gillian reached the top of the drain. He tried to tug his leg free but found it rooted to the spot.

"Son of a—!" he exclaimed.

Gillian glanced back to see what the problem was. "Jake?"

"Don't wait for me!" he said. "Go!"

"Rubbish." Coaxing one last spurt of flame from the torch, she sliced through the thick white strand holding Stone in place, then hurled the still-hot torch at the spider. Her wild throw missed, but it struck a hanging sheet of cobwebs instead, setting it ablaze. The fire leaped from web to web, spreading quickly through the underground chamber. Chittering in panic, the spider retreated from the flames, even as they began to eat away at the wooden timbers supporting the ceiling. Smoke filled the ancient cistern, hiding the spider from sight. Acrid fumes stung Stone's eyes and throat.

"Oh my," Gillian said. "I didn't mean to do that."

"Doesn't matter," Stone said. "We're leaving anyway."

Between the fire and the frantic spider, there was no time to dawdle. He shoved Gillian headfirst through the drain opening, then dived in after her.

Geronimo, he thought.

The tunnel was steeper than he expected, and slimier, too. Muck and algae greased the curved walls of the chute so that he and Gillian shot down the drain as though riding the world's least sanitary waterslide. Their screams echoed in their ears as they hurled faster and faster down the tunnel, tearing through random webs and roots and weeds. The beams from their headlamps danced wildly, doing little to combat the utter blackness of the tunnel, as Stone squeezed his eyes shut and waited tensely for the heart-stopping ride to end.

Whose bright idea was this again?

For a second, it felt like they were going to go spilling down the pipe forever, but they burst through one last curtain of hanging roots and reeds to splash headlong into the deep, dark pool at the base of the hill. Gillian hit the chilly water first, followed almost immediately by Stone. With no chance to hold his breath, he swallowed a good chunk of the pool before kicking to the surface and gasping for breath. Paddling in the water, he glanced back toward the exposed end of the storm drain to make sure the spider wasn't still pursuing them, but he saw no sign of the creature. With any luck, it was toast or buried alive by now.

"Gillian?"

"Over here!" she called, making her way toward the tall reeds marking the shore. "God, this water is cold!"

He paddled after her and, within moments, collapsed onto the muddy bank beside her, crushing the damp reeds beneath him. They were both soaked to the skin and shivering. Fall in North England was no time for a refreshing dip outdoors, even with the sun coming up. The cold and damp chilled them to the bone.

On the bright side, they didn't smell like vinegar anymore.

"We did that wrong," she said, cuddling up to him for warmth. "I'm supposed to come tumbling after you."

He drew her closer. "I went off-script . . . just like Mother Goose."

"Yes, about that . . ."

"Later," he promised. "Preferably in front of a warm fire."

She shivered in agreement. "My place or yours?"

"I'm guessing yours is closer."

Despite the appealing prospect of cozying up with Gillian somewhere warm and dry, Stone kicked himself for letting Mother Goose abscond with another third of the book, bringing her one step closer to putting Humpty Dumpty back together again. He hoped his phone had also survived the crone.

Sorry, team, he thought. *Watch out for that witch.*

18

※ *Oregon* ※

The Dead Man's Chest was gaining on Baird.

Intent on devouring the Golden Fleece, the ambulatory treasure chest chased Baird through the Library, practically chomping at her heels. Baird could feel the chest's hot breath, redolent of rum and gunpowder, at her back, even as the fleece thrown over her shoulder felt as though it was getting heavier by the moment. *At least the Argonauts had a ship to transport the fleece,* she thought crankily, *instead of having to schlep it halfway across a magic library.*

To make matters worse, she couldn't even *try* to get too far ahead of the hungry chest for fear of it abandoning the chase to go after easier, more stationary prey. She needed the chest to keep pursuing her until she had it where she wanted it, assuming she could keep a few steps ahead of the chest until then, despite her aching legs and straining lungs. Sweat glued her clothes to her body. Her feet pounded against the hardwood floor of a seemingly endless corridor deep within the labyrinthine bowels of the Library.

I swear, I do more running as a Guardian than I ever did hunting terrorists.

Still, she was pretty sure she was heading the right way. She might not know the Library as well as Jenkins or Flynn, and she might even still get lost if she strayed into some of the more esoteric, less frequented galleries and collections, but she'd been a Guardian for a couple of years now. As long as she stuck to the areas she knew, she should be able to get where she was going.

In theory.

She entered a long hallway lined with closed doors hiding various special sections of the Library, some of which she was actually familiar with. She ticked them off in her head as she sprinted past them.

The Sun Room . . . no.

The Frozen Land of Giants . . . no.

The Lost Jungle . . . no.

The Hive of Giant Bees . . . hell, no!

Glancing back over her shoulder, she saw that the chest was only a few yards behind her and showed no sign of slowing. She envied its preternatural persistence; she was running on fumes and adrenaline at this point, all while being acutely aware that this whole sideshow with the run-away goose and the treasure chest was keeping her from finding Flynn and focusing on the larger threat posed by Mother Goose and Humpty Dumpty, as insane as that still sounded to her.

The chest clattered after her. In a pinch, she could always save herself by ditching the fleece and letting the chest de-vour it while she got away, but what kind of Guardian threw a literally legendary relic under the bus just to keep from being chomped on? Digging deep, Baird pulled out a fresh burst of speed, increasing her lead on the treasure chest, but not by too much.

Just a little bit farther, she promised herself. *Almost there . . . I think.*

Her doubts were dispelled when, moments later, a sealed wooden door came into view at the end of the hallway. A bronze plaque confirmed that she had at last reached her destination:

The Ozymandias Room.

"About time," she gasped. Despite her relief, an involuntary shudder ran through her as she recalled the time that she and Flynn had gotten trapped in this very same room while desperately attempting to shore up the Seven Pillars of Wisdom. That had been a close one. . . .

But now was no time to stroll down memory lane (which was actually two floors down on the southeast side of the Library). Reaching the closed door, she turned to face the oncoming treasure chest. Her hand rested tensely on the knob as she waited for the voracious artifact to catch up with her. She took a deep breath to clear her head and steady her nerves. This was going to take split-second timing . . . and some seriously bad weather.

Drooling rum, the chest scuttled toward her as fast as its ridiculous peg legs could carry it. Iron-edged jaws snapped incessantly, eager to tear into the fleece as well as anything and everybody that got between it and all that yummy gold. Baird remembered the fifteen evil spirits trapped inside the chest and wondered if they were the source of the chest's insatiable lust for gold or its victims or both.

She'd have to ask Jenkins about that . . . later.

"C'mon," she muttered. "Let's get this over with. I've got Librarians to look after."

Drawing closer, the chest sprang at the fleece and Baird, who yanked open the door and jumped to one side, shielding herself behind the door as a ferocious sandstorm blew out of the Ozymandias Room into the hallway. A hot, desert wind flung a barrage of sunbaked yellow grit at the startled treasure chest, sandblasting it. Baird could feel the blistering heat and force of the storm even through the sturdy wooden door protecting her. The howling wind drowned out the rapid beating of her heart. Anxious to see if her plan was succeeding, she peered cautiously around the edge of the door to see the beset chest vanishing beneath the sheer accumulation of sand piling up in the hall. More sand blew into the chest's gaping maw, faster and harder than it could possibly swallow.

"Choke on that," Baird said.

Within moments, the chest had disappeared completely beneath a newly born sand dune. Taking no chances, Baird waited until the chest was entirely covered before, shoving her shoulder against the door with all the strength she could muster, she struggled to push the door shut again. The storm fought her every inch of the way, but finally the door clicked back into place—and the howling winds and flying sand ceased at once.

Whew!

Panting from exertion, she leaned against the closed door while keeping watch over the out-of-place sand dune, just in case the inundated chest tried to dig itself out, but nothing stirred beneath the piled sand. The storm appeared to have been too much for the chest, just as she'd planned.

Makes sense, she thought. *How else do you dispose of a treasure chest?*

You bury it.

"Look on my works, ye mighty, and despair," she murmured before scooting past the dune to head back the way she came, leaving the Dead Man's Chest safely buried behind her. *That should hold it for the duration*, she hoped, *or at least until we have Mother Goose under wraps as well.*

Now if only Jenkins had dealt with that other goose in the meantime. . . .

Uncertain where to find Jenkins and the goose, she headed back toward the Annex. If the goose was indeed looking to escape the Library, it was bound to find its way there eventually. And if, alternatively, Jenkins had already dealt with the goose situation, the Annex would be the logical place for her to meet up with him and regroup.

"Jenkins?" she called out as she retraced her path through the Library, carefully avoiding any potentially confusing detours. "Jenkins? You within earshot?"

Nobody responded at first, but as she neared the front of the Library, it was hard to miss the strident honking of an upset goose, along with the annoyed utterances of a certain immortal caretaker.

"Get down from there, you infernal creature! I have better things to do than round up an ungrateful egg-laying machine!"

Sounds like Jenkins still has a goose problem on his hands, Baird thought, *and could probably use some backup.*

Following the commotion to its source, she arrived at the Library's main entrance hall: a vast, cavernous chamber with vaulted barrel ceilings. Dark wooden bookcases and wainscoting lined the walls, while row after row of glass display cases held some of the prizes of the collection, including the Spear of Destiny, the Shroud of Turin, a crystal skull, and the Philosopher's Stone. A pair of life-sized gold lions guarded the stone steps leading up to the frosted glass door barring the way to the Annex. Bird droppings and golden eggs, scattered randomly about the premises, testified to the goose's incursion.

Ignoring the fantastic relics and marvels on display, which were old news to Baird by now, she instead scoped out the chaotic scene playing out in the hall. To her surprise, she saw that Jenkins had traded in his oversized butterfly net for . . . a squirt gun?

A super-soaker-sized squirt rifle, to be precise, which Jenkins was firing at the squawking goose flying back and forth overhead. Unfortunately, the hall's high ceilings meant that the bird was out of range of the squirt-rifle, so that the pressurized streams of water fell short of their avian target, spilling back down onto the floor and furnishings. Baird had to jump backward to avoid being splattered herself.

"Watch yourself, Colonel," Jenkins warned, noting her arrival. The front of his suit and shirt were shredded as though by fierce claws, making Baird wonder what else he might have run into since they split up. "Trust me when I say you don't want to get doused with this particular water."

Baird attempted to bring herself up to speed. "And that would be bad because . . . ?"

But Jenkins was too busy to offer an explanation, which, given that he lived and breathed exposition, meant he was busy in the extreme. "Hold this if you please, Colonel," he instructed as he thrust the half-empty squirt-rifle into her hands and turned to retrieve another item that Baird had overlooked before: an old-fashioned jet pack (!) resting on the floor at the base of a glass display case containing the Maltese Falcon. The gleaming silver gadget looked like something straight out of an old, pulp-era comic strip, complete with twin gas cylinders mounted to a stainless steel backpack and harness.

We have one of those? Baird thought. *And where on Earth did we get it from? If it is from Earth. . . .*

With his hands now free, Jenkins pulled the jet pack on over his usual gray suit and buckled the straps before reclaiming the squirt-rifle from Baird. "I'll take that back now, thank you."

Baird gaped at the unlikely sight of Jenkins decked out like a pin-striped Buck Rogers. "A jet pack . . . seriously?"

"Borrowed from the Retro-Futurist collection, naturally," he said blandly, as though that went without saying. "I anticipated that this highly inconvenient interlude might come down to a matter of altitude."

She noticed something missing. "No crash helmet?"

"Immortal, remember?"

"Right. As you were."

"If you'll pardon me, Colonel." He stepped away from her in the interest of safety. "All systems, as they say, are go."

Clutching the plastic yellow squirt-rifle, he activated the jet pack and blasted off from the floor atop a column of swirling orange vapor that smelled like Tang, the one-time drink of astronauts. Coughing on the fumes, Baird blinked and covered her mouth as she tilted her head back to watch Jenkins rocket after the goose.

Alarmed by the blast-off, the soaring bird attempted evasive maneuvers high above the floor of the Library, but Jenkins zipped after it, trailing streamers of citrus smoke. The goose flapped its wings frantically in hopes of escaping its airborne caretaker, but Jenkins had the bird in his sights. Squeezing the trigger, he nailed the goose with a well-aimed stream of water.

"That should dampen your wanderlust," he said. "And none too soon."

The squirt had an immediate effect. The large white goose shrunk in midflight, its feathers blurring into a soft yellow down, the soaring wings contracting into stubby little limbs that were wildly inadequate for flight, no matter how hard or how fast they were flapping. Booming honks were dialed down to cheeps. As Baird gazed upward in amazement, a full-grown goose transformed into a cute baby gosling—and began to plummet toward the floor.

"Jenkins!"

"Have no fear, Colonel." He discarded the empty rifle, letting it fall onto the top of a tall oak bookcase, and dove after the falling bird. "I have the matter in hand . . . or soon shall."

Accelerating past the terrified gosling, he reached out and caught it with both hands before it could hit the ground. He cradled the chick against his chest as he reversed his orientation in the air and slowly descended to the floor, touching down only a few feet away from Baird, who was still trying to process what she had just seen.

"How in the—?" she began, appropriately boggled.

"Water from the Fountain of Youth." Jenkins kept a firm but gentle grip on the squirming gosling. "I thought it would make the goose easier to manage, at least until it wears off."

Baird recalled that the Fountain of Youth gurgled elsewhere in the Library, not far from Noah's Ark, and she thanked her lucky stars that she hadn't been splashed accidentally. She wasn't quite sure how long the water's rejuvenating magic lasted, but the Librarians didn't need a Guardian who was back in diapers again.

"Creative," she said.

"And the Dead Man's Chest?" he asked.

"Buried . . . outside the Ozymandias Room."

He nodded in approval. "That should keep it contained for the time being, although I'm not looking forward to sweeping out that corridor at some future date."

Baird recalled the flooded Greco-Roman collection. "Someone's going to need to mop up Antiquities as well."

He arched an eyebrow. "Neptune's trident?"

"Got it in one."

He sighed, but heroically refrained from scolding her. "Well, I'm sure it couldn't be helped." He handed the chirping chick over to her as he shrugged off the jet pack and placed it securely on a nearby shelf. "Congratulations, Colonel, on a job well done."

Baird appreciated the kudos, but she could savor her triumph over the treasure chest later. She had bigger things on her plate.

"What's going on with our Librarians?"

19

The door opened readily, admitting Cassandra and Cole into the Hell Room, which turned out to be just as spooky as one might expect. Black curtains shrouded all six walls, while a six-legged table occupied the center of the chamber, where a large pentagram ominously adorned the parquet floor. A silver candelabra holding six black candles rested on the ebony table. A chill ran down Cassandra's spine as she saw that there were *two* chairs set at the table. One for Ezra Wilshire, and one for . . . a guest? The upholstery on one of the chairs, she observed, was badly scorched. And was it just her screwball senses or was there still a trace of sulfur lingering in the air?

"I don't know about you," Cole said, "but I'm having second thoughts about finding this place."

Cassandra couldn't blame him, but, in her experience, dangerous magic relics weren't always found in cozy settings. More often than not, you had to venture into a forgotten dungeon or dragon's lair.

"Let's just find those pages and get out of here," she said. "No need to stay here any longer than we have to."

"Amen to that," Cole said.

They swept their beams around the room, searching for another clue. Cassandra was tempted to light the candles on the table, but thought better of it; the last thing they needed was to summon an unwanted visitor. Peering at the floor, she noted that it was charred at one point, breaking the protective seal. That probably hadn't boded well for Ezra Wilshire.

"Yo!" Cole said. "Looks like there's another way in."

His beam spotlighted another door on the opposite side of the room. Because it was painted black, she had almost missed it among the sable drapes.

Cassandra's brow furrowed in confusion. "That's not possible." She didn't conjure up her mental model again, but she remembered it well enough. "There's simply no room, spatially, for another stairwell."

"You sure of that?" Cole crossed the room and took hold of the doorknob. "Then where does this go?"

He pulled open the door, letting in the wind. A six-story drop to the ground waited beyond the doorway.

"Nowhere," she said. "Another door to nowhere."

"No lie." He shut the door and stepped away from it. "Guess there's only one way in or out, unless you're in the mood for a one-way trip."

"I don't think we're quite that desperate yet," she quipped, as her beam lighted upon an antique grandfather clock resting in one corner of the chamber. As with every other clock she'd spied tonight, its hands were stuck at midnight. *Want to bet*, she thought, *that's the exact time that Ezra Wilshire's luck ran out?*

She forced that sinister supposition from her mind in order to focus on the puzzle at hand. The crooked man rhyme

had led them to the Hell Room, but what about the other
rhyme they had stumbled onto, the one on the crooked page?

"Hickory, dickory, dock," she recited. "What does that even
mean, anyway? Are they just nonsense words or some sort
of code?" Anxious to solve the mystery, she brainstormed
fiercely. "Hickory, dickory, dock abbreviates to H-D-D, and
if we replace each letter with the corresponding number of
the alphabetical sequence that gives us 7-4-4, or seven hundred and forty-four, which is the sum of four consecutive
prime numbers . . . or am I overthinking this?"

"Maybe a little," Cole said.

"Okay, back to square one," she said. "Hickory, dickory,
dock, the mouse ran up the clock." She drew nearer to the
grandfather clock. "What if that wasn't just referring to
the clock tower, but a clock in the tower?"

"Like that one?" Cole strolled over to examine it as well.
"How's the rest of the rhyme go? 'The clock struck one, the
mouse did run,' etcetera." He contemplated the unmoving
hands on the clock face. "This dinosaur isn't striking one
anytime soon."

"You're right. This clock hasn't moved past midnight in decades, if it ever did at all." Cassandra's eyes narrowed suspiciously. "Let's remedy that, why don't we?"

Holding her breath, she reached out and moved the hour
hand from twelve to one. At first nothing happened, and Cassandra feared that she had jumped to the wrong conclusion;
then rusty hinges squeaked like a startled mouse, and a wooden
panel slid open beneath the clock face revealing a hidden
niche nestled in the trunk of the clock. Twin flashlight beams
converged on the concealed hiding place, which was found to
contain a single hardcover book.

"Hot damn, little—"

She shot him a warning look.

"I mean, Cassandra," he corrected himself. "Remind me to ring you the next time I misplace my car keys!"

"Well, this *is* my job." She rescued the book from the clock and lifted it up to read the title on the front cover:

Mother Goose's Melodies. Volume Three of Three.

"Mission accomplished," she said with relief. This was one part of the spell book that wouldn't be ending up in Mother Goose's clutches. "Now I believe I said something before about not sticking around longer than necessary?"

"That was the plan," Cole confirmed. "Let's get the hell out of the Hell Room."

"My thoughts exactly."

Cassandra tucked the book under her arm as they started for the real exit, as opposed to the suicide door. They only got a few steps, however, before the trick door slammed open behind them, causing them to spin around in surprise. Cassandra's eyes widened and her jaw dropped.

"Oh no," she whispered.

Mother Goose stood framed in the open doorway, cackling jubilantly. A cold wind rustled her shawl and skirts. A gnarled wooden cane rested on the floor before her, as though the old woman had just dropped it. Cassandra had not yet met Mother Goose in the flesh, but she recognized her at once from the storybooks.

"Who the—?" Cole blurted. "How?"

Good question, Cassandra thought. Peering past the crone, she looked for Mother Goose's gander but caught no glimpse of it in the open air beyond. So how exactly had Mother Goose reached the tower room by way of the suicide door?

"That's her?" Cole asked. "Mother Goose?"

"Or a reasonable facsimile thereof." Cassandra clutched the book to her chest, unwilling to surrender it without a fight. She glared defiantly at the crone. "If you're here for the book, think again."

"But you did all the thinking for me, Cassandra," the older woman said, taunting her. "Well done, my dear. I knew that if anybody could crack this Puzzle House—and find me the last part of my book—it would be you."

That Mother Goose knew her by name was troubling, and that she seemed to be implying that she already had the other two-thirds of the spell book was even more so, but Cassandra didn't let that rattle her. "Sorry, I didn't find this for you." She nudged Cole toward the door. "Come on, Georgie. We're leaving."

"That's what you think!"

Moving surprisingly quickly for an old woman, Mother Goose sprang forward and snatched the silver candelabra from the table. Her voice rose as she chanted:

Jack be nimble,
Jack be quick,
Jack jump over the candlestick!

With a sudden whoosh, the black candles ignited. Gripping the central column of the candelabra, she pointed it at the open door. Flames sprayed across the room. A wall of fire erupted in the doorway, barring the way to the stairs.

"Jump over that, children, if you dare!"

Cassandra and Cole looked at each other in dismay. Roaring flames stood between them and escape, trapping them in the Hell Room with Mother Goose, who swung the lighted candelabra toward them, brandishing it like a weapon. Cassandra knew a magical flamethrower when she saw one.

"Change your mind about giving me my book," Mother Goose said menacingly, "or shall we see how high this Jack can jump?"

Cassandra hesitated, torn between the immediate threat and the greater danger of allowing Mother Goose to get the final piece of the spell book. She suspected she knew what Jenkins would advise, but he wasn't the one facing imminent incineration—and the person responsible for putting Cole in this position in the first place. Her gaze fell upon the scorched chair at the table and she realized she had no choice. Humpty Dumpty was a theoretical threat; George's life was in danger right this very moment.

"Sorry, universe," she murmured as she stepped forward and laid the book on the table in front of Mother Goose. "Go ahead. Take it. One Librarian or another will outsmart you in the end; scarier bad guys than you have learned that the hard way."

"We'll see about that, dearie." Mother Goose snatched the book from the table and held it up victoriously. "At last! I am complete again . . . and nothing is beyond the power of my rhymes!"

Cole looked at Cassandra. "Let me guess. Our goose is cooked?"

"I'm afraid so," she said. "Sorry."

Baird would try to disarm Mother Goose somehow, Cassandra assumed, but hand-to-candlestick combat was not exactly her forte. She was trying to calculate some kind of workable solution to the problem when things got . . . stranger.

"Enough dillydallying," Mother Goose said, her voice sounding much more hoarse all of a sudden. She hurled the candelabra away from her. "Time to fly away home!"

Feathers sprouted from Mother Goose's clothes and face as the crone underwent an abrupt metamorphosis. Her craggy face elongated, forming a large beak, which plucked the book from her fingers a heartbeat before they transformed into the wing tips of an enormous goose, albeit one wearing a hat and shawl. Gripping the stolen book tightly in her beak, while a pair of scaly orange feet took hold of the fallen cane, Mother Goosier turned around and took off through the suicide door into the open air. Immense white wings carried her aloft, taking volume three of the spell book with her. A loud honk taunted Cassandra as the goose flew beyond their grasp.

Cole blinked and rubbed his eyes. "Did I really just see that?"

"I'm afraid so." Cassandra was a little less floored by the transformation, having witnessed equally miraculous things in the past. She ran forward to stamp out the fallen candles. "It could be that her spells are getting more and more powerful, especially now that she has all three parts of her book."

Just like Prospero grew stronger, she thought, *as he reacquired his lost objects of power.*

Although she managed to extinguish the burning candles, the fire in the doorway was still blazing—and spreading. The flames ignited the thick black drapes on the walls, threatening to turn the chamber into an inferno. The Hell Room was rapidly living up to its name, which meant that she and Cole had to make a hasty exist if they didn't want to go the way of the late Mr. Wilshire.

Cole contemplated the wall of flames between them and

the stairs. The heat from the blaze drenched his face in per-spiration. He took a hesitant step toward the doorway.

"Maybe if we make a dash for it . . . ?"

Cassandra doubted they could make it through the fire un-scathed. She dragged him toward the other door instead, the one that led to nowhere . . . yet.

"I may have a better option," she said, working her phone, "if somebody picks up in time."

Fortunately, she had the Annex on speed-dial. Even still, she anxiously watched the spreading flames while listening impatiently to the ringing at the other end of the line.

Come on, come on, she thought. *We haven't got all night here. . . .*

Smoke and flames filled the Hell Room, making her grate-ful for the fresh air blowing in through the suicide door. Any chance of making it through the other doorway had gone up in flames by now, so they had run out of escape routes—unless somebody picked up the damn phone already!

Ring after ring chipped away at her odds of surviving. Then, just as she was starting to fear that she would be shunted to voice mail, Baird's voice picked up at the other end of the line.

"*Cassandra? What's up?*"

"No time to explain!" Cassandra said, coughing through the smoke. "I need you and Jenkins to open the Magic Door now." She took a moment to visualize a globe, then zeroed in on their exact location in terms of longitude and latitude. "I'm sending you the coordinates . . . and a photo of the door, too." She snapped the pic and sent it along with specs. The smoke invaded her throat, making it hard to speak. "Hurry, Eve!—*cough*—We haven't got a lot of time. . . ."

"*We?*" Baird asked. "*What's happening? You sound terri-ble. . . .*"

"The Door! Please!"

She lowered the phone and stared expectantly at the open doorway, which still offered nothing but a straight drop to oblivion. Cole was right beside her, backed up to the brink of the drop-off by the encroaching flames. The wind coming through the doorway slowed the flames, even as it fed them as well.

When the wind blows, she thought.

"What's going on?" Cole asked urgently. "What Magic Door were you talking about?"

She doubted that a stiff breeze could save Cole this time. "Wait and see. Any minute now. . . ."

Caught between the fire and the fall, she prayed that Baird could get the Magic Door open in time—and in the right place. The Magic Door had gotten more reliable over the years, as she and Jenkins had fine-tuned its targeting mechanism, but it was still only *approximately* accurate sometimes, and the Wilshire Puzzle House had a lot of doorways to latch on to, sensible and otherwise. She really hoped it found the right door this time, before she and Cole not-so-spontaneously combusted.

"Do we jump?" he asked, peering over the edge. "Don't tell me we're jumping."

"Wait for my signal . . . and believe in magic."

The six-legged table had become a bonfire. The grandfather clock was being burned at the stake. The fire was practically licking the trapped pair's heels when, just in time, a blinding flash of white light illuminated the doorway. Eldritch energy crackled almost as loudly as the flames consuming the chamber.

Thank you, Eve. Cassandra took hold of Cole's hand. "Now! Jump!"

He balked at the brink. "But—"

"You just saw a woman turn into a goose!"

"Good point."

Escaping the hungry flames, they leaped through the doorway. . . .

20

. . . and landed in the Annex.

Cassandra gulped in the slightly musty air of the Library, which tasted wonderful after the suffocating inferno of the Hell Room. Soot and a distinctly smoky aroma still clung to her hair and clothing, which were only slightly singed. Cole gasped beside her, no doubt surprised and relieved to find himself alive and well, as opposed to splattered on the ground outside the crooked house. He let go of her hand.

"Hot damn!" he exclaimed. "That's some primo magic!"

Baird and Jenkins and the rest of the team were already present, along with two strangers whom Cassandra assumed were the Daughters Goose. Everyone was staring at her and Cole as they made their dramatic entrance, reeking of smoke. A chick in a birdcage, which now occupied the office for some reason, cheeped in excitement.

"Cassandra?" Baird said anxiously. "Is everything all right? You sounded like you were in trouble."

"*Were*," Cassandra stressed. "Not anymore, thanks to you."

"But what was—?"

"Just a minute." Cassandra dialed Miami on her phone.

"Hello, 911. I'd like to report a fire at the old Wilshire estate. . . . Oh, you know about that already? The trucks are on their way? Glad to hear it. No, I don't want to leave my name or number."

She hung up and put away her phone. She had done her part; it was up to the Miami Fire Department now. She hoped they could save the Puzzle House, but given the mansion's history of hellfire and brimstone, she wouldn't be surprised if the house suffered the same fate as the late Ezra Wilshire— that is, reduced to ashes. There would, perhaps, be something fitting about that.

"Sorry," she said to Baird and the others. "Where were we again?"

"Forget that." Cole gaped at his new surroundings. "Where the hell *are* we anyway?"

"Oops, where are my manners?" Cassandra said, sympathizing with his confusion. Mere moments ago, he'd been in a burning clock tower on the other side of the continent. "Welcome to the Library."

"Oh joy," Jenkins said, frowning. "Another visitor. I was unaware that this was Bring a Goose to Work Day." He swept a disapproving gaze over Cole and the other two guests. "If I'd known we were expecting this much company, I would've straightened up more. Perhaps ordered some light refreshments?"

His sarcasm was not lost on Cassandra. "Jenkins—"

"Might I remind you all," he said sharply, "that the Library is *not* a safe house, let alone a shelter for wayward strays."

"Hey!" Cole protested. "Who are you calling a stray, Bow Tie?"

"My thoughts exactly," said the older of the two women, whom Cassandra deduced to be Mary Simon, the children's librarian from Ohio. "That's hardly what I call a hospitable attitude, Mr. Jenkins."

"You tell him, Mary," added the younger woman, whose English accent pegged her as Dr. Gillian Fell of Northumberland. "I expected better from a man of your obvious breeding and culture."

"No offense intended, ladies, gentleman," Jenkins said. "My issue is with certain reckless Librarians, not your good selves."

"I'm sorry, Jenkins," Cassandra said, "but I didn't have any choice. This secret room was on fire and—"

Jenkins wrinkled his nose at the sooty odor emanating from her clothes. "I appreciate the extremity of the situation, Miss Cillian, but the security of the Library is no small matter. This institution is not open to the public for a reason."

"I'll vouch for Gillian," Stone said, standing close enough to her to make Cassandra raise an eyebrow. Something about their body language made her wonder what exactly had gone on between them over in the UK. Certainly, it wouldn't be the first time Stone had his head turned by a pretty face.

None of my business, Cassandra thought, *as long as she doesn't turn out to be a master assassin like Lamia. . . .*

"And Mary is all right by me," Ezekiel said, "for a stubborn old lady, that is."

"I'll take that remark in the spirit in which I hope it was intended," Mary Simon said. "But I've still got my eye on you, you young scamp."

"And you can trust George," Cassandra stated, realizing as she said it that she couldn't imagine Cole having any ulterior motives. He had been nothing but straight with her all the way through the crooked house. "And I'm guessing that the others had good reasons for bringing their guests to the Library, just like I did."

"Be that as it may," Jenkins said, "there is still the matter of security. It's all very well and good that you each trust your respective charges, but—"

Cassandra cringed inside, fearing that he might bring up that one time, back in the beginning, when she had betrayed the Library in a moment of weakness. A great deal of water had flowed under the bridge since then, and she liked to think that she had fully regained her teammate's trust, but Jenkins had a *very* long memory.

"—this sets a dangerous precedent," he concluded, not mentioning her past treachery at all.

Cassandra felt a warm glow of relief. Maybe all was forgiven after all?

"Look, Jenkins." Stone placed a protective arm around Gillian's waist. "I get that you're just trying to protect the Library, and that we've been double-crossed before, but Mother Goose has already targeted these people once already. We can't leave them unprotected while she's still out there. . . ."

"Plus, we might need their help," Cassandra argued. "I couldn't have found that last part of the book without Cole . . . even if we weren't able to hang on to it."

"Ditto with me and Gillian," Stone said.

Various eyes turned toward Ezekiel, who shrugged.

"Well, I absolutely could've found it on my own," he insisted, "because I'm just that awesome but, sure, Mary knows her stuff where all this Mother Goose business is concerned."

"Humility is a virtue, Ezekiel Jones," she chided him, "but ours *was* a successful collaboration, at least up until the end."

"Very well," Jenkins conceded, surrendering to the inevitable with a world-weary sigh. "You're the Librarians. Ultimately, it's your call." He wagged a finger at them nonetheless. "But let's not make a habit of it, shall we?"

"That won't be an issue," Baird pointed out, "unless we can stop Mother Goose from putting Humpty Dumpty back together again . . . and unmaking the universe in the process."

Cole did a double take. "Say what?"

"I may have left that part out," Cassandra admitted. "Let me try to explain. . . ."

———

"Make no mistake," Jenkins said, addressing all present. "The situation is dire."

He stood facing the Librarians, their Guardian, and the three Goose heirs, who were seated at the conference table. Jenkins was still not entirely happy about the visitors' presence in the Annex, let alone including them in the briefing, but he conceded that they had a stake in the proceedings as well. There was, he reflected, something of precedent in that regard. Past Librarians had worked with Mother Goose and her heirs to resolve previous crises, including the delicate negotiations that resulted in the Treaty of 1918, which had held for nearly a century . . . until the current unpleasantness put the entire cosmos in jeopardy.

"Despite our efforts, best or otherwise, the individual purporting to be Mother Goose is in possession of the entire spell book now, granting her the means to reassemble Humpty Dumpty, aka the World Egg, and give birth to a new Creation."

"Yeah, about that," Ezekiel interrupted. "Are we sure we're not overreacting here? I mean, Humpty Dumpty is going to reverse the Big Bang? Even by Library standards, that seems like a stretch."

"Would that it were so, Mr. Jones. Alas, I have been monitoring the situation while you and your confederates were gallivanting about the globe, making new friends, and I can assure you that the evidence increasingly bears out my initial suspicions."

To be more precise, he had been conducting certain investigations since the disturbances at the Library had been dealt with, but Jenkins saw no need to muddle matters by mentioning his earlier difficulties with the amuck goose, the Lion, the Unicorn, and the Dead Man's Chest. Those were not germane to the present crisis, or so he rationalized. Nor was the question of why there was now a caged gosling chirping in the background.

"What sort of evidence?" Baird asked.

"Omens and portents of impending doom, as we were wont to call them back in my salad days." He had set up a vintage slide projector on the table to better illustrate his discoveries. "Lights, please?"

Baird obligingly lowered the lights even as Ezekiel scoffed at the antiquated device. "A slide show, mate? You do know we have PowerPoint presentations now?"

"I was present at the invention of the printing press, Mr. Jones, so I have some appreciation for the impact of new technologies, but this is no ordinary slide projector. You've heard of magic lanterns? Well, this particular projector more than lives up to that quaint description."

He pressed the clicker on a handheld remote and a holographic projection of the night sky manifested above them, not unlike a celestial light show at a planetarium. Constellations burned bright in the heavens.

Too bright, in fact.

"This was the sky only a few hours ago," he stated. "Here's what the same sky looks like at this very minute."

Another click brought forth an even brighter sky, in which

the stars were noticeably larger and more luminous than before. The difference was enough to provoke gasps from the Librarians and their associates.

"Damn!" George exclaimed. "Twinkle, twinkle, little stars!"

Mary rubbed her eyes and looked again. "I take it that's no optical illusion or photographic hocus-pocus?"

"Hold on." Gillian stared at Jenkins. "I'm still back on the printing press thing. Did he just say that he was there when it was—"

Jenkins moved on with his briefing.

"As you can see," he elaborated, "the very stars are appearing larger and closer as the universe begins to contract."

Cassandra raised her hand like a well-mannered schoolgirl.

"Yes, Miss Cillian?"

"That doesn't make any sense," she protested. "It takes millions of years for the light from distant stars to reach us. There's no way we could discern any noticeable changes in their position or luminosity right away."

"And you just crossed from Miami to Portland in a single step," he reminded her. "Your point?"

Cassandra shrunk back into her seat. "I withdraw the question."

"Nor is this troubling stellar phenomenon the only warning to present itself tonight," Jenkins said, picking up where he'd left off. "I call your attention to the following YouTube video, posted only twenty minutes ago from Racine, Wisconsin."

A click replaced the planetarium show with a floating screen roughly the size of a deluxe seventy-inch television set. Captured on the screen was a view of a radiant full moon, which was also disturbingly large and bright for this time of year. Jenkins was briefly reminded of the ominous Skull Moon of 1548 before clearing his mind of those dismal recollections. That tragic victory had no bearing on the present crisis, save as an unwelcome reminder that happy endings were not always in the cards. He prayed no such sacrifice would be required this time.

"What are we looking at here?" Stone asked. "Is it just that the moon is also shining more brightly than usual?"

"Wait for it," Jenkins advised.

An object abruptly entered the frame, appearing to arc over the lambent moon. Jenkins froze the image and used the special properties of the projector to zoom in on the UFO, which turned out to have big brown eyes, a patchy brown-and-white hide, cloven hooves, and udders.

"Whoa!" Baird blurted. "Is that actually—?"

"A cow jumping over the moon?" Jenkins said. "Why, yes, that's precisely what it is, Colonel."

"Oh, man," Stone said. "Just when I think this deal can't get any freakier."

"Keep watching," Jenkins said, operating the remote.

The video resumed, pulling back to its original parameters, as the gravity-defying bovine arced over the moon and out of the frame. A plaintive moo lingered behind on the video's audio track, accompanied by the startled gasps and interjections of whoever was recording the images. Off-screen hilarity joined the hubbub and the camera panned to the right to reveal a small French bulldog gazing up at the sky and laughing uproariously—just like a human being.

"Oh for Pete's sake!" Stone exclaimed. "You've got to be kidding me!"

Jenkins bestowed his most funereal expression on the (much) younger man. "Do I look as though I am kidding, Mr. Stone?"

"'And the little dog laughed to see such sport,'" Cassandra recited.

"Exactly, Miss Cillian." Jenkins clicked the video away. "There has also been a marked uptick in reports of dishes and spoons going missing, often in tandem."

"Runaway cutlery," Ezekiel said incredulously. "Okay, that's new."

Baird flipped the lights back on. "So, is that it? Are we too late?"

"Perhaps not, Colonel. I believe these are but portents, heralding the restoration of Humpty Dumpty, but not ensuring it. A magic of this magnitude needs must occur at the appointed time and place, when all the essential elements are in conjunction."

"And when is the proper time?" Baird asked. "Just how much time do we have left to stop this?"

As ever, Jenkins admired her ability to stay on point and focused on the mission at hand. The Library had chosen wisely in recruiting her as a Guardian.

"The dawn of a new Creation needs to take place at sunrise." He consulted his pocket watch. "Which is at approximately 6 A.M. this time of year."

Cassandra gazed upward at empty air. "6:08, to be precise."

"And the place?" Stone asked. "I mean, it's always sunrise somewhere on the planet, but you said this spell has to be performed at a specific locale as well?"

"That is correct, Mr. Stone." Jenkins glanced at Baird. "Would you care to hazard a guess, Colonel?"

"No guessing required," she said. "We're going back to Mother Goose's Gardens. That's where Humpty Dumpty is waiting to be put back together, symbolically, magically, whatever."

"Same difference." Jenkins consulted his pocket watch. "And the sun rises on the East Coast in less than an hour."

He looked at Cassandra, who did not disappoint.

"Thirty-two minutes, fourteen seconds," she clarified. "Just so you know."

"In other words, the countdown is on." Baird struck a resolute tone. "The time difference *would* have to be against us, damn it."

Stone put on his game face. "Then let's get this over with."

"One more thing," Ezekiel said before Jenkins could declare the briefing adjourned. "Do we have any idea yet who 'Mother Goose' really is?"

Jenkins wished he had an answer to that query.

"That, Mr. Jones, remains to be determined."

21

Unnaturally bright moonlight flooded Mother Goose's Magic Garden as Baird and the Librarians stepped through the front door of the giant shoe into the derelict theme park. It was light enough that there was no need for a flashlight app. She glanced anxiously to the east, relieved to see that they had indeed beaten the sunrise by a brief margin at least. Streaks of red, visible through the denuded trees, were already climbing above the horizon, but the sun had yet to poke its blazing head up.

Good, Baird thought. That meant they still had time to stop Mother Goose, spell book or no spell book. How exactly they were going to do that, however, was still a work in progress. *Rushing in without a plan is Flynn's approach, not mine.*

"Wow." Cassandra took in the desolate remains of the park. Deteriorating displays and mannequins greeted her. Dead leaves blew past her ankles. "I can't decide if this is creepy or sad or both."

"I'm voting for creepy," Stone said. "Hard to imagine that people used to bring their kids here for fun."

Ezekiel made a face. "What a dump. Just for once, can't we avert an apocalypse on the Riviera or in Monte Carlo?"

"Maybe next doomsday," Baird said, "but no promises."

It occurred to her that none of the Librarians had visited the park yet, aside from Flynn at some point in the recent past. At her insistence, they had left the three Goose heirs back at the Annex under Jenkins's watchful eye. Gillian, Mary, and George had protested strenuously at being excluded from the mission, but Baird had overruled them; she trusted the Librarians when it came to their visitors being legit, but there was too much at stake to risk including three unpredictable civilians in the operation. There were enough question marks hanging over her head without adding any more variables to the equation.

Besides, she had reasoned, *they're only a Magic Door away if we need them.*

Dawn was getting closer by the minute, which meant there was no time for sightseeing. She took out the same handheld magic detector she had used before and pointed it in the general direction of Humpty Dumpy. To her alarm, the needle swung all the way to the right, to the far end of the red zone, while the scanner's probes spun like egg beaters on meth. Smoke rose from overheated circuits. Sparks flared as the detector blew a fuse. Baird tossed it away to avoid getting a nasty electrical shock. The device landed in the weeds, where it sputtered briefly before dying.

"Okay, that's not a good sign," she said, "although it looks like we're definitely in the right place."

Not that she had ever really doubted it. According to Jenkins, the Humpty Dumpty ritual required an appropriately symbolic site, imbued with just the right energies, and Mother Goose's Magic Garden fit the bill perfectly. Decades of visitors, all enjoying the park and reciting the rhymes, had charged the grounds with a critical mass of Mother Gooseness, conveniently atop the juncture of some freshly reactivated ley lines. And with wild magic seizing every opportunity to manifest these days, the once-harmless park had become a genuine place of power.

"This way," she said, retracing her path from before. "And be ready for anything: blackbirds, a giant spider, flame-spewing candles, a hungry pirate chest, whatever."

Cassandra didn't miss that last bit. "A hungry pirate chest?"

"Tell you later," Baird promised. "The point is, we have no idea what tricks Mother Goose may have up her sleeves, so keep frosty, okay?"

"Don't need to tell me," Stone said. "We've all seen what that witch can do."

Ezekiel flashed a cocky grin. "She just caught me off guard last time. I'm ready for her now."

"Let's hope so," Baird said, "for all our sakes."

The night was not getting any younger, so they started out across the park. Dilapidated cottages and moldy mannequins marked the overgrown path, contributing to the eerie atmosphere of the ruins. An unsettling feeling came over Baird, raising the fine hairs on the back of her neck.

We're being watched. I know it.

Rather than discount the feeling, Baird trusted her instincts, which had kept her alive through some very hairy situations in hot spots all over the globe. Her gaze swept from side to side, scanning for hostiles, but all she saw were the rotting mannequins posing still and silent alongside the path.

Or maybe not so still?

She detected a hint of movement out of the corner of her eye. Turning quickly in that direction, she saw that all Three

Men in a Tub were now looking directly at her, which she could have sworn they weren't doing a moment ago. Their leering expressions also struck her as possibly more malevolent than she remembered. Surely they hadn't always looked so sinister, back when this was a kids' theme park? She doubted that they were *supposed* to be nightmare material.

"Um, gang." She nodded at the mannequins, which were sharing a mildewed claw-foot tub that now resided in a thick patch of brambles. "Don't look now, but I think we've been made."

All heads turned toward the mannequins, who turned their own heads to look back at them. Watching the moldy fiberglass figures come alive was one of the creepier things Baird had seen in a while, and that was saying a lot. She had, after all, recently dealt with an outbreak of vampire yogurt.

"Yeah," she muttered. "Should've seen this coming."

One by one, the Three Men clambered out of the tub and marched toward Baird and the Librarians, clearly looking for trouble. The Butcher, sporting a bloody smock, brandished a gleaming meat cleaver. The Baker, who wore a high chef's hat and flour-white apron, gripped a raised rolling pin. The Candlestick Maker, who, surreally, had a wax candle sprouting from his cap (so visitors could more easily identify him?), was armed with a heavy brass candlestick. All three figures displayed obvious signs of deterioration: scratches, dents, faded and chipped paint, greenish-white splotches of mold that no empty tub could wash away. Dirt and decay gave them a vaguely leprous quality that made Baird's skin crawl. She didn't want to touch them—or let them touch her.

"Another candlestick?" Cassandra said. "Really?"

"Just be thankful there aren't any nursery rhymes about chainsaws," Stone said, "or Uzis."

"You know, I never really got this one," Ezekiel said. "Why three men in a tub? Was there a water shortage or something? And why are they fully dressed?"

"Originally, the rhyme was about three women sharing a bath," Stone informed them, "but it got cleaned up for the storybooks."

"Too bad," Ezekiel said. "That would have made this a lot more entertaining."

Men, Baird thought, rolling her eyes. "Enough with the chatter. Looks like we're going to have to fight our way to Humpty."

"Fine with me." Stone clenched his fists. "Bring it on."

Cassandra cringed. "Not so much for the fighting, actually."

"I *can* fight," Ezekiel maintained, "but it's a sorry waste of my talents."

"Don't think we've got any choice." Baird drew her sidearm. "But at least we outnumber them."

Stone stiffened and glanced around. "Umm, I wouldn't be so sure of that."

Bushes rustled all around them. Twigs snapped and fallen leaves crackled as more mannequins emerged from the murky woods and gardens. Jack Sprat and his much heftier wife stomped toward the intruders armed with table forks and knives. Little Jack Horner and Little Boy Blue had teamed up to take on the Librarians and their Guardian. Even Little Miss Muffet had abandoned her tuffet . . . whatever the hell a tuffet was.

"Ouch!" Ezekiel yelped as Jack Horner hit him with a fake plum pie that was as hard as a rock. The missile struck Ezekiel in the shoulder. "That hurt, you dummy!"

The mannequins closed in on them.

"Any tactical advice?" Stone asked Baird.

"Retreat is not an option," she said grimly. "Hit 'em hard and try not to get killed."

———

Past experience had taught Baird that bullets were seldom of use against magical menaces, but she figured it was worth a try. A warning shot blasted the candle off the top of the Candlestick Maker's cap, but did nothing to discourage the Three Men, who kept on coming.

"Back off," she said. "This is your final warning."

The silent mannequins ignored her command, leaving her no choice but to fire again. The sharp report of the second gunshot disturbed the stillness of the morning as she blew a hole in the Candlestick Maker's fiberglass face, but the animated mannequin barely missed a step, keeping pace with his tub-mates, none of whom had anything resembling vital organs to aim at. The head shot hadn't even slowed them down. They appeared impervious to fear or pain.

So what else is new? Baird thought. *God, I miss terrorists sometimes.*

A third shot dislodged the candlestick from its Maker's grip, but by then the Three Men were upon her, forcing Baird into close-quarter, hand-to-hand combat. The trick to taking on multiple opponents, she knew, was to keep moving and stay on the offensive; unfortunately, chokes, strikes, pressure points, and other conventional attacks were likely no good where walking mannequins were concerned, so she had to rely on speed and leverage and takedowns instead. Ducking beneath the Butcher's swinging cleaver, she swept the Baker's leg out from under him and tossed him into the unarmed

Candlestick Maker, sending them both tumbling to the ground. They landed hard, in a tangle of sculpted limbs.

Two down, she thought, *for the moment.*

That left just the Butcher to deal with. Moving in too close for him to use his weapon, she executed a flawless shoulder throw that hurled the Butcher to the ground as well. He landed on his back, hitting the path with a thud, but almost immediately sat up again—like a hockey-masked madman in a slasher movie.

Great, Baird thought. *Now what?*

None of her martial arts moves were going to slow down the Three Men for long. She liked to think that the mannequins lacked her training and experience in hand-to-hand combat, but there were three of them and they were armed, so she looked about for something to even the odds, even as all three climbed back onto their feet and came at her from different directions. A length of rusty rebar, jutting from a nearby heap of debris, caught her eye and she somersaulted past her foes to wrest it from the trash. The thirty-inch metal rod felt good in her hand; it wasn't a weapons-grade steel baton, but it would do.

I can do some serious damage with this.

Rod in hand, she hurled herself back into the fray, employing the improvised weapon for both defense and offense simultaneously. The rebar deflected the Butcher's cleaver, even as she dodged the Baker's rolling pin and shattered the Candlestick Maker's right knee on the back swing. The crippled figure toppled over onto one side and couldn't get back up again. Bits of pulverized leg littered the path.

Okay, Baird thought. *Now we're talking.*

She saw how this had to go.

"You can't kill them or knock them out!" she shouted to the others. "You have to smash them to pieces!"

She whacked away at her remaining opponents, swinging the rebar like a sledgehammer. The Butcher's cleaver went flying, along with his hand, as she brought the steel rod down on his wrist with all her strength, breaking it off from his arm. Undaunted, he kept coming at her, as did the Baker. This was going to be a workout.

Disarm and demolish, Baird thought. *That's the ticket.*

But how long was that going to take? The end of the world was dawning and they had better things to do than take some magic crash dummies apart!

———

Jack Sprat and his wife were the original odd couple. He was a tall, rangy string bean clad in vaguely "old-timey" garb while she was short and squat in the extreme. Neither appeared particularly interested in eating fat *or* lean at the moment, only in stopping Stone and company from getting to Humpty Dumpy in time to save the universe.

Nothing doing, Stone thought. He hadn't hopped back and forth across the world and nearly gotten eaten by an "itsy-bitsy" spider just to get stalled at the last minute by a couple of nursery rhyme characters with strict dietary restrictions. *Hell, I took out the Big Bad Wolf once.*

Sprat rushed ahead of his lumbering spouse, trying to jab Stone with his pointy cutlery. Stone ducked and weaved, dodging the skinny mannequin's thrusts. Stone's fighting moves weren't as slick as Baird's, but they usually got the job done. He'd won his fair share of bar brawls even before he'd signed on with the Library, even if this fight was more annoyingly

ridiculous than most. This wasn't even the first time somebody had come at him with a fork. He still had a scar where
that jealous waitress in Tulsa had poked him a few years back.

But then, I probably had that one coming.

Sprat lunged at Stone, but Stone was ready for him. He
blocked Sprat's knife arm with his own forearm and seized
the fork hand by the wrist, then butted Sprat with his head
just like he would with a flesh-and-blood opponent.

But Sprat wasn't flesh and blood. Stone grunted in pain as
he slammed his head into the solid fiberglass head. The impact was enough to stagger Stone for a moment. His head
swayed limply atop his neck. An ugly bruise began to blos-
som on his forehead.

Okay, bad idea, Stone thought. *Let's not do that again.*

Still grappling with Sprat, he lost track of Mrs. Sprat—until
a fork jabbed him in the back. Stone yelped and kicked backward with one leg to fend her off. He hoped to knock her over,
but her center of gravity was too large and too low; all he could
do was force her back a few steps and keep her from jamming
the fork in any deeper. She swung at his leg with her knife,
but her chubby arms were too short to reach him. Stone
thanked whatever unknown sculptor had molded those arms
years ago.

*On second thought, maybe I underestimated these two. I'll
take the Big Bad Wolf any day.*

Trapped between the Sprats was no place to be; he threw
his full weight against Jack Sprat, knocking the less-centered
mannequin onto his back. Eerily, Spratt issued no sound—no
grunts or groans—as he fell, but stayed utterly silent as he
struggled to employ his weapons. Letting go of Sprat's arms,
Stone sprang away from the fallen figure while dashing out
from under Mrs. Sprat's slashing blade as well.

"Uh-huh," Stone said. "Keep your silverware to yourself."

Jack Sprat's fingers grabbed his ankle, impeding his escape. Swearing, Stone had to sacrifice his left cowboy boot to break from the mannequin's grasp, yanking his foot free of the boot and hobbling awkwardly away from his foes with one boot on and one boot off, which certainly sounded like something from a nursery rhyme even though it took him a moment to place it. *Diddle, diddle, dumpling . . . oh, the hell with it.*

Staggering away from the Sprats, Stone stumbled into the tangled remains of an untended garden. Instead of silver bells and cockle shells, ragweed, thistles, and brambles had overrun the flower beds. He tripped over something in the dark and swore out loud as he hit the dirt. Glancing back, he saw that he'd run afoul of a long-forgotten garden hoe lying in the weeds. He mentally cursed whatever careless gardener had left it behind.

As relentless as a bad dream, the Sprats pursued him into the garden. Reaching back, he yanked the fork out of his aching trapezius, which stung like blazes. Scrambling to his feet, he looked from the fork to the oncoming mannequins and wondered how the hell he was supposed to stop them.

"You can't kill them or knock them out!" Baird called out. "You have to smash them to pieces!"

With a fork?

Risking a glance at Baird, Stone saw her whaling on the Three Men from the Tub with a sturdy piece of rebar she'd scrounged from somewhere. Fiberglass limbs shattered as easily as bone when hit by rebar as Baird went to town on the mannequins, smashing them to bits. A two-handed swing amputated the Baker's right arm, rolling pin and all. Chips and flakes went flying.

Now there's a sight for sore eyes, he thought.

He didn't see any rebar in his immediate vicinity, but there was the hoe. Discarding the fork, he dived for the tool and grabbed on to its long aluminum handle just as the Family Sprat caught up with him. A pronged metal blade jutted transversely from the end of the pole. He gripped the hoe like a weapon as he faced off against his lean and not-so-lean opponents.

"Batter up," he muttered.

———

Little Miss Muffet skipped merrily toward Cassandra, all molded pigtails and pinafores. Cobwebs clung to the mannequin in a case of life imitating rhyme. It wasn't armed with anything besides a large wooden spoon, but it was still as spooky as could be, Cassandra thought, like a possessed doll or ventriloquist dummy in a horror movie she regretted watching when she tried to get to sleep afterward. Cassandra had no intention of letting the lifelike figure get its clutches on her, and not just because the prospect of being beaten up or worse by Little Miss Muffet of all characters was too embarrassing to contemplate. . . .

"I don't suppose we can just talk this out," she suggested, "maybe over some yummy curds and whey?"

Miss Muffet picked up a rock and threw it at her.

"Hey, watch it!" Cassandra flinched as the rock whizzed past her ear. "That's not very nice at all!"

Looking for a weapon of her own, she ran over to a rickety white picket fence near a picnic area. Braving splinters, she pried loose one of the surviving slats and charged at Miss Muffet, swinging the slat like a club.

No more nice Librarian, she thought. *Tough it, Miss Muffet.*

The slat connected with the mannequin—and broke apart.

The fencing, that was, not Miss Muffet

Cassandra's face fell. *Right*, she thought. *I should've considered the relative density of rotting plywood versus molded fiberglass. . . .*

Undeterred by the blow, Miss Muffet kicked Cassandra in the shin.

"Oww!"

A wooden spoon smacked Cassandra repeatedly. Greedy fingers grabbed on to the hem of her skirt. Cassandra threw herself backward, tearing from the mannequin's grip.

No fair, she thought. *I liked that skirt.*

Baird may have said "no retreat," but Miss Muffet had Cassandra on the run. Limping, Cassandra retreated to the picnic area, where Miss Muffet chased her around the weathered tables and benches. The bratty mannequin was fast and determined, so Cassandra had to sprint to keep a step or two ahead of it, which wasn't getting her or the other Librarians any closer to Humpty Dumpty, which was what really mattered. Miss Muffet was just a distraction, a delaying tactic on the part of Mother Goose. Cassandra wracked her brain for a way to solve this frustrating story problem.

Maybe this is like fighting a Fictional, she thought, *and you have to turn their own narrative against them?* She ran through the rhyme in her head:

Little Miss Muffet sat on a tuffet,
Eating her curds and whey,
Along came a spider, who sat down beside her,
And frightened Miss Muffet away.

Cassandra didn't have any spiders on hand, and wasn't inclined to go foraging for one, but maybe she didn't have to. Climbing up onto one of the picnic tables, she feigned horror (which was not too difficult under the circumstances) and pointed frantically past Miss Muffet.

"Eek!" Cassandra screamed. "A spider!"

The bluff worked like magic. Just like that, Miss Muffet threw up her arms in fright and ran madly away, vanishing into the premorning gloom as fast her little legs could carry her. Cassandra grinned in satisfaction, feeling very much a Librarian.

Who needs to clobber things when you can research an answer instead?

Surveying the scene from atop the table, she saw that Baird and Stone had almost finished disposing of their own adversaries in their own inimitable styles. Broken pieces of mannequin twitched and vibrated harmlessly upon the ground. Hopping on one foot, Stone retrieved a boot from the rubble and pulled it back on. Baird maintained her grip on a lethal piece of rebar. Cassandra started to look for Ezekiel when Stone called out a warning.

"Heads up, folks! We're not done with these characters yet . . . and I do mean 'characters'!"

More of Mother Goose's army arrived on the scene, including Wee Willie Winkie in his nightgown, Tweedledum and Tweedledee, Old Mother Hubbard, the King and Queen and Knave of Hearts, the Three Wise Men of Gotham, Little Tommy Tucker, Mary and her Little Lambs, Tom the Piper's Son, clutching a stolen pig under his arm, and several more that Cassandra couldn't immediately identify. The Three Little Kittens, still missing their mittens, extended their claws as they guarded the path leading to Humpty Dumpty. Sharp teeth were bared beneath the Kittens' whiskers. Cassandra found herself wishing that Mother Goose hadn't been quite so prolific.

A little case of rhymer's block would have made our job so much easier.

But where was Ezekiel? The last she'd seen, Jack Horner and Boy Blue had been converging on him. Fearing for his safety, and knowing that he would never willingly desert them, she raised her voice.

"Ezekiel? Answer me if you can!"

———

An earsplitting air horn responded to her plea, followed by the unexpected sight of a hot-wired John Deere bulldozer crashing through trees and shrubbery with Ezekiel Jones at the wheel. Leaning on the horn to warn his compatriots, he steered the noisy tractor straight for Mother Goose's reinforcements while Stone and Baird dived out of the way. The 'dozer's heavy metal blade slammed into the mannequins, knocking them over like bowling pins, just as it had done with Jack Horner and Boy Blue earlier, bits of whom were still wedged into the tractor's reinforced steel treads. Yet more fiberglass crunched loudly as the army of figures were also ground to pieces beneath the 'dozer's tread. Ezekiel backed the vehicle over them again, just to play it safe, before shifting the engine into neutral. He leaned out of the cab to shout to the others, who were all gaping at him in surprise.

"What?" he asked glibly. "They were scheduled for demolition anyway."

"Jones?" Stone asked in disbelief. "What the hell are you doing in a bulldozer?"

He sounded more cranky than grateful; Ezekiel figured Stone was just annoyed that he hadn't thought of it first.

"Please!" the thief said, offended. "I boosted my first

construction vehicle before I even got my learner's permit. They're great for carrying off ATMs and soda machines."

He was about to invite the others to climb aboard, or maybe follow behind him, when the tractor's engine started choking loudly. Oily black smoke erupted from the exhaust pipe and steam billowed up from the engine. He frantically worked the gear shift, trying to get the chug-chugging engine running properly again, but it faltered and died. Hissing steam taunted his efforts.

"Damn it, Jones!" Stone complained. "You overheated the engine."

"Did not!" Ezekiel hit the gas and ignition, but the tractor remained stubbornly inert, like a lock that refused to open no matter how many times you entered the right combination. "It must be . . . magical sabotage . . . or something. From all the bad mojo in the air, you know?"

"Bad mojo?" Stone threw down a garden hoe in exasperation. "Do you even hear the words coming out of your mouth sometimes?"

Ezekiel got down from the cab. "Like you could have done any better?"

"You bet I could. I've worked more construction sites than you've—"

Baird whistled loudly to get their attention. "That's enough, boys. Save the sibling rivalry until after we've saved the universe."

To the east, the sky was getting even brighter and ruddier.

Ezekiel knew a red-alert signal when he saw one. This was the part in a heist when the alarms went off and everything went pear-shaped.

"So what are we waiting for?" he asked.

22

They made good time crossing the grounds without running into any further obstacles along the way. Baird wanted to think that Mother Goose had run out of tricks, but she knew better than to count on that. Too many battles had been lost by underestimating the enemy, so Baird had held on to her rebar. She and the Librarians were almost to the Humpty Dumpty tableau when she signaled the others to stop. She lowered her voice to avoid being overheard—by the mannequins or anyone else.

"Okay, here's the plan. If Mother Goose is already at ground zero, I'll try to hold her attention while you three circle around behind her and try to get those books away from her. Got it?"

"I guess," Stone muttered. "But I don't like the idea of you putting yourself in the line of fire."

"She hasn't attacked anybody directly yet," Baird said. "Frontal assaults don't seem to be her style. I just need to keep her talking long enough for you folks to sneak up on her."

"Er, she did turn a candelabra into a flamethrower," Cassandra pointed out, "and threaten me and Cole with it."

"True," Baird said, "but from what you said, she didn't blast either of you when she had a chance, before or after she got the book. And in any event, I'm the Guardian. Drawing fire while you three pull a rabbit out of the hat is my job, basi-cally, so let's get on with it . . . before it's too late to argue about it."

The Librarians scattered into the woods and gardens ahead while Baird hurried around the corner and down the path to where Humpty Dumpty still rested in pieces, if only for the moment. The mannequin's decapitated body sat atop the brick wall, while his bisected head rested at its base. A wide gap a few feet across separated the two halves of his face.

So far, so good, Baird thought. *He's not back together again yet.*

There were, of course, other Humpty figures to be found around the world; this particular effigy was not literally *the* original World Egg, but, according to Jenkins at least, it was a suitably symbolic representation of the same. The way he explained it, they were talking sympathetic magic here, as with, say, a voodoo doll or a cursed waxwork dummy. Baird wondered why Mother Goose had chosen this particular Humpty, but only for a moment, because of a matter of much more immediate concern.

Humpty was not alone.

"You again, Guardian?" Mother Goose greeted Baird. "I thought I warned you to mind your own business and stay away from my Garden!"

The crone stood atop the brick wall, next to the headless figure, looking just as she had the last time Baird had encoun-tered her, despite having been last seen in the form of an actual goose. Human once more, Mother Goose held one of the purloined books in each hand, while a third volume hov-ered in the air before her, levitating. Angry winds whipped up abruptly, roiling the dry, fallen leaves. Tree branches shook

and swayed. Thunder rumbled from a clear sky that was growing lighter by the moment. Dawn was almost upon them.

"Sorry, not happening." Baird advanced cautiously. "Guess
you don't know me as well as you think you do."

"I wouldn't be so sure of that, Eve Baird!"

With a dramatic gesture, Mother Goose slammed the three
slender books together with a bang. A blinding white flash
made Baird blink and look away; when she looked back, the
three books had merged into a single large volume floating
open in the air. Pages magically flipped themselves until they
reached the right spot in the text.

"Ah, there's the whole rhyme at last," Mother Goose said,
cackling. Her exaggerated Boston accent grated on Baird's ears.
She grinned at the rising dawn as she started in on the spell:

> Humpty Dumpty sat on the wall,
> Humpty Dumpty had a great fall . . .

"Uh-uh," Baird interrupted, dropping the rebar and drawing her gun. Blue spots danced before her watery eyes as they
recovered from the flash. "That's far enough. Turn over the
book, Mother Goose, if that's really your name."

It still felt wrong to pull a gun on Mother Goose, even
knowing what Baird knew, but the sun was rising and they
were running out of time. With any luck, the mere sight of
the firearm would be enough to distract Mother Goose long
enough for the lurking Librarians to make their move.

"A gun, truly?" Mother Goose shook her head sadly. "I'm
disappointed in you, Eve. You're far too clever a girl to resort
to such pedestrian means."

"Sorry to let you down," Baird said, "but that doesn't change
anything. Surrender the book or—"

A loud honk came from above, startling her. Glancing up, she saw the giant gander swooping down at her while squawking up a storm. She started to adjust her aim and swing her sidearm toward the diving bird, but the gander was too fast. Its beak bit down on her wrist, causing her to cry out. She lost her grip on the gun, which went flying into the bushes. A flapping wing buffeted her, knocking her to the ground. She punched, trying to get it to release her wrist, but she couldn't get a good blow in. Feathers smacked her in the face.

Damn, Baird thought. *Where's a squirt-gun full of magic rejuvenating water when you need one?*

"That's enough, my pet!" the crone called out. "No need to damage the poor dear. She's having a bad enough morning as it is!"

Heeding its mistress's command, the gander let go of Baird's wrist and flapped back up into the trees overlooking the scene. The disheveled Guardian scrambled to her feet and glanced around fruitlessly for her weapons, both of which were lost somewhere in the thick weeds and underbrush. Spitting a small white feather from her mouth, she mentally kicked herself for forgetting about the gander—and for getting disarmed by a bird!

"You know," Baird said, glaring at Mother Goose, "ordinarily I wouldn't want to get rough with a woman of your advanced years, but you're not getting the senior citizen treatment anymore." She clenched her fists, while keeping one eye on the sky in case the gander took another run at her. "Get ready to cash in on your Medicare benefits."

"Stay back, Eve!" the crone said menacingly. "And that goes for the rest of you, too." She swept her gaze over the surrounding shrubbery. "You might as well come out of hiding. This is my Garden and my eyes are everywhere. I have nothing to fear from anyone, least of all an impudent pack of apprentice Librarians!"

"Apprentice?" Ezekiel popped out from behind a nearby tree. "Who are you calling an apprentice?"

"Says the thief who doesn't even know how to use a card catalog," Mother Goose mocked him. She spun around atop the wall, pointing here and there. "And the roughneck, and the waif . . ."

"Waif?" Cassandra emerged from hiding, her cover obviously blown. "I haven't been a waif in years. . . ."

"You tell her, Cassie." Stone rose up from behind a bush across from her. He cracked his knuckles in anticipation of a brawl. "We've taken on tougher customers than her. Let's cook this Goose."

They converged on her warily, but Mother Goose was quick on the rhyme:

Ring a ring of roses,
A pocket full of posies,
Ashes, ashes,
You all fall down!

Baird's legs turned to rubber and she collapsed onto the ground, landing facedown a few yards away from Humpty Dumpty's shattered remains. Fallen leaves cushioned her landing, but the impact still knocked the wind out of her. Loud crashes, shouts, and curses signaled that her Librarians had hit the ground as well. She tried to spring back up to her feet, but her limbs failed to respond. It was all she could do to lift her head high enough to see what was happening. Ashes fell from the sky like snowflakes, weighing her down and tickling her nose.

"Stone?" she called out. "Cassandra? Ezekiel?"

"I'm down!" Stone shouted back. "Trying to get back up again, but I haven't got the strength. Feels like that heavy-gravity trap back in that secret lab outside Peking. . . ."

"That was an artificial dark-matter event horizon," Cassandra corrected him from a few yards away. "This feels more like the world's worst case of the flu. I feel too weak and heavy to move."

"Whatever," Ezekiel said impatiently, "we've all face-planted . . . and we can't get up!"

Baird remembered hearing somewhere that the "ring around the rosie" rhyme actually had to do with the Black Death back in the Dark Ages. A chill ran down her spine.

"Crap!" she blurted. "She gave us the Plague!"

"Nonsense!" Mother Goose said. "My rhyme has nothing to do with the Plague; that's a spurious bit of poppycock no serious scholar believes." She turned back to the levitating spell book. "Now then, if you don't mind, where was I?" She peered over the top of her spectacles at the page before picking up the rhyme where she left off:

All the king's horses and all the king's men,
Couldn't put Humpty together again.

That should have been the end of the rhyme, but Mother Goose kept going, reciting secret verses Baird had never heard before:

Humpty Dumpty, together once more,

Humpty Dumpty, open the door,
A new day is dawning, happy birthday to you,
Out with the old world, in with the new!

The spell kicked in at once. Suddenly, there was something electric in the air, like before an approaching storm. A rosy glow enveloped the two halves of Humpty's head as they began to stir of their own accord, drawn toward each other as though by some magnetic force, while the headless figure on the wall came to life as well, reaching out expectantly for his missing head. Rocking upright, the right and left halves were reunited at last, colliding together to form a large ovoid head with the wide end on the bottom. The egg's painted features awoke. Humpty's wide grin broadened in a way that made Baird's skin crawl. A dish-sized eye winked at her as she looked on helplessly, pinned to the ground by a children's nursery rhyme of all things.

"Stop this!" Baird shouted at Mother Goose. "We know what you're planning and—"

"Plan?" Mother Goose sounded offended. "I don't plan, I act. I go by rhyme, not reason. I do as the spirit moves me. I am my own muse, the one true Mother Goose. No plans for me, only inspired flights of fancy!"

Sounds like something Flynn would say, Baird thought, then froze upon the ground as the stray observation echoed in her head.

Like something Flynn would say . . .

Her heart skipped a beat. A wild, utterly crazy idea stampeded across her brain, knocking over all the furniture as it abruptly burst out into the open from wherever it might have been hiding in the back of her mind. She remembered the old vacation photo Jenkins had found in the Mother Goose folder back at the Library, and she suddenly knew in her heart who the little boy in the photo was and why he had looked oddly familiar. She gazed in shock at Mother Goose.

"Flynn?"

23

※ *A few days ago* ※
Oregon

Flynn Carsen ran into the Annex as though the Curse of the Seven Hells was chasing him, which, in fact, it was. A jade dagger whizzed past his head, following him through the Magic Door as he dashed from the Even More Forbidden City, deep in the Jiangsu Province of mainland China, into a cluttered office on the opposite side of the globe. Mystic lightning crackled in the doorway as he left his pursuers and the Far East behind. The flying dagger thwacked into a polished wooden railing across from the entrance, lodging deeply in the wood. Flynn wondered if the esoteric weapon had any historic value in its own right or was just for killing intrepid Librarians venturing into forbidden tombs in search of hazardous magic.

I'll have to consult Dragomiloff's Guide to Lethal Implements *with regard to that dagger,* he thought, *when I have a free moment.*

Skidding to a halt, Flynn paused to catch his breath. A lean, slightly gawky fellow whose boyish visage and manner belied his forty-some years, he was dressed for desert grave-robbing in a pith helmet, jodhpurs, knee-high hiking boots, and a rumpled safari jacket that had seen plenty of action over the years. Said jacket was also slightly shredded at the moment, due to the vicious claws of the angry terra-cotta cat currently trapped in the plastic pet carrier Flynn was holding on to with one hand. Furious at its confinement, the ceramic feline hissed and snarled and scratched at the interior of the carrier, despite having been made of fired clay more than two thousand years ago. Its violent tantrum rocked the carrier, making it harder to hold on to.

Good thing terra-cotta cats didn't weigh that much.

"Bad kitty!" Flynn scolded. "Just a few more minutes and you can take a nice long catnap again."

He placed the carrier down on the nearest available surface, which just happened to be the conference table. In his other hand, he clutched an ancient bamboo scroll, which he unrolled with a flick of his wrist. His late Han Dynasty Mandarin was a little rusty, but he could decipher the characters on the ancient scroll without too much difficulty. Clearing his throat, which was as dry as the forgotten tomb he had just escaped from, he recited an arcane incantation that had not been spoken aloud since the Great Wall was just a fence:

[REDACTED PER LIBRARY PROTOCOL]

A flash of azure light lit up the pet carrier from inside. The terra-cotta cat let out one last plaintive meow before going stiff and toppling over onto one side, no longer animated by primordial magic. The unmistakable odor of oolong tea lingered in the air.

"Whoa." Flynn wrested the knife from the door and gave

it a quick flip. "That was trickier than I expected. Who knew ceramic cats wouldn't come when called?"

He brushed the dust of ages off his shoulders and hat before stowing the cat and carrier in a supply closet until he had the time and energy to schlep it all the way over to the Artificial Pets and Wildlife collection elsewhere in the Library. He tossed the displaced dagger into the closet as well. He tried not to think about just how closely the knife had whizzed by his head.

Occupational hazard, he thought.

In retrospect, though, he probably should've recruited some backup for this mission. He was trying to be a better team player these days, out of respect for Eve and the new crop of Librarians, but sometimes he still liked to fly solo on a case just for old time's sake. And a routine, seemingly by-the-numbers tomb excursion had hardly seemed like a job for the whole team.

Speaking of whom . . .

"Hello?" he called out. "Anybody home?"

He soon discovered that nobody was present to greet him, let alone congratulate him on yet another death-defying job well done, but then he realized that China was fifteen hours ahead of Portland, which meant it was—he did the calculations in his head rather than cheating by looking at a clock—roughly 3:45 in the morning, Pacific time.

No wonder the place is so deserted.

He glanced around at the empty office, which was literally quieter than the tomb he had just vacated. Given the lateness of the hour, it was no surprise that nobody else was on hand. Neither the Librarians nor their glamorous Guardian actually lived at the Annex, even though it often felt that way. Flynn assumed that even Jenkins had retired for the night, assuming the ageless caretaker actually required slumber the way mere mortals did.

Does Jenkins ever sleep? Flynn wondered. *Never occurred to me to ask.*

For himself, he was far too wired to turn in, not to mention fifteen hours out of sync with the local clocks, so he figured he might as well take advantage of the peace and quiet to get in a little "me time" while he had the Annex to himself. The more he thought about it, in fact, the more this seemed like an ideal opportunity to kick back, chill out, and maybe catch up with the news.

Yep, he thought, *that's just the ticket.*

He hung his (slightly battered) helmet on a hat rack, next to an industrial hard hat, a deerstalker cap, a red velvet fez, a Native American headdress, a scuba mask, a samurai helmet, a Venetian plague-doctor mask, a bishop's miter, a pair of night-vision goggles, and a stylish black silk top hat, suitable for formal occasions, that had also been known to generate a rabbit or two under certain extraordinary circumstances, before trading his shredded outerwear for a comfortable burgundy smoking jacket.

That's better, he thought. *Less like a doomed archaeologist and more like a scholarly gentleman of leisure, settling in for a relaxing evening.*

Slightly ruining the effect was the portable magic detector still clipped to his belt. Flynn didn't like to rely on the gadget too often for fear of losing his edge, but it had come in handy when tracking the ceramic feline through the labyrinthine tunnels and secret passages of that particular cursed tomb. He unhooked the device and laid it down on the table where the cat carrier had briefly rested.

"And now," he loudly informed the Library, "I am officially off duty."

He peeked apprehensively at the Clippings Book, just in case it had other plans, but apparently it was on the same page, as it were. Reasonably confident that he would not be disturbed, he wandered over to the Annex's well-stocked news stacks, where he picked up the evening edition of *The New York Courier*. The Library subscribed to pretty much every newspaper and periodical on the planet, including those serving the dragon, leprechaun, and cryptid communities, but Flynn was still a New Yorker at heart and had been reading *The Courier* since before most kids his age even knew how to read. It was still his hometown paper, even if he was based out of Portland these days.

Could be worse, he reflected. *Could have been Antarctica.*

Paper in hand, he strolled back to the desk he shared with Eve and sat down to peruse. Ezekiel often mocked Flynn for still reading "dead tree" newspapers in the digital area, but Flynn didn't care. He still enjoyed making his way through pages of folded newsprint, just as he still preferred bound paper books to their electronic equivalents. Sometimes it was just more relaxing to read the old-fashioned way.

You can take the bookworm out of the twentieth century, he thought, *but you can't take the twentieth century out of the bookworm.*

Also relaxing? Catching up on current events that had nothing to do with perilous quests and supernatural menaces. Flynn enjoyed his job and wouldn't have traded it for all the Jewels of Opar, but it was nice to take a break now and then, if only to remind himself that life still went on as usual for most of the world, even with all the wild magic running loose these days, reactivating dormant ley lines and long quiescent artifacts. With all due respect to the Clippings Book, he was looking forward to unwinding with some totally mundane news items.

The more ordinary, the better.

He skimmed past the front-page news and world affairs in search of more low-key stories. Turning to the local news, he stopped and stared as an unexpected headline caught his eye—and brought a pang to his heart.

"No Happy Endings. 'Mother Goose' Theme Park Scheduled for Demolition."

"Oh, my," he murmured, shaking his head sadly. Bittersweet nostalgia drove him to retrieve an old photo album from the bottom drawer of his desk, where he kept various personal mementos, including twenty-two diplomas, a high school yearbook, and a blue ribbon he won in a spelling bee back in fifth grade. Most people would keep such souvenirs at home, he suspected, but, honestly, the Library had been his only real home for more than a decade now, so he kept his most precious possessions there, along with all the other relics.

He dusted off the album, feeling vaguely guilty that he hadn't looked at it for so long. Years had elapsed since his mother had passed away, but old memories reminded him how much he still missed her. He flipped through the album until he came to the photo he was looking for: himself as a small boy, grinning in front of a life-sized Humpty Dumpty figure atop a decorative brick wall.

A wistful smile lifted the corner of Flynn's lips. He remembered that afternoon. Located just across the river from Queens, where he'd grown up, Mother Goose's Magic Garden had been a favorite summer excursion back in the day, both before and after his father died. Flynn sighed, recalling how simple life had seemed back then, before he'd grown up and discovered that myths and magic and fairy tales were real, and that Mother Goose was far more than just a storybook character.

Mother Goose . . .

It occurred to him that the Mother Goose Treaty, which Judson had once told him about, was coming up on its one hundredth anniversary. Flynn had never actually inspected the Treaty, which was the work of a much earlier Librarian, but was it possible that there was an expiration date on the Treaty, or perhaps some special clauses or riders that kicked in after a full century?

Couldn't hurt to check it out, he thought. *And I do need to file the Bamboo Sutra anyway.* . . .

Putting away the photo album and newspaper, he exited the Annex and made the long trek across the Library to Subsection IX of the Archives, where were kept rare, often one-of-a-kind documents and records that were unlikely to be consulted on a regular basis, such as the Ultra Charta, The Arcturus Compact, The Transubstantiation Proclamation, the original deed to the Library of Alexandria, and, in theory, the celebrated Mother Goose Treaty of 1918.

Look at me, he thought proudly, *getting out ahead of a potential situation for once. Eve will be impressed.*

Actually locating the Treaty proved harder than expected, however. He knew where it was *supposed* to be, but recent events had resulted in a certain degree of disarray at the Library. Random hallways and wings had rearranged themselves, doors and carpets had changed color without warning, cross-referenced materials had literally crossed over from one collection to another, certain artifacts had gone missing before being recovered. Flynn liked to think that everything was back where it belonged, kinda sorta, but the Library was a big place and sorting through the older Archives had not been a top priority.

So would the Treaty be under "Goose, Mother" or "Mother Goose"?

For the second time today, he found himself playing archaeologist, rooting through dusty old files and folios in search of the elusive Treaty. A lesser Librarian might have given up, but the challenge only invigorated Flynn, increasing his determination to track down the Treaty.

The game was afoot!

It wasn't easy, but at last he stumbled onto a neglected filing cabinet tucked away in an inconspicuous corner of the Archives. Riffling through the hanging files, he found a sealed folder filed under "Pacts, Poultry."

Seriously?

A familiar rush of excitement greeted his discovery. Flynn lived for moments like this, when the buried secrets of the past were unearthed. The mouth of the folder had been sealed with wax, but he sliced through the seal with the tip of his pocket knife.

"Voilà!"

Occult energy flared and popped as he broke the seal, startling Flynn, who gasped in surprise as the liberated Treaty shot from the folder into the air, making a break for it. Dropping the folder, he grabbed for the Treaty without success.

The wild magic, he guessed. There was much more ambient magic in the atmosphere today than there had been when the Treaty had been hermetically sealed away almost a century ago. Breaking the seal had exposed the Treaty to the magic, triggering an immediate reaction, or at least that was the best explanation Flynn could come up with at the moment. *Mother Goose's magic has woken up—and it's trying to break free!*

The flying parchment wafted erratically around the Archives like a paper airplane, blown about by an unnatural breeze. Kicking himself for not anticipating any magical complications, Flynn took a running leap and snagged the fugitive Treaty in midair, only to have an electric jolt run down his arm and along his entire nervous system. Landing flat-footed on the floor, he twitched and jerked as the captured Treaty furled itself tightly within his grip, transforming into a gnarled wooden cane. Flynn tried to let go of the cane-slash-treaty, but it was like holding on to a high-voltage electrical cable: his fingers refused to cooperate.

Okay, he deduced, *this isn't good.*

He could feel the forbidden magic coursing through him, eagerly seeking expression after being curtailed for so long. He sensed the fractured spell book yearning to be made whole once more. Magic potent enough to reshape reality escaped the Treaty that had bound it for nearly a century. There was great work to be done, and somebody needed to do it. . . .

A blinding flash of light lit up the Archives, hiding what transpired from even the Library's view. When the glare faded, Flynn was no longer to be seen; in his place was a wizened crone clad in a bonnet, shawl, and skirts. She held up her cane in exultation. A gleeful cackle echoed off the walls.

"High diddle diddle!" she exclaimed. "I'm back . . . and fit as a fiddle!"

Mother Goose basked in her newfound freedom. For too long had her magic and merriment been barred from the world by fainthearted legal quibbles and caveats. For too many generations had her spells and legacy been divided between

unworthy pretenders to her title. No longer was she con-
strained by that picayune Treaty. Mother Goose was reborn,
with power enough to restart all of Creation.

Once she had her book back and in one piece again,
of course.

The time had come to regain what was rightfully hers, and
she knew just where to begin. She held out an open hand.
Magic flashed and a photo appeared in her hands: a picture
of a young boy posing before Humpty Dumpty's wall. The
crone contemplated the photo, oddly troubled by the sight of
the child, before averting her eyes.

The boy doesn't matter, she thought. *That's my Garden,
not his.*

An empty folder lay upon the floor where the Librarian had
dropped it. Taking a moment to tidy up, Mother Goose placed
the photo in the folder and filed it back where it belonged.

"A place for everything and everything in its place," she
said, chuckling. "And those baby Librarians will be none the
wiser!"

Eager to be on her way, she hurried through the sleeping
Library to the Annex on her way back to the world. Flynn's
magic detector beeped in alarm as she strode past it, much
to her annoyance. Scowling, she turned toward the device,
ready to banish it to the bottom of the deep blue sea, but
paused and thought better of it. The clever contrivance might
well prove of use where she was going, if only to trace the unseen currents of magic flowing through the world outside as
she went about reclaiming her spells.

"Waste not, want not."

She tucked the scanner under her arm before heading out
the Magic Door.

Her Garden awaited . . . as did her destiny!

24

⁂ New Jersey ⁂

"Flynn?" Baird repeated. "Is that you?"

The very idea was insane, but the more she thought about it, the more it added up:

Mother Goose knew them all by name, and seemed to have a bit of an attitude regarding the new crop of Librarians . . . just like Flynn used to.

Mother Goose had pedantically corrected her regarding the Black Death . . . which was just what Flynn might have done.

Mother Goose's hammy Boston accent was about as subtle as Flynn's atrocious Elizabethan dialect had been that one time they'd traveled back in time and met Shakespeare.

Mother Goose was manic and reckless and out of control . . . just like Flynn had been when under the pernicious influence of the Apple of the Discord, which had amplified that aspect of his personality. And there was certainly a part of Flynn, the boundlessly curious, wildly foolhardy part, who just loved magic and marvels and arcane lore and secrets for their own sake, who never met a code he didn't want to crack or a forbidden tomb he didn't want to open, and who might not be able to resist putting Humpty Dumpty back together just to see what happened next.

And *somebody* must have left that photo in the Library's files as a clue to Mother Goose's true identity. . . .

Could it be?

She peered into Mother Goose's eyes, looking for a glint, a trace, of a man she liked to think she knew better than most. And, yes, there it was: an unmistakable intelligence, along with a slightly lunatic spark of genius, that couldn't belong to anyone else.

"It is you, isn't it? Underneath all that . . . goosieness."

"Nonsense!" the crone replied. "I'm Mother Goose . . . as any fool can plainly see." She shook her cane at the grounded Guardian. "Now be a good girl and let me get on with my work. I've no wish to hurt you, Eve."

"That's right!" she said. "You've never actually hurt anyone, even as Mother Goose. The 'attacks' on Gillian and Mary and George . . . those were frightening, but they left your 'victims' alive and well. If you'd really wanted to eliminate the competition, like you thought you were doing, you've been doing a pretty sucky job of it. And later, when you ambushed the other Librarians, you always left them a way out, knowing they'd be able to save themselves."

No wonder I could never bring myself to shoot her, Baird thought. *Maybe deep down I always sensed who "she" really was.*

"Hell, you even left us a clue to figure out who you really are, so we could free you from whatever spell you're under." *Typical Flynn,* she thought. "You're still in there somewhere, Flynn, trying to stop this. You know you are!"

"I know nothing of the sort," Mother Goose insisted, perhaps a bit defensively. She shook her cane at Baird. "You've

clearly taken leave of your senses, Eve Baird! You're mad, mad
I say!"

"Excuse me," Cassandra interrupted. Like the other Librarians, she remained pinned to the ground by a nursery rhyme.
"Am I following this right? Mother Goose is Flynn?"

Baird was certain of it. "He's under a spell or possessed or
something, like that time you turned into Prince Charming,
or when Shakespeare was accidentally transformed into his
own creation!"

It had taken the combined efforts of three Librarians to
turn the wizard Prospero back into William Shakespeare. She
was surely going to need their help to restore Flynn to himself as well.

"We need to snap him out of this!" she urged the others.
"All of us, together, before it's too late!"

She glanced up at the sky. The sun was rising higher in the
east, a rosy glow encroaching on the moon and stars, which
were looking ever larger and closer than before. The universe
was shrinking, just like Jenkins had predicted. *Red sky at
morning, sailors take warning*, she recalled. *Isn't that a Mother
Goose rhyme, too?*

Baird wasn't sure.

Worse yet, Humpty Dumpty was coming together again.
She watched in horror as the reformed egg bounced off the
ground and back onto the headless mannequin's empty shoulders. Humpty's gloved hands reached up to fit his head back
on. Mother Goose cackled and clapped her hands at the sight.

"That's it, that's a good egg! Pull yourself together!"

Baird's heart sank.

"I don't understand, Flynn!" she said urgently. "Why are
you doing this? The whole universe is collapsing, everything
you've fought so hard to protect all these years!"

"Can't make a new Creation without breaking an egg." The crone cackled at her own joke. "You see what I did there?"

"But think of all that will be lost," Baird said. "The books, the learning, the obscure facts and history, everything you've devoted your life to." She looked to the others for assistance. "Back me up here, people!"

"Art, architecture, form, function," Stone chimed in. "The Taj Mahal, the Parthenon, Angkor Wat, Notre Dame, the Sistine Chapel, Impressionism, Surrealism, Dadaism, Michelangelo, Da Vinci, Rembrandt, Van Gogh, Picasso, Dali, Rockwell, Frazetta—"

"Algebra, trigonometry, calculus," Cassandra called out. "Differential equations, Einstein's Theory of Relativity, quantum physics, superstrings, brane theory, mathemagics—"

"Still not a thing," Baird muttered under her breath.

"The Hope Diamond, Fort Knox, the Crown Jewels," Ezekiel added. "Secret codes and passwords and puzzles and riddles, with shiny prizes just waiting to be found if you're quick and clever enough. . . ."

Very good, Jones, Baird thought, impressed. *You've got Flynn's number all right.*

Their combined efforts seemed to hit a nerve. A look of uncertainty came over Mother Goose's face. The levitating spell book rocked in the air, its pages flipping randomly. Her cane drooped in her grip.

"No," the crone muttered, her fake accent slipping. "You'll not dissuade me from my course. A new age dawns, the age of Mother Goose . . . the only true Mother Goose." Her conviction faltered. "Or am I?"

"It's working!" Baird shouted. "We're getting through to him. Keep it up!"

"The Alhambra!" Stone shouted. "Hagia Sophia, Stone-henge, the cave paintings at Lascaux!"

"Inverse hyperbolic functions!" Cassandra yelled. "The double helix, Gödel's theorem, superconductivity!"

"Treasure maps!" Ezekiel said. "Secret rooms, hidden vaults, booby traps, alarms!"

"Hush!" Mother Goose's cane slipped from her fingers. She clapped her hands over her ears. "Still your tongues, you insolent brats, or I'll whip you all soundly and send you to bed!"

The floating spell book crashed to the ground, as though her power was weakening. Confusion contorted Mother Goose's features. She reeled unsteadily atop the brick wall, clutching her head. A low moan escaped her lips.

"Listen to me, Flynn," Baird pleaded. "Not just with your brain, but with your heart. Remember all the people and places most dear to you, everyone and everything that wants you back: the Library, Judson, Excalibur . . . and me."

The crone's face rippled and blurred, growing translucent enough that you could almost see another face behind it. A face Baird knew up close and personal. A familiar voice emerged from Mother Goose's mouth.

"Eve?"

Hope flared in Baird's heart as she recognized Flynn's voice.

"That's right, Flynn. You can beat this. Come back to me, to all of us!"

The faltering crone looked down at herself in disbelief, as though for the first time. She reached up and felt her own face, exploring its contours with both hands. Startled eyes—Flynn's eyes—bulged behind Mother Goose's wavering, insubstantial countenance.

"This is all wrong," she said. "This isn't who I—"

A blazing blue fireball consumed Mother Goose, flaring brighter than the rising sun. A shock wave radiated from the blast, sending Baird and the others tumbling across the ground, rolling over the weeds and underbrush. The impact knocked the wind out of Baird and left her ears ringing.

Damn it, she thought. *Why does the big magic always have to be so . . . pyrotechnic?*

But had it worked?

Although battered by the blast, she realized that her arms and legs were no longer weighed down by magic. Scrambling to her feet, despite various scratches and bruises, she looked anxiously at the wall to see:

Flynn Carsen, not Mother Goose.

The witch was gone, replaced by the restored Librarian, who gazed down at himself with a dazed expression. A burgundy smoking jacket looked much better on him than Mother Goose's shawl and skirts. Unruly brown hair was adorably mussed. He shook his head to clear it of any lingering identity crises.

"Okay, that was . . . different."

Mother Goose's cane had transformed, as well, into a furled sheet of parchment that started to blow away in the breeze.

"Oh, no you don't!" Flynn hopped off the wall and stepped on the parchment to keep it from getting away. "You're not going anywhere except back into the Archives!"

The missing Treaty, Baird guessed. *So that's what happened to it.*

Flynn looked up at Baird, their eyes meeting across the short distance between them. "Thank you," he said softly, even as the other Librarians rushed toward him, now up and about as well.

"Flynn!" Cassandra squeed, hugging him. "It is you! You're back!"

Stone slapped him on the back. "Good to see you again, man!"

Typically, Ezekiel played it cool. "You owe me a drink, mate, for that business with the blackbirds. . . ."

"I'm so sorry, everyone!" Flynn said, contrite. "You know that wasn't really me, right? It was the spell and the rhymes and . . . whoa, did I really turn into an actual goose at one point?"

Cassandra nodded. "And flew off into the sky."

"And, boy, are my arms tired," Flynn said with a cheesy grin. "Sorry, had to say that."

Baird wanted to join in the reunion, but their mission wasn't completed yet.

"No time to celebrate, people. Looks like we're still on the clock."

She had hoped that breaking the spell over Flynn, and exorcising Mother Goose, would end the crisis, but Humpty Dumpty had not gone anywhere. Looking past Flynn and the others, Baird saw that Mother Goose's explosive transformation had failed to dislodge Humpty from his perch atop the wall. His great head rotated east to watch the sunrise. He grinned in anticipation.

Mother Goose's big spell is still playing out, Baird realized. *If Humpty hatches, it's the Big Bang all over again.*

Racing forward, she rescued the fallen spell book from the ground and thrust it at Flynn.

"Welcome back," she said. "Can you stop this?"

"I'm not sure." He cracked open the book, but peered down at the pages in confusion, as though he didn't even know where to begin looking for a counterspell. "The spell has been cast, events have been set in motion, taking on a life of their own, and I'm not Mother Goose anymore. I don't think I can halt this."

Baird started to despair until she saw a sudden inspiration light up his eyes. He smiled encouragingly.

"But I think I know who can!"

25

❉ *New Jersey* ❉

The rising sun hurt Flynn's eyes as the Magic Door deposited
him, Baird, and the three Goose heirs back in the park, outside Peter the Pumpkin Eater's colossal pumpkin shell of a
house. White light filled the doorway behind them, vanishing almost as quickly as it appeared.

Baird looked about, orienting herself. "The pumpkin, not the
shoe?"

"This way is faster," he replied. Mother Goose's spell book
was tucked under his arm. "Trust me."

Mary, Gillian, and George, less accustomed to instanta-
neous cross-continental travel, needed a moment to adjust to
their new surroundings. Both wonder and trepidation played
across their features.

"Another pumpkin," Gillian said with a shudder. "Lovely."

"But just a fake," George pointed out, "and more rundown
than my first car."

"Just as long as any nasty rodents are purely decorative as
well," Mary said. "I left my carving knife at home."

Flynn flinched inside, recalling the trials he'd inflicted on

Mary and the others as Mother Goose. He'd have to make it up to them somehow, *after* they saved the universe.

Assuming they were up to the challenge.

"Come along, come along!" he urged them. "Time—and Humpty Dumpty—waits for no man, or woman, or combinations thereof."

Mary eyed him warily. "Who exactly are you again?"

"Just another Librarian," Baird said, ducking the issue to a degree.

"Well, maybe not *just* another Librarian," Flynn objected.

He appreciated that Baird wanted to avoid getting into the whole "temporarily possessed by the magic of Mother Goose" thing, but he *did* have a certain degree of seniority where the Library was concerned. . . .

"You sure we never met before?" George peered at Flynn. "'Cause there's something about you. . . .'"

Flynn tugged nervously on his collar. "Just have that kind of face, I guess."

"No, it's not that," Gillian said. "I feel certain that I know you from somewhere, but I can't quite place—"

"We can sort that out later," Baird interrupted, coming to Flynn's rescue. "Flynn's right. There's not a moment to lose!"

Truer words were never spoken. Arriving back at Humpty Dumpty's wall, they found the other Librarians struggling to keep a teetering Humpty from taking another fall—and cracking open again. Stone had Humpty in a headlock, while Cassandra and Ezekiel shoved against Humpty, trying to hold the animated mannequin in place, despite the fact that Humpty was not making it any easier for them. Unhappy at being restrained, he kicked and swatted at the Librarians. His painted face expressed his displeasure. His smile flipped into a frown. Glossy black eyebrows tilted angrily. Jagged streaks of red painted his big eyes bloodshot.

"Hey!" Ezekiel yelped as a gloved hand slapped him in the face. "Watch it, you crazy . . . egghead! Do you want to fall and go boom?"

"Think that's the general idea," Stone said, grunting. "He's raring to hatch!"

"No! This isn't how it's supposed to go." Cassandra strained against the weight of the toppling egg man. Her feet skidded backward across the ground. "It . . . everything . . . can't end like this. By every reasonable cosmological hypothesis, our universe still has billions of years left to go. This is too soon. We can't let the whole cosmos die young—because of a stupid nursery rhyme!" She glanced up at Humpty. "No offense."

"I'm trying!" Ezekiel was right beside her, shoulder to shoulder. "Not sure how long we can keep this up, though. Frankly, we could use all the king's horses and all the king's men at the moment!"

Flynn appreciated their strenuous efforts, but winced at the sight.

"Careful there!" he shouted. "Don't crack the shell!"

"Easier said than done," Stone said. "You try wrestling this thing!"

Not up to me anymore, Flynn thought. He turned to the Goose heirs, who were gaping at the bizarre scene. They huddled together, united by circumstances as well as blood.

"Oh my," Mary said. "Am I seeing things?"

"I wish." George shook his head. "Man, that is seriously messed up."

"You took the words right out of my mouth," Gillian said before looking helplessly at Flynn and Baird. "I still don't quite understand. What on Earth do you expect of us?"

"You said it yourself," Flynn answered. "I need words straight from your mouth, from all three of you. You're the legitimate heirs to the title of Mother Goose. You're the only ones who can reverse this spell . . . by composing a new rhyme!"

Shock and disbelief registered on their faces.

"You can't be serious," Mary said. "I can't perform actual magic. I'm just a small-town librarian."

"I'm an academic," Gillian said.

"And I'm just a rapper-slash-tree-trimmer," George said. "You've got the wrong crew, dude."

Flynn shook his head. "Not from what I've seen . . . I mean, heard. You can absolutely do this if you work together. Forget the Treaty. Forget the old dynastic rivalries that divided your ancestors." He held out the reassembled spell book: *Mother Goose's Melodies*, complete in one volume. "This book, the power, the legacy . . . it belongs to you three."

Even if I temporarily usurped it when I wasn't quite myself, he thought.

"So you say," Gillian said uncertainly, "but still . . ."

"Listen to him, Gillian," Stone encouraged her. "You know this stuff better than anyone. You've studied for this for your entire life. If anybody can do it, you can."

"Thanks for the vote of confidence," Gillian said. "I can't deny it's much needed at the moment."

"That goes for you, too, Mary." Ezekiel glanced back at her over his shoulder. "I hate to admit it, but Flynn usually knows what he's talking about and, honestly, we could use some help here."

"Manfully admitted, Mr. Jones," Mary said. "And far be it for me to disagree."

"And you, George . . . Bo-Peeps," Cassandra said. "You're a born rapper, remember? Rhyming is in your blood."

"Damn straight it is!" He accepted the book from Flynn and held it out to his long-lost cousins and fellow heirs. "All right, ladies, let's get our Goose on."

He placed his right hand atop the book, as though being sworn in, and Mary and Gillian placed their hands over his. Magic flared as the embossed golden type on the book's front cover took on a dazzling glow.

"Well, I'll be damned!" Gillian gasped. "Did we do that?"

"I do believe we did, dear," Mary said, her eyes wide behind her glasses. "My husband is not going to believe any of this."

"It's just what I'm always saying," George said. "Magic is out there. You just got to look for it!"

The spell book cracked open of its own accord. Startled, the heirs yanked their hands away, but the book remained levitating in the air between them. Its pages turned, past rhyme after rhyme, until it reached Humpty Dumpty. Flowing ink rearranged the type on the page, creating an empty space at the bottom, just waiting to be filled with new verses.

"Well, that's not intimidating at all," Gillian said.

"No time for rhymer's block." Flynn fidgeted restlessly behind them, peering over one shoulder after another. "The clock is ticking . . . and the egg is hatching."

Glancing over at the wall, he saw that, despite the other Librarians' exertions, cracks were appearing in Humpy Dumpty's shell. The light of a new day—and a new Creation—seeped through the cracks, growing brighter by the second. Humpty's eyes took on a manic gleam. He grinned gleefully. The spreading cracks scarred his face, making him look like the Egg of Frankenstein. He was about as cute as doomsday.

"He's cracking open!" Cassandra shouted. "We can't stop it!"

Baird scanned Humpty with a new and improved magic detector, which was beeping like a Geiger counter on top of a nuclear test ground. Her eyes widened in alarm at the readings she was getting.

"Anytime now, people!" she prompted.

George nodded. "You heard the lady. Let's freestyle the hell out of this egg-pocalypse!"

He started them off:

"Humpty Dumpty, stay in your shell," he rapped.

"Humpty Dumpty, all will be well," Mary continued the rhyme.

"Sleep deep and long, all night and all day," Gillian added.

The words wrote themselves on the page as they were spoken. The trio looked at each other in amazement as the final verse came to them all in unison:

"Rest safe on your wall until Judgment Day!"

The verses lit up on the page, glowing brighter than the dawn, before fading away. A hush fell over the park. The wild winds abated, the thunder muted, swirling leaves settled back onto the trees, flailing trees fell still and silent. The universe stayed right where it was, basking in the morning light. Birdsong started up, welcoming a new day.

No Big Bang? Flynn thought. *That's encouraging.*

He looked at Humpty Dumpty. As hoped, the mannequin was no longer flailing or cracking. Its weathered white shell had been restored, as was its blandly smiling, immobile expression. It sat securely on the wall just as it had back in the good old days, as it did in the snapshot from his childhood. Humpty's right hand was raised again, as though waving to him from the past.

Flynn's throat tightened a little.

"Is that it?" Mary asked. "Did we do it?"

"Naturally." Flynn suppressed a sigh of relief. "Never doubted it for a minute."

Baird scanned Humpty with her detector just to be sure. "No more magical energy spikes," she reported. "All clear. You can stand down, folks."

The other Librarians let go of Humpty and cautiously stepped away from the figure, as though afraid that it might be playing possum, but Humpty wasn't going anywhere, not anymore.

"Whew," Stone said, wiping his brow. "That was one tough egg."

"Eh." Ezekiel shrugged. "I wasn't worried."

"Yeah, right." Stone smirked at his friend. "Tell me another."

Cassandra looked worriedly at the sky. "What about the stars? Is the universe still contracting with Humpty Dumpty put together again?"

"Nope." Flynn said with confidence, walking over to the wall. "The spell has been broken. That isn't the World Egg anymore—or, to be more precise, it doesn't represent the World Egg anymore. It's just a forgotten old mannequin." He rapped it with his knuckles to prove his point. "Ouch, that's harder than it looks."

Baird joined him by the figure. "Just the same, we should probably cart Humpty off to the Library, wall and all. Why take chances?"

"A reasonable precaution," Flynn agreed. "It's not like we don't have the space."

"Good job, everyone," Baird said. "Mission accomplished. And thanks for the timely assist," she added, addressing the Goose trio. "We couldn't have done it without you."

"But what about that other Mother Goose?" Mary asked, holding on to the spell book for the others. "Isn't she still on the loose?"

Flynn gulped and glanced down at his shoes, unsure how

to respond. Mother Goose's reign of nursery-rhyme terror weighed on his conscience, even though he wasn't really to blame.

It could have happened to anyone, he thought, *assuming they were messing with a magical peace treaty from a hundred years ago. . . .*

"You don't have to worry about her anymore," Baird said diplomatically. "She's been . . . dealt with."

"But how?" George asked. "What happened to her?"

"And who was she anyway?" Gillian asked. "Another distant relative . . . and heir to the title?"

"Nothing of the sort," Baird assured them. "She was an imposter, a pretender, but she's out of the picture now."

"How so?" Mary persisted. "Where is—?"

"I don't think we need to get into that right now," Flynn said.

26

※ *Oregon* ※

"Are you quite certain about this?" Jenkins asked.

"Absolutely." Mary turned the restored spell book over to Jenkins, while George and Gillian looked on, nodding in agreement. The Goose heirs, along with the Librarians and their Guardian, had returned to the Annex after concluding their business at Mother Goose's Magic Garden. "We talked it over, the three of us, and concluded that it would be a shame to split the book up again after going to so much trouble to recover the hidden pieces." She sighed wistfully as she let go of the book. "And as much as I would personally love to add this precious volume to my own library back home, I suspect it will be somewhat safer in yours."

"Same with my college," Gillian said.

"And my apartment," George joked, "which isn't exactly Fort Knox."

Jenkins accepted the book with all due dignity. "Rest assured that it will be safe in our hands," he said, "and that we fully appreciate the honor and responsibility you're entrusting to us."

"And don't you forget that, Mr. Jenkins." Mary stepped

back, relieved of her burden, and took a moment to admire the Annex's full shelves and old-fashioned card catalogs. "You do have quite a nice library here, but I don't suppose you offer story time for the kiddies?"

"Heaven forbid." Jenkins shuddered at the very idea before looking pointedly at the Librarians. "I have enough unruly youngsters on my hands."

Mary shrugged. "Your loss."

With the final disposition of *Mother Goose's Melodies* settled, the Librarians and their charges milled about in the Annex, celebrating their last-minute rescue of everything under the sun. Cradling the long-lost "ghost volume" in the crook of his arm, Jenkins was equally relieved that a new Creation had been postponed indefinitely. As far as he was concerned, there was still considerable work to be done when it came to tidying up the current model, even if the goose, the lion, and the unicorn were now back to normal and residing peacefully in their respective stalls, while Arthur's Crown was back where it belonged as well.

All's well that ends well, he thought, *for now.*

He looked forward to shelving *Mother Goose's Melodies* in the appropriate section. Perhaps alongside *The Secret Memoirs of Tom Thumb* and *Rip Van Winkle's Dream Journal?*

"Good job back there at the park," Stone congratulated Gillian as they retreated to a secluded corner of the office that was still not as private as Stone would have liked. "Seems to me that saving the universe deserves a dinner at least, and maybe some drinks and dancing afterward?"

"Consider it a date." She glanced back over her shoulder at

the Magic Door of the Annex. "And given that handy portal of yours, you have no excuse for being late . . . unless, of course, you're urgently needed in Atlantis or wherever."

"Thought you didn't believe in Atlantis," he teased her.

"After what I've seen since we met, I'm ready to believe in everything from faeries to Brigadoon."

"Funny you should mention faeries," he began. "As it turns out—"

She placed a finger over his lips. "Save it for the date."

"I was pleased to see you applying yourself at the wall," Mary said to Ezekiel. "Perhaps there's hope for you yet."

"Just another day doing the impossible," Ezekiel said, as though it was no big deal. "And doing it with style." He leaned against an overstuffed bookcase as he relished his latest amazing victory. "And who knew you were such a kick-ass librarian yourself?"

"Please," she replied, "I was a librarian while you were still a naughty child shoplifting candy bars or whatever else you surely got up to. Still, I admit that this unlikely adventure has boosted my confidence somewhat, enough so that I'm thinking of writing down my own stories and trying to get them published. Maybe carry on the family tradition by becoming a children's book author as well as a librarian . . . minus any sightless rodents, of course."

"Go for it," Ezekiel said. "Although I'll wait for the movie version."

Mary rolled her eyes. "Young people these days . . ." She smiled at him nonetheless. "You take care of yourself, Ezekiel Jones, and try to stay out of trouble."

He grinned back at her.

"Where's the fun in that?"

––––––

Jenkins raised his voice to get the room's attention.

"Mrs. Simon, Dr. Fell, Mr. Cole," he addressed them from the navigational apparatus by the Magic Door. "At the risk of calling short these celebrations, the exit is primed and ready to go, per your instructions."

"Looks like Bow Tie is giving us the bum's rush," George said to Cassandra. "Gotta jet, little lamb. Peace out."

She hugged him good-bye. "You get down with your bad self, Bo-Peeps. And keep slammin' your def phat flows. Represent!" She cringed at the words coming out of her mouth. "I really can't pull that off, can I?"

"Stick to the brainy science girl talk," he advised her. "It's working for you."

"Well, I like to think so. . . ."

Letting go of him, she escorted him toward the Magic Door, where the others were converging as well. "So I guess you're heading back to Miami now?"

"Not just yet," he said, joining Mary and Gillian before the door. "The three of us, we're taking a detour to Boston first."

"Boston?" Baird asked. She stood beside Flynn, holding his hand as though to keep him from running off again anytime soon.

We'll see how long that works, Cassandra thought.

"One-time home of Elizabeth Goose," Flynn deduced, figuring it out. "The last true Mother Goose."

"Right on the money," Gillian said. "After all of this, we thought we should make a pilgrimage to her grave and pay our respects . . . together."

"Something of a family reunion," Mary explained, "as well as a chance to get to know each other under slightly less tumultuous circumstances."

"Just try to avoid igniting any new family feuds," Jenkins cautioned. A tinge of melancholy entered his voice. "Trust me when I say that bonds of blood can break more catastrophically than most."

"Not going to happen, man," George said confidently. "You know what they say, nothing brings kin back together like saving the entire freaking world from one bad egg."

"That's what we thought in Caerleon," Jenkins murmured softly before inhaling deeply and returning to the task at hand. "In any event, ladies, gentleman, I wish you all good fortune and a safe journey. May you carry on the illustrious tradition of your forebears with both wisdom and imagination, jointly or separately as fate will have it."

"And that goes for the rest of us," Baird said. "Big time."

Jenkins opened the door. Supernaturally white light spilled into the Annex.

"Brilliant," Gillian said in a hushed tone. "Literally brilliant."

George gestured toward the glowing doorway. "After you, ladies."

"No." Mary joined their hands, with her in the middle. "All at once."

They stepped out the Magic Door together.

"Finally!" Jenkins said with visible relief. "With all due respect to our recent guests, I wish to remind you all again that this Annex, let alone the Library, is for Librarians only." He tipped his head toward Baird. "And their esteemed Guardian, of course."

Baird appreciated the nod, as well as his understandable concerns regarding the Library's security. She had no intention of adopting an open-door policy at the Library, except under extreme circumstances. She preferred to run a tight ship, too.

"Roger that," she said. "And don't worry about it. After running around the globe trying to put out this Mother Goose fire, I doubt that any of us are up to diving into another crisis right away. We could use some time off from relic runs and impending doom." She pulled Flynn closer to her. "And that goes for you, too, Librarian."

"Fine with me," he said. "Unless something comes up, that is."

She gave the Clippings Book a warning look. "Don't even think about it."

"Amen to that." Stone yawned and stretched. "I don't know about the rest of you folks, but I figured we're entitled to a day off . . . or three."

"Not going to argue with you there, mate," Ezekiel said. "I've been bouncing around so much I'm not even sure what day it is."

"Sunday morning, 7:12 A.M., Pacific time," Cassandra supplied. "Not that it really matters what time it is. I feel like I could sleep for a week."

"I'm oddly exhausted as well." Flynn glanced down at his restored form as though he was still trying to wrap his head around his recent transformations. "So, I *really* turned into a goose . . . not a gander?"

"Don't think about it." Baird started herding them toward the front door, the one that led to plain old Portland instead of quests on the far side of the globe. "Lord knows I'm trying my best not to."

"And that's a wrap," Stone said. "See you folks on the other side of some serious R&R."

"Ahem."

Jenkins cleared his throat loudly. Turning around, Baird and the others saw him emerging from a discreetly unobtrusive supply closet with an assortment of brooms and mops. He regarded their dismayed expressions with bemusement.

"What?" he asked. "We still have to clean up after the goose."

ACKNOWLEDGMENTS

The third season of *The Librarians* has just wrapped filming, even as I'm finishing up this, my second novel based on the television series, so it strikes me as the ideal time to give credit where credit is due.

Thanks to my editor, Christopher Morgan, and my other friends and colleagues at Tor Books, whom I'm proud to have been associated with for even longer than Flynn Carsen has worked for the Library.

Thanks also to Dean Devlin, John Rogers, Rachel Olschan-Wilson, and the whole crew at Electric Entertainment for allowing me to play in their sandbox and for all their help and cooperation along the way. I've been a big fan of the series and its characters since that first "Quest for the Spear" way back in 2004 and am looking forward to enjoying the Librarians' future onscreen adventures.

I'm also grateful to my agent, Russell Galen, for handling the contractual end of things with his customary aplomb. And, as always, I'm thankful for my girlfriend, Karen, for her ceaseless support, and for her willingness to listen to me ramble on about Mother Goose for months on end. And I'm thankful for our sweet dog, Lyla, who sadly passed away during the writing of this book, after sharing our home and lives for ten precious years, and for her feline big sister, Sophie, who is still very much with us.

On to Book Three . . . !

ABOUT THE AUTHOR

GREG COX is the *New York Times* bestselling author of numerous books and short stories. His previous novel, *The Librarians and the Lost Lamp*, is already shelved at the Library. (Really. I have photographic proof.)

In addition, he has written the official movie novelizations of such films as *War for the Planet of the Apes, Godzilla, Man of Steel, The Dark Knight Rises, Ghost Rider, Daredevil, Death Defying Acts*, and the first three *Underworld* movies. He has also written books and stories based on such popular series as *Alias, Buffy the Vampire Slayer, CSI: Crime Scene Investigation, Farscape, The 4400, The Green Hornet, Iron Man, Leverage, Planet of the Apes, Riese: Kingdom Falling, Roswell, Star Trek, Terminator, Warehouse 13, Xena: Warrior Princess, The X-Files, X-Men*, and *Zorro*. He is also a consulting editor for Tor Books.

He has received three Scribe Awards from the International Association of Media Tie-In Writers and lives in Oxford, Pennsylvania.

Visit him at: www.gregcox-author.com.